CW00456476

Breaking free

Book 2 of the Abigail's Fate series.

By Adele Lea

Copyright © 2017 Adele Lea

The right of Adele Lea to be identified as the author of this work has been asserted by her in accordance with the Copyright, Designs and Patents Act 1988. All rights reserved. This book is sold subject to the condition that it shall not, by way of trade or otherwise, be lent, resold, hired out or otherwise circulated in any form of binding or cover other than that in which it is published and without a similar condition including this condition being imposed on the subsequent purchaser.

This is a work of fiction. Names, characters, places, and incidents either are the products of the author's imagination or are used fictitiously. Any resemblance to actual persons, living or dead, businesses, companies, events, or locales is entirely coincidental.

Cover design Reform Creative
Copyright©2017. Used by permissions. All rights reserved.

To my husband

Dedicated to Andrew for putting up with me, listening to my rant's! For giving me the encouragement to continue, when at times all I wanted to do was to throw my laptop through the window, but most of all for convincing me that there was a light at the end of the tunnel.

Thank you.
Adele -x-

Chapter 1

I open the door and he's standing there, looking at me, his head cocked to one side. He looks friendly and happy to see me. I say nothing, just smile as he opens his lips to talk.

Abigail," he says, his eyes scanning me. I gesture with my hand to invite him in. I like what I'm seeing.

"Edward, please do come in. I'll just get my bag."

I turn away with the biggest grin on my face; my tongue's practically hanging out. God, he looks handsome! He's wearing distressed blue jeans, a grey T-shirt and a light-grey fitted V-neck cashmere jumper. I can see the shape of his chest through the wool; he looks toned and strong. His hair is tousled over to one side, and a light stubble covers his chin, making him look rugged and masculine. He looks like a playboy, a rich playboy. My playboy. *Goodbye, Mr Olympus and hello ... Mr Scott!*

I can't quite believe he's here in the flat, taking me out. Lucky me! Alison comes out of her bedroom, dressed in a skirt and jumper.

"Hi Edward," she says.

"Hi Alison. How are you? Are you out with Tom tonight?"

She nods but he doesn't notice – his eyes are on me, gliding over my body and occasionally up to my face. They're piercing, and a little menacing. I want to giggle – with nerves.

"Yes, I'm staying over at his place tonight."

She winks as I pull my lip in tight, rolling my eyes at her, mouthing, "Stop it, that's enough."

She grins, completely ignoring me.

"Have a wonderful time on your date."

I'm going to kill her. My face is flushed, and Edward hasn't moved his eyes from me as Alison goes into her bedroom, giggling. He walks towards me, shaking his head and smiling slowly.

"Abigail, you look gorgeous. I don't think I've ever seen anyone more stunning."

I smile nervously back at him, thinking he certainly knows how to charm.

He leans over and kisses me on the cheek. "Are you ready?"

I nod.

He looks around, then continues inquisitively, "Don't you like flowers?"

"Yes, I like flowers," I say, puzzled. "Why?"

"Well, I sent you some flowers, but as I arrived I noticed they'd been thrown next to the bins."

I gasp, putting my hand to my mouth.

"They were from you?"

He nods, and I bite my lip.

"I'm so sorry, I thought they were from …" I raise my eyes. "I wouldn't have thrown them out, honestly, if I'd known they were from you. Let me go and get them. I feel dreadful."

He takes my hand.

"It's fine. It's just a misunderstanding, that's all. I'll just have to buy you some more."

I pull a sad face, and he smiles.

"Come on, let's go. I'm starving. Are you hungry?"

"A little," I say, grabbing my bag, then shouting goodbye to Alison.

"Have fun, you two!" she replies from her room.

"Thank you," I say, turning to look at Edward, who's watching me, his eyes smiling. I breathe in deeply. He nods his head sharply and firmly, his voice confident, knowing what he wants.

"Abigail, let me take you to dinner," he finishes, all macho.

We leave the flat and go down the corridor and out into the car park. I look around but don't see the black BMW.

"Are we walking?" I ask.

"No," he says shaking his head. He removes his keys from his jeans pocket and presses the fob. The lights of a British racing-green Aston Martin flash on.

My eyes nearly pop out of my head as the penny drops. "It was you!" I blurt out.

He nods. "I was coming round to see you, to explain that I had to go away, but you ignored me—"

"No, I didn't," I interrupt. "I just didn't know it was you driving the car or beeping your horn at me."

"Well," he continues, "I turned around and followed you, but then I saw you with James."

"Oh, don't," I say with a grimace. "He makes my flesh crawl."

He closes his eyes briefly, accepting my explanation.

"I know that now but at the time I didn't. I was annoyed and jealous, so I drove off."

I'm a little shocked by his response.

"Then I rang the ward and left you a message and my mobile number, but you didn't ring. On Saturday night, I received a text from you."

I shake my head, but he continues. "You texted: *Don't ever speak to me again or get in contact with me.*"

I'm stunned at first, then alarmed.

"That wasn't me! I didn't send you a text, I … I wouldn't, and I didn't get your message, either. Who did you leave it with?"

He doesn't answer, but raises his eyebrows again.

"I also know that now, and it's been sorted."

I frown at him, but he won't be drawn on the issue. "I've dealt with it, Abigail."

"No, tell me Edward!" I grit my teeth. "Was it Darcy, by any chance?"

He shakes his head. "I said it's been dealt with."

I'm cross that he won't say, but I'm also wondering if he doesn't want me to make a scene. I leave it because it's clear he won't budge and I don't want to argue with him, not about her, the scheming little cow. I'll deal with her later.

"Well, will you at least tell me where you've been?"

"My grandfather was ill. They didn't think he was going to make it. It was a heart attack."

"Oh, I'm so sorry." I frown, and he smiles at my concern.

"Thank you. He's on the mend now, and out of intensive care. I came back on Wednesday to try to sort things out and to get him transferred to HDU so that I could keep an eye on him. He's very stubborn. I called at your flat before I left for home on Wednesday, but you were out. I left you a note in your postbox."

"A note? I didn't get that either. Was it in the right mailbox?"

I'm so angry that I'm shaking a little. That bitch! I remember the conversation I overheard in the toilets between Darcy and Emily: *I've sorted it. She'll not cross me again in a hurry.* So that's what she meant. He knows that I know what's going on. I'm still annoyed, but I smile at him. It's not his fault. All this, and because of her.

"Are you okay?"

"Yes." But I know full well that I'll pay her back. "Did you manage to get your grandfather transferred?"

He nods, a little relieved that I'm not pursuing the Darcy thing.

"Yes, although it took some persuasion. They moved him today. What are you grinning at?"

"I bet it didn't take that much persuasion."

"Meaning?"

"Oh, I think you know what I mean. Do you always get your own way?"

"Pretty much." He laughs and winks. "So you like the car then?"

"Yes, I love the car." I point at the plate. "Scott 85?"

"My date of birth. Do you want to drive it?" he asks, grinning at me.

"Oh, yes!" Then I glance down at the shoes I'm wearing, "Well, maybe not tonight, but another time?"

"Another time, meaning more than one date?"

"That's rich coming from you!"

He doesn't reply, but a slight grin flickers on his face. He puts his hand in the small of my back and slides his fingers under the material, touching my bare skin and sending jolts of electricity through my body like a pinball in a machine. I shiver at his touch.

"Are you cold?" he asks as he guides me towards the car door.

I shake my head at him, and he raises an eyebrow. "You've got goosebumps."

He knows the effect he has on me. He opens the car door, gesturing with his hand.

"Get in."

I slide into the passenger side, enjoying the scent of new leather. The seats are comfortable, the upholstery a soft cream, but it's cold against my back.

He closes the car door and walks around to the driver's side, climbing in and putting the key into the ignition. He turns the key and the engine fires up, then purrs like a panther.

"Belt up, Abigail."

I giggle, wondering if he means that literally. I'm in a bit of a quandary now as I don't know whether to look at the beautiful specimen driving or the car itself. I'm well and truly in a fix.

He drives away from the car park, heading out of the hospital grounds.

"Where are we going?"

"The Drake. I've made a reservation."

"The Drake? I'm not dressed for the Drake."

"I'm a member and, trust me, you're dressed just fine. You look amazing."

I make a non-committal noise and roll my eyes. The bloody Drake. I've heard about it – it's very exclusive.

Gran and Grandad went there a few times but Grandad, being Grandad, would say it was a little pompous for his liking, and how could they justify the prices they charged for a spoonful of veg and a miniscule steak?

Gran would reply, "Oh, you're just tight, George."

He'd shake his head, and continue, "I didn't get where I am today by spending my money on nouvelle cuisine. They must think people are daft – nothing on your plate and paying a fortune for it. What a silly fad! Hell, lass, can you imagine charging those prices in the delis? We'd give our regular old dears heart failure!"

Gran and I would just raise our eyebrows at him as he continued to mutter under his breath about prices and small portions, though he did admit it was a beautiful place. To hear him talk, you'd think he'd not had two pennies to rub together, when in fact, if he'd wanted to, he could have bought the place.

I start fidgeting, working myself up into a right state. Here I am in ripped jeans. Fabulous.

Edward turns into the long gravelled drive that leads to the imposing mansion house. Lights are discreetly set along the edge of the drive but the mansion is lit up with spotlights. I'm starting to feel decidedly inferior, dressed as I am. We pass a sign halfway up the drive: *The Drake. Five-Star Country Club. Members Only.* I seriously doubt they'll let me in dressed like this.

We reach the entrance and Edward brakes, pulling the car to a stop. He removes the keys and starts to get out of the car. A young man approaches, dressed in black trousers, white shirt, maroon jacket and a tie.

"Mr Scott, very nice to see you again," he says politely. "Any bags, sir?"

Edward throws his keys to him as he's walking around to my side of the car to open the door for me. I take off my seatbelt, and he holds out his hand to me. He helps me out of the car and guides me towards the steps at the entrance.

Then he turns to the man. "Paul, don't go too far in it this time. I've a young lady to take home tonight," he says, laughing.

"You're not staying over, Mr Scott?"

Edward doesn't answer him, but gestures me up the steps.

Great, is this where he takes all his dates so they can stay over with him? However, it's clear that I'm not staying over. He's taking me home; he's just said so to Paul. Or was that a ploy? Well, if it was then I'm still not staying over. I start to second-guess myself. What if he doesn't want me to stay over? What if he's having second thoughts? I look at his face but I can't tell anything from his expression.

We enter the huge lobby and my heels sink into the carpet. It's opulent but elegant. A woman behind the reception desk looks up and smiles at Edward.

"Mr Scott, it's very nice to see you again. Are you staying over with us, sir?"

There it is again – staying over!

All of a sudden, I feel cheap as the receptionist stares pointedly at me. My face burns cherry red. Edward takes my hand but I wiggle out of it and he throws me a surprised look. The receptionist waits for Edward to reply but I speak before he can.

"Can you please tell me where the ladies' is?"

She points the way, and Edward frowns at me. I turn away without speaking and start off towards the bathroom. I hear Edward speak.

"I have a dinner reservation."

I feel like a cheap date. I knew this was a bad idea. I walk into the ladies' toilets and find the room surprisingly busy. All the women there are wearing nice dresses. I muster a smile, and they smile back politely, but they look me up and down at the same time, and one raises her eyebrows at me. I hurry into a cubicle, lock the door and shut my eyes.

"Did you see her, Lottie? She was wearing ripped jeans! What on earth is this place coming to, letting in that sort of woman? She's obviously come with a member."

They laugh nastily.

I'm livid. Do I go out and give them a piece of my mind, or do I sit here and wait for them to leave? I choose the latter, not wanting to make a scene.

They finally go, and I step out of the cubicle, feeling self-conscious. I walk to the mirror. My face is red and my eyes look glazed. I wipe them with my finger, then go out onto a long corridor where I see the same two women talking to Edward. One has her hand resting on his arm, and it's apparent from the way she's looking at him that she's flirting with him. That's when I realise that Edward is wearing jeans too, but this doesn't seem to bother them at all. Maybe it's because he's a man, or because he's so good-looking, or, just maybe, money talks. I want to turn back into the ladies' and make a run for it but it's too late. Edward has seen me, and quickly calls me over.

"Abigail, there you are."

The woman with her hand on his arm removes it and digs the other woman in her side. They both look in my direction. I have no choice but to walk over to them.

"Hi, I'm Lottie," she says with a false smile, holding out her hand to shake mine. I look at Edward and he grins at me. "Edward was just telling us about your jeans. I can't believe they're charging nearly two thousand pounds for denim! What make are they?"

I'm confused now, but Edward interrupts before I can answer.

"They're Prada." He winks at me, but she doesn't notice. "Honestly, Lottie, do you know nothing at all about fashion?"

he gently chides. She looks embarrassed, and he just shakes his head in mock disapproval.

The other woman pipes up, "I knew they were Prada! They look expensive."

I think, yeah, really – weren't you the one that was just implying I was cheap? *Ripped jeans! What on earth is this place coming to?*

"No, you didn't, Victoria!" Lottie says, rolling her eyes. "You were the one telling Edward all about the shocking girl in the toilets with the ripped jeans."

Edward laughs in an over-the-top way, and we all look at him with wide eyes. When he speaks, his voice is loud, with a hint of sarcasm.

"Oh, dear. Ladies, you've no idea who this woman is, do you?" He shakes his head and huffs dramatically. "And you call yourself socialites?"

He takes my hand and guides me in the direction of the dining room. I can hear the two women gossiping as we walk away.

"Who is she?"

"Oh, I think I know. Isn't she Prada's latest model? Now I think about it, I'm sure I've seen her as a guest on that show, *Britain's Next Top Model*. She's been on the billboards in Times Square."

"I think you're right! She's shorter than you'd expect for a model, but stunningly beautiful."

Edward sniggers, squeezing my hand.

"Sorry about that but I couldn't resist it. They make me sick. They think they're so much better that everyone else – a lot of the wives here do. They're very shallow."

Adam and his mother Margo would fit in nicely with their crowd, I think to myself.

"That was naughty of you, but funny!" I say, squeezing his hand back. It was nice of him to stick up for me like that.

We enter the dining room and a man greets us formally. "Your usual table, Mr Scott?"

Edward nods. "Thank you, Norman."

He walks us over to the far end of the dining room where there are around ten or twelve private booths.

This must be the members' section, as I can see Lottie and Victoria waving at two men and walking over to one of the booths. I hope they haven't seen us because I don't think I could keep a straight face if Edward started with his stories again.

"Sit, Abigail."

I shuffle myself around to the middle. The table has been set for two. I smile as there's a party going on in one of the booths and it's very noisy.

I look around and grin as I see another couple literally eating each other.

Edward looks in their direction and laughs. "That's members for you!"

He glides around and sits beside me, and I smile at him.

All the booths are full. I spot another couple arguing, and watch them for a moment or two. I can't make out what they're saying because of the noise coming from the party, but I can see their mouths going hell for leather. Edward squeezes my hand as Norman speaks.

"Would you like to see the menu, sir?"

"No. We'll have two of the specials, please."

"Wine?" Norman looks at me.

"Please," I reply, praying he doesn't ask me which one. Edward jumps to my rescue.

"Just bring the wine that suits the specials."

Norman nods and walks off.

I sit back and study Edward. They all know him by name. How often does he come here, and how often with other women?

"I know what you were thinking when we arrived," he says, suddenly, "and I'm sorry about that. Yes, I have stopped here many times, with many women."

Has he just read my thoughts? I don't know why he would bring me to a place where he brings other women. It's embarrassing. The scene in the lobby was humiliating. He's made me feel cheap again.

"I don't want to know," I reply, deflated. "I think we should just eat dinner and leave. I don't want to make a scene, so I'll sit here quietly, if you'll let me."

"Are you ever going to listen to me?" he asks curtly.

"Stop it, please. People are looking."

"Nobody is looking."

"Stop it!"

He's doing it again, overpowering me and forcing me to listen to what he has to say. I can leave if I want to, but do I want to? I go to stand. He grabs my wrist, pulling me back down.

"Sit down!"

My eyes have gone wide.

"No! Let go of my wrist."

"Please, Abigail," he begins, letting me go. "Don't leave. Sit back down and let me explain everything to you. If you don't like what I have to say then I'll take you home, but sit, please."

He does seem to want to explain, but does he really care? I suppose if he didn't then he wouldn't be trying to explain at all. He would've just let me leave. I nod slowly, and sit back down.

"Thank you," he says with a relieved smile. "This might take some time. I'm not used to explaining myself; I've never had to. I'm always the one in charge, calling the shots."

I raise my eyebrows.

"Really? I'd not noticed."

He laughs.

"The first time I met you … remember the car, the lights?"

I nod. "Yes, you were very angry!"

"I was, but then you called me a Richard Cranium and I laughed all the way to work. I couldn't get your face out of my head, and when I walked into the handover and you were sitting there, I couldn't believe my luck. You blushed when you saw me, and it turned me on. I pictured me fucking you over the table, you screaming for me to take you harder and harder."

My eyes nearly pop out of my head as he continues with not a care for who's listening or watching.

"Then, when you fainted, I felt bad. I picked you up from the floor, and, God, you affected me. I wanted you, I wanted to take you there and then. But then you started with your clever talk again, and I couldn't understand what I was feeling. You annoyed me so much, but you also excited me."

I hear somebody cough; I daren't look up to see who it is.

"Sir, would you like to try the wine?"

Oh, dear Lord, how long has Norman been standing there?

Edward's voice is snappy when he replies, and it's obvious he doesn't like being interrupted.

"Just leave it!"

Norman places the bottle on the table and walks off.

My face must be a picture. I grab the bottle and pour myself a glass, drinking it straight down.

Edward looks at me, surprised. "Another one?"

I'm too stunned to answer, so he pours me another glass, and then one for himself. He continues, "I tried to apologise to you. I came to your room, but you were in the shower. I waited a few minutes to speak to you. I'll be honest, I wanted to go into the bathroom to see what you were doing, as you were making some strange noises."

I blush hotly.

"But I didn't. I'm not a pervert!"

My voice is croaky. "I'm glad to hear it."

He laughs, smiling at me. "I tried again to talk to you, but you wouldn't talk to me. Though I didn't like it, I tried to understand. Then you left the ward and went to stay with Alison. Tom told me what had happened at the house with your husband. I wanted to come and talk to you. I felt sorry for you. Then when Tom rang me ..."

He breathes out sharply. "When he thought you'd taken the pills, for the first time in my life I was scared, and I'm never scared.

The thought of you trying to harm yourself was too much for me. Finding you as I did in the shower made me so annoyed with you. I was confused about what I was feeling; I've never felt like this about anyone. Then you told me to leave, and I admit I was cross with you. I thought I knew what you were going through, what had happened in the treatment room. I was so angry with Darcy for hurting you. But then, again, you wouldn't speak to me. The things you said that I overheard?"

I roll my eyes.

"I can't blame you for thinking those things. I've acted like a complete arse towards you. I'm surprised you even agreed to come out with me tonight.

The other things ... me going away – I'm sorry you didn't get my message. When I spoke to Tom on Wednesday he said you seemed upset, but I thought you weren't interested in me because of the text I'd received. Although," he adds, "I must say, it did come as a bit of a shock."

I shake my head. "Stop. Please don't carry on, Edward. It's been a bit of a disaster, hasn't it? For us both. I was upset when you left without a word. I'm sorry, too, for the things I said. I'll be honest though – I did think those things at the time, but I never meant for you to hear them. I was confused, upset, and fighting against my own emotions. I wasn't sure how I felt towards you. I'm going through a lot at the moment, and you've turned my world upside down."

His eyes bore into mine.

"That night you found me in the shower, and then later in my room – I didn't want you to leave, but I couldn't let you stay. It wasn't the right time for me."

"And now?"

I smile.

"I'm not a very nice person at the moment. I say all the wrong things at all the wrong times. I don't mean to, it's not me, I'm just in a tricky place right now."

I feel emotional. I really do like him – a lot – even more so now that he's explained his feelings and apologised.

"So, what do you want to do?"

"I don't know. What do you want to do?"

He doesn't think about his answer; he knows exactly what he wants to do.

"I'd like us to try, Abigail. This is new to me." He laughs, and I give him a puzzled look. "I mean seeing someone more than once!"

Without thinking, I blurt out, "Not a one-night stand then?"

He shakes his head.

"I would never want you to be a one-night stand."

Hmm, that sounds nice. That's different, especially coming from the master of one-night stands. I smile at him.

"Let's start again then, but can we please take it slowly?"

He nods and pecks me on the cheek.

"We'll start again, and if you want to take it slowly then I'll try!" He smiles at me with a devilish grin, and I think to myself that his version of slowly might be a little different to mine. With that in mind, I change the subject quickly.

"Please, call me Abbie."

"Move your arm, Abbie," he says with a laugh. "Your food is here."

I look at the food and burst out laughing. Norman looks shocked.

"Is everything all right, madam?"

Edward starts to laugh too.

"I think I should have asked what the specials were," he comments, amused.

"Hmm … that would have been a good idea."

"Does madam not like mushroom risotto?" Norman asks, perplexed. The poor man, he looks so put out that I feel quite sorry for him. I smile kindly.

"I'm sorry, Norman. It's a long story. Could you please take mine away?"

He nods and removes my dish.

"Mr Scott?"

Edward looks at me.

"You eat yours. I'm fine, honestly."

"No, take mine too, Norman. Can we order steak instead? Is steak okay with you, Abbie?"

"Steak is perfect, thank you."

Norman leaves the booth with our dishes and I giggle.

"I'm sorry, I don't think I could ever eat rice again!"

He stares at me fondly as he moves closer to me, slipping his arm around my waist and pulling me tightly to him.

I stop laughing, and I feel my body flush at his closeness. My pulse elevates as he moves his mouth close to my ear. His voice a seductive whisper.

"You're beautiful when you laugh. Kiss me!"

I crumble. I move closer to him and kiss him on the cheek. His voice is sharp. "Is that it?"

I look around to see if anyone is looking, but they're not. I roll my eyes at him to stop, but he pulls me in tighter still, slipping the palm of his hand through the back of my top and leaving it on the small of my bare back. It sends tingles coursing through my body. My hearts began to race at his touch, and my cheeks burn.

His voice is louder now. "I said kiss me, and I meant it!"

"Edward, we're in public."

He raises his eyebrows at me.

"Stop it. I know what you're doing."

"I said kiss me."

I glance nervously around the room, but still no one is watching. I look back to him, seeing the amusement in his eyes. He has no idea what I want to do to him at this particular moment in time. I don't think I'd be able to stop kissing him once I started.

He raises an eyebrow at me as though to say, *Well? I'm waiting.* He's so cocky, but it's such a turn-on.

I give in; I can't help myself. I move my mouth to his and close my eyes. Our lips touch, and he groans. It sounds primal and sexy.

He forces my lips open with his tongue, and I'm nearly panting as he invades my mouth, searching for my tongue. His fingers move gently across my back, tickling and tantalising me. I wriggle in his arms, and as I do my breasts slightly rub his chest. I hear him moan in response. Our mouths and lips are entwined, moving slowly, each of our tongues gliding over the other's. He starts to suckle my tongue, and my breathing accelerates as I lose myself in his kiss. And, boy, can he kiss! I've never been kissed like this before. He moves his hand slowly around to my waist, groaning seductively. He pulls away from my mouth, leaving me red faced and panting.

He moves to my ear, nipping it with his teeth and whispering against my skin, "The things I want to do to you, Abbie!"

I feel as if I'm going to faint. My face is scarlet, my pulse has just reached maximum overload, and he groans deeply again into my ear.

"You're going to beg me to do them to you!"

A nervous whimper leaves my throat. Oh my God, he's so kinky and blunt. His words make my body tingle all over. I close my eyes. He has to stop before I throw myself on the table and offer myself to him. *Take me, you bad boy!*

A dry cough brings me suddenly out of my erotic trance, and Edward breaks away from me.

"For fuck's sake! Norman, is there something wrong with your throat?"

I'm speechless. Bloody hell, he sounds furious. Either that or he's frustrated. I don't need to ask which, as his face says it all.

I look up and see Norman trying his best to remain calm.

"Your steaks, sir."

Edward glares at him.

Norman remains professional, but I can't help but feel a little sorry for him. He places the plates on the table in front of us – the steaks and a small side salad. Edward frowns at the food.

"No potatoes or vegetables, Norman?"

His reply is polite, with only a hint of sarcasm.

"The dish came with rice, sir, so I took the liberty of removing it before bringing it to your table. I thought that might be preferable for the young lady."

I start to laugh. I think Norman is funny; he reminds me of Hobson from the film *Arthur*. Edward looks at me. Norman looks at me. And I realise with horror that some of the diners are also looking at me. Great, nobody pays the slightest bit of attention to people shouting, or couples making out in the booths, but someone laughs and they all bloody look. I can feel my face going red. I shrug my shoulders and gesture towards Norman.

"He's very funny, you know …" I nod my head slightly manically to hide my embarrassment. "Ask him to tell you a joke!"

I look at Edward but he doesn't seem amused. Neither does Norman, for that matter. Whoops, no sense of humour then! I grin at them both sheepishly.

"The food smells lovely."

I pick up my knife and fork, wondering why I can't just keep my mouth shut. Norman walks away and I wait for

Edward to blow a gasket, but he continues to watch me with a straight face.

"Abbie," he murmurs, shaking his head.

I smile sweetly at him, batting my eyelashes and hoping to calm his temper, despite what I'm about to say.

"I'm sorry, Edward, but you were very rude to him, and he's only doing his job. I think I would've said the same thing in his situation, and I'm damn sure you would have."

He lets out an exasperated huff.

"I'll apologise on the way out if you want me to."

"No," I say, much to his surprise. "I'd only want you to apologise if you meant it, or there's no point."

"Is it any wonder I snapped at him?" he says with a sigh.

"Why? Because he coughed at an inconvenient moment?"

He nearly chokes.

"Are you serious, Abbie?"

I nod, and he tilts his head to one side to observe me. I try my best not to laugh at him, but he's noticed the effort. I'm so busted!

"I think you're playing a dangerous game with me, lady," he says, his voice low and seductive.

I giggle. We both know perfectly well why he snapped at Norman. His eyes are suddenly dark and serious, his come-to-bed look, and it's as hot as hell. I shrug my shoulders at him and try to look innocent.

"I don't know what you mean. Anyway, eat your steak. It's getting cold."

He coughs, and I can't resist the opportunity to tease him.

"Gosh, it seems to be catching!"

He laughs. "You're going to be so sorry, lady, for the things that come out of that mouth of yours."

"Really? What comes out of my mouth? And what about what comes out of your mouth?"

"That's a fair comment. I can't seem to help that though, not since I met you. You bring out my dark side."

"I'm sorry," I say with a nervous smile.

He shakes his head. "Don't be sorry! You're a breath of fresh air." He grins. "You frustrate me, you annoy me, and you bloody irritate me!"

I cough now, and he laughs pointedly at me.

"But you also fascinate me. You intrigue me and entice me."

He falls silent and watches me. My attraction to him is intense, and I enjoy his bluntness, his honesty about what he wants to do, his goddamn ability to make me crumble and melt with just one touch. I don't know how to reply to him, so I lean to the side and knock his shoulder with mine.

"I can't wait to get to know you better, Abbie," he says playfully.

"I can't wait either! This is nice, the two of us laughing, talking, having a nearly normal date. It's new to me too, you know, having a friend."

He raises an eyebrow at me. I feel impossibly shy talking to him like this.

"I mean a friend that's …" I hesitate.

"A friend that's what, Abbie?"

Just say it to him, since you mean it.

"A friend that I like a lot. That I want to spend time with."

"Quite right too!"

I knock his shoulder again, and we both laugh, enjoying the flirtation. It feels wonderful and carefree.

"Come on," he says. "Eat your food. I bet you've not eaten all day."

I realise I haven't. We both eat our steak and salad, and when Norman comes for our plates, asking if we'd like dessert and coffee, Edward apologises to him. Norman looks stunned, and I can't help but smile.

We order cheesecake and two coffees. I don't want to leave now. We talk all though the remainder of our meal and our coffee.

Then Edward gets up.

"Ready, Abbie?"

I nod and stand, and we both start to leave the dining room.

"I won't be a minute." He walks over to a desk and signs a receipt while talking to the concierge.

Norman approaches me and I smile at him.

"I'm sorry about before."

"No need to be sorry, madam. I've known Mr Scott for a long time and I'm used to his ways."

I raise my eyebrows at him, and he smiles at my confusion.

"Although I have to say, I've never known him to apologise before. I think you might be good for him and I think he's sweet on you."

He winks at me before turning away and leaving me to wait for Edward. I see Edward stop Norman as he's walking past. He says something to him, and they shake hands. Edward pats him on the shoulder, and then walks back to me, looking pleased with himself.

"What did Norman say to you?" he asks probingly.

"Nothing much," I reply casually.

His eyebrows raise.

"Well, I think he was just making sure I wasn't upset about the rice, that's all."

He gives me an inquisitive look, then smiles as he puts his arm around me, kissing the top of my head. I lean into his chest, and he pulls me closer to him.

I find myself thinking, *Yes, Norman, I think I'm sweet on him too.*

Chapter 2

We leave the dining room and head down the lush corridor towards the exit. Edward still has his arm around me. We don't speak; we just smile at each other. I wonder what he's thinking. Is it the same as what I'm thinking?

I'm nervous. What if he wants to come back to the flat when he drops me off? I know I'm not ready for that. If he kisses me again the way he did in the dining room, but with no possibility of any interruptions this time, then I know I won't be able to resist him. I'm drawn to him … my spider. I'm already past looking into his parlour, and I'm making my way into his den. But I'm scared he's going to hurt me, take me, devour me, and then wrap me up in a cocoon of heartache and sorrow.

I think of the countless women Edward must have been with, and of everything I've been told about him. Women fall at his feet, and he expects them to. One-night stands, all of them, and if he said jump, I'm sure they asked how high. But I won't jump, and I can't do casual.

The next time, I … well, I want to be sure, and I want it to be special. I've never had special. I've never had love. I think I'd like to date someone, to have a boyfriend and do all the things you're meant to do when you're young and in love. I don't believe that's too much to ask, is it? I like Edward, I like him a lot, but I hardly know him. We need to take it slowly. I can't afford to be wrong, not after Adam. I got that one so wrong. I'm confident that I won't allow myself to make the same mistake twice.

I jump suddenly as Paul calls to us, quickly bringing out of my daydream.

"Your keys, Mr Scott. I've brought your car front, sir."

"Thank you, Paul." Edward looks at me. ' okay? You seem quiet, and a little jumpy."

I nod.

"Are you cold?"

I nod again, not quite trusting myself to speak as I mull over my thoughts.

He takes off his jumper and places it around my shoulders. Then he runs his hand over my back, rubbing it, trying to warm me up. I smile at the thoughtful gesture, but I feel confused, wondering whether I'm over-analysing everything. I look at him, and wish dearly that I could read his mind.

We walk out into the cold night air, and I shiver.

"You are cold. Come on. Let's get you warmed up." He grins, then winks as we get into the car and he puts the heater on. "Better?"

I smile, nodding my head.

He looks quizzical. "Have you lost the ability to talk?"

"No," I reply slightly nervously.

"Good, because I thought I'd upset you in some way."

"No, I'm just tired." I can't tell him what I'm really thinking, so I make up a weak excuse for being so quiet. "All that laughing has made me, well … a little tired, but I've had a lovely night. Thank you!"

"You're very welcome," he says, nodding in response. "It's been lovely."

As we drive back to Alison's flat, Edward talks about his grandfather.

He'd been a heart surgeon, but had since retired. Edward rolls his eyes at me, saying, "Ironic really," but then he grows silent. I put my hand on his knee to comfort him, because I can tell he's worried about him, and that he loves him a great deal – it's evident in his voice. I tell him about my gran, and we both agree that they're a worry, and that they have a lot in common, especially when it comes to being stubborn.

I ask Edward whether it was his grandad who'd got him interested in surgery and becoming a doctor. He nods. I don't push the issue and he changes the subject quickly, asking me about my past. I'm vague, as I always am. I don't really trust people's intentions; I tend to assume the worst although I can tell from his expression that he knows I'm holding back.

I guess it's obvious from my answers, although to my surprise he doesn't pursue it either. I smile at him, grateful for his sensitivity, and he smiles kindly, as if to say, let's give it time. I nod in response.

We enter the hospital grounds and I feel jittery. My thoughts are running away with me again. What if he asks to come in and I can't say no? What if he kisses me? What if he wants coffee? My hands are a little shaky, and my brain can't keep up with my emotions.

Edward pulls the car to a stop outside the flat and removes the key. Oh hell! I think he's expecting coffee. I smile at him, and then panic. Should I have done that? Will he take it as an invitation?

He gets out of the car, walks around it and opens the door for me as I'm taking off my seatbelt. He holds out his hand for me to take and as they meet, I instantly feel a familiar rush.

Oh Lord, he can't come in, though I'm crumbling from just one touch of his hand. I know I'll struggle to say no to him; I don't think I'm capable. My body overrules my brain every time he touches me.

"I'll walk you to your door."

He smiles. If he's experiencing any of the same emotions as me then they're not showing on his face or in his voice. I nod as casually as I can, trying to enter the key code with my shaking hand. The door opens and he follows me in. The corridor stretches on endlessly, and my nerves are out of control by the time we reach the door to the flat.

Edward leans against the wall, and I watch him mutely. "Your keys, Abbie?"

"Umm, yes," I reply timidly as I reach into my bag. I pull them out and drop them on the floor because my hands are still shaking. He notices and bends to pick up the keys.

"Abbie, are you scared of me?" he asks gently.

"Yes!" I blurt out without thinking. He steps back, shocked by my admission. "I mean, no. I'm scared of myself!"

He nods, slowly passing me the keys.

"Open the door. Let me see you inside and then I'll leave."

I've upset him now; I knew I would.

He walks me into the empty flat. Then he switches the light on and studies my face. He can tell I'm nervous and scared. He takes me in his arms and I close my eyes. I'm trembling.

"Hey, you said you wanted to take things slowly, and I respect that. I'm not going to bite you. Is this why you've been quiet?"

I smile, starting to relax.

"I'm sorry, Edward, it's just—"

He doesn't let me finish, but places a finger tenderly to my lips.

"It's okay, I understand. But can I at least take your number, please?"

"Yes. Sorry."

We exchange numbers, and he kisses me on the lips. It's gentle, caring and respectful, not lustful or passionate.

"I'll see you at work tomorrow," he says, tracing a finger gently down the side of my cheek.

I nod and my heart feels full of joy.

He moves towards the door.

"Edward ..."

He turns, smiling at me as I remove his jumper from my shoulders.

"You keep it," he says kindly before walking out through the door. "Goodnight, Abbie," he whispers, and closes it softly behind him.

"Night," I reply to the closed door. I lean against it and hold his jumper close to me. It feels soft as I brush it against my cheek, and I can smell his clean, fresh scent on it. I rub my lips together, still feeling the pressure of his mouth on mine, that gentle, lingering kiss. I'm falling for him fast, and with no parachute or safety net.

I walk into my room with the most ridiculous smile on my face and start to get undressed, hanging Alison's clothes up, then put on my pyjamas, making my way to the bathroom, washing the makeup from my face, then clean my teeth, use the loo and wash my hands.

I hear my phone beep as I go into my bedroom. I scoop it up along with Edward's jumper and climb into bed. I hug the cashmere and smile as I eagerly swipe the screen. It's 11.15 p.m.: *Goodnight, and sweet dreams.*

I reply a minute later. *Goodnight, and thank you for a wonderful night. Sweet dreams! xx*

I close my eyes, wearing the biggest smile on my face that I've had for years. I think about Edward; I can still feel his kiss as I run my tongue over my lips. I keep his jumper close and drift off to sleep.

I wake early the following morning. It's still dark outside. I have the same silly grin on my face that I went to bed with. I stretch out my arms and legs as I look at the clock; it's only 5.30 a.m. I decide to get up anyway as I don't feel tired. I shower and then eat my breakfast – porridge with honey – at the table.

I can't stop smiling to myself as I think about last night. I finish my porridge, wash the dish and tidy up. Then I go and sit back at the table, waiting for the time to pass. My bag's packed, ready for work. A bleep sounds from within it. I take out my phone and smile as I see Edward's name. I swipe the screen.

6.35 a.m. *Good morning, Abbie. I hope you slept well!*

Reply: 6.36 a.m. *Good morning, Edward. Yes, I did sleep well ... thank you. Curled up with your jumper! xxx*

Edward: 6.37 a.m. *I'm glad you did. Did you dream of me? I dreamt of you, but I can't say what it was about. Well, not in a text.*

I laugh, as I reply at 6.38 a.m. *I can imagine, Edward! You're very naughty. You do know that, don't you? You're far too suggestive for 6.38 a.m. xxx.*

Edward: 6.39 a.m. *That I am, but I can't get you out of my head. Can we do lunch today?*

Reply: 6.40 a.m. *That would be lovely, but I'm working until 2.30 p.m. if that's okay? xxxx.*

Edward: 6.41 a.m. *I'll sort it. See you at some point today on the ward. I'll have to go now. I'm just setting off for work.*

Reply: 6.42 a.m. *Drive carefully, and don't skip any red lights. xxx.*

Edward: 6.43 a.m. *Excuse me! I rather think it was you who skipped the red lights, dear. But I'm sure I'll be quite safe on the roads this morning, knowing that you're walking to work and not DRIVING!*

I laugh.

Reply: 6.45 a.m. *Touchy ... See you at work. xxx.*

I'm still laughing as I return my phone to my bag, then go off to make myself another coffee. I feel so happy – texting Edward has been the perfect start to the day, although I know it's going to feel strange when I see him on the ward later and he takes me out for lunch. We're getting to know each other. I grin happily. Hmm ... I could get used to this.

I think about how my first impressions of him were so wrong. This is the second time I've done this in a week, but I'm glad that Edward has proved me wrong. He's turning out to be full of surprises. Edward Scott, you're an enigma! A wonderful one, nevertheless, and one I can't wait to find out more about.

I leave the flat and walk to the ward, smiling to myself all the way. I arrive early and sit in the staff room. I take my phone from my bag and text Edward at 7.10 a.m.

Hi. Have you arrived safely? I'm sitting in the staff room, thinking of you! xxx.

Edward, 7.11 a.m. *I'm getting changed into my scrubs. I've an early start today because I've a hot date at lunchtime and I think she'll get very cross with me if I'm late!*

It's 7.13 a.m. and I'm beaming from ear to ear as I reply, *Oh dear ... I'd better let you go then. I don't want to get you into trouble. A hot date at lunchtime, you say? Where're you taking your hot date and what time? I'll have to look out for her. xxxx.*

Edward: 7.15 a.m. *About 3 p.m. I'm picking her up from her place.*

Reply: 7.16 a.m. *Does she know this? xxx.*

Edward: 7.17 a.m. *Not sure. If you see her, can you tell her?*

Reply: 7.18 a.m. *Sure. What does she look like? xxx.*

Edward: 7.19 a.m. *Sorry, I can't think about that right now. She's far too hot! I need to compose myself for surgery.*

I giggle, blushing.

Reply: 7.21 a.m. *I'll tell her. 3 p.m. on the dot. I know you don't like to be kept waiting. Have a good day. I have to go into handover now. xxx.*

I make my way into the handover. Sister's already in and talking to the night nurse. I spot Alison, head over to her and sit at her side. She's grinning.

"Nice time, last night?"

"Umm, yes, thank you! And you?"

She raises her eyebrows at me, as though to say, *I asked first.*

"Did he stay over?"

"No!"

"I'm kidding!" she says with a laugh.

We have the handover from the night nurse, and I wonder if Sister is going to mention anything about what happened yesterday. I'll be working with her again today, as Darcy doesn't appear to be in, which I'm glad about. I certainly don't want another scene like that at work.

That was unprofessional of her, and truly uncalled for. I'd understand if Edward was her boyfriend, or if they had a history together, but they don't.

What she did, stealing my mail, was completely out of order. I huff under my breath. That's something I'll rectify, but not here, not on the ward. I'll sort her in my own good time.

I get up to leave with Alison, but Emily stops me and asks if she can have a word. Sister nods her head at me, as if it's already been discussed by them both beforehand. Alison leaves the room with the other staff as Sister chaperones them out.

I'm alone with Emily and I watch her in silence, waiting for her to speak. She looks uneasy. The atmosphere is tense, and when she speaks she sounds weary.

"Abigail, I want to apologise to you for everything that's happened."

I raise an eyebrow at her.

"I know I've behaved badly towards you, and I'm sorry. I took the message from Mr Scott on Thursday, and, yes, I should have passed it on to you."

I'm livid with her, she must be able to see that, unless she's blind. "Darcy saw the message, and that it had Mr Scott's number on it. She snatched it out of my hands and said she'd pass it on to you." She's practically squirming as she tries to worm her way out of it. I knew that something had happened yesterday while Alison and I were still in the canteen. I don't know what Edward said, as he won't tell me, but I'm starting to get an inkling. It must have been bad if she feels the need to apologise.

I put my hand up to stop her from continuing.

"I'll stop you right there, Emily. Darcy might not have taken the message – you said yourself that it was you. She never passed the message on to me, but I think you know that too, don't you?"

She doesn't say anything, so I continue.

"You had the chance to come and tell me about the message, but you didn't. I also overheard you and Darcy in the staff room on Wednesday."

Her face drops.

"And by the look on your face, I don't need to remind you what was said."

She looks worried now, and so she should be.

"You were happy enough to spread her lies at the nurses' station, backing up her story about Mr Scott being on the ward on Monday and Tuesday, when you knew damn well he wasn't." I shake my head at her, and she stares mutely at me. "I don't know how, or why, you think you can treat people this way. You're obviously not a very nice person, and I won't accept your apology.

Yes, I think that Darcy coerced you into doing those things, but you're a grown woman in a responsible, caring profession. You can make your own decisions, but you chose to make bad ones."

I don't know how I'm keeping my cool, but eventually she speaks.

"You're right, but I just want you to know that I really am sorry, Abbie."

"Then I think you need to choose your friends a little more carefully in future, Emily. You've behaved so spitefully – presumably out of jealousy, I don't know. But from now on, unless its work related, I'd appreciate it if you didn't talk to me."

I leave the room, breathing out long and hard, somehow keeping my temper. I know why she's apologising: because she's been caught out. She may not have done the damage, but she certainly didn't try to stop it either.

I go to find Sister.

"All cleared up, Abigail?"

I smile back at her. *Are you kidding? I've not even begun yet.*

I'm given my tasks for the day, and to my surprise I find that I enjoy working with Sister. She's strict but very good at teaching.

Lunchtime arrives and I meet Alison. We each get a sandwich and a drink, and sit by the window in the canteen. It seems very quiet today.

"Have you seen the staff rota?" Alison asks keenly. I shake my head. "Darcy's not in for the rest of this week. Her shifts have been blanked out."

"Really?" I reply, unconcerned. "To be honest, I'm not interested in her or what she's doing."

"I know, I just thought you might want to know."

"Thank you."

"Anyway, Tom said Variety are on again at the club on Saturday, and asked me to see if you and Edward would like to make a foursome."

"I'd love to, but I don't think Edward will go. I've been told he doesn't go to the functions at the hospital, but I'll ask him anyway."

"Yes, do. It will be really good fun."

"I will," I say, nodding. "Come on. Let's get back."

"How you finding working with Sister?" Alison asks as we head back to the ward.

"Pretty good. Surprisingly, I quite like her, although she's strict and doesn't give much leeway. But it's good."

When we reach the ward, we put our things away and I go to find Sister. She's at the nurses' station, taking a call, so I stand to the side and wait for her to finish. She turns and sees me as she's replacing the receiver.

"Ah, good, you're back. We've a patient to receive from theatre." She comes round from the station. "Come on. Let's go and get them."

I smile inwardly, thinking I might get to see Edward. He's been so busy in theatre that I've not yet seen him on the ward today. I've already seen how many patients have returned from surgery to the ward, and I wonder if that's what he meant when he said he'd "sort it". I smile as I follow Sister down the corridor, out of the ward, and into the lift to the top floor.

We enter through a door hung with a sign.

STRICTLY NO ADMITTANCE UNLESS AUTHORISED.

I smile again. I'm entering Edward's domain. I suddenly feel anxious and I'm not sure whether it's because I might see him, or because I'm coming to understand the importance of his job.

We wait in an authorised area. Sister explains about the red line on the floor – that only the theatre staff who're dressed in scrubs are permitted to pass it. I'm both curious and anxious to see what's beyond that red line. I look down a bright corridor; there are several sets of double doors on each side and each have a light on over them.

"They're the operating theatres," Sister explains. "When the red light's on, no one's allowed to leave or enter through those doors, as the patient is still inside on the table. When surgery is finished and the surgeon is happy with the patient, they then come from theatre to the recovery room to be monitored, before being discharged back to the ward. That's where we take over. Have you ever been to theatre, or had an operation, Abigail?"

I nod silently, hoping she'll not ask why. I don't remember any of this, even though it was in this hospital. She's about to enquire when, thank goodness, the red light goes off in theatre two.

"Look," she says, breaking my train of thought. "They'll be bringing a patient out very soon."

I watch for the doors to open. When they do, a trolley is pushed out by a member of staff. It's a little boy with a blanket over him. An oxygen mask covers his mouth, but you can still hear the whimpering noise he's making.

"Aww … bless him, little love," I say aloud. He's so tiny – he can't be more than three years old – and looks so lost on the huge trolley. I want to go over to him and cuddle him. I watch as he's pushed down the corridor and out of sight.

I turn back to Sister, and find Edward looking at me. I smile at him, admiring his appearance. He's in pale-green scrubs, and a little of his chest is exposed by the V-neck of his top. His skin is olive toned, and he looks very much the hot-to-die-for surgeon, which of course he is. He's *my* hot-to-die-for surgeon. He looks amused as I gape at him. Wow, I think. And he must know what's going on in my head as my face is as red as can be.

"Tonsillectomy, Nurse Baxter," he says calmly.

I pull a sad face. "Will he be in pain?"

He smiles at my concern. "For a few days, but if they keep on top of the painkillers, he'll be okay. And I'm sure his mummy and daddy will spoil him."

"I'd spoil him if I was his mummy."

Sister looks at me pointedly, reminding me that we have a job to do.

I nod ruefully. "Oh, but he's so tiny."

"Yes, he is," she agrees with a smile. "Mr Scott, please excuse us. Our patient is here."

He lets us go, and I smile at him as I follow Sister towards our patient. I turn to look back at him and he winks at me. Sister has her back to him, and doesn't see. My heart jumps and I want to run over and hug him, but I can't. He turns with a grin and disappears into the changing rooms.

My shift is over, and Sister says I can go. We say goodbye, and I grab my bag from the staff room and leave the ward.

I run back to the flat, strip off quickly and jump into the shower. Then I dress in my jeans, a jumper and my Converse pumps, apply some makeup, spray on some perfume, and I'm done with five minutes to spare. My God, I've never gotten ready so quickly before! I giggle out loud as I check my appearance in the mirror. "Speed dressing!"

There's a knock at the door, and I rush to open it.

"You're a little over-dressed for lunch, Edward! Or am I under-dressed?" I say, grinning at him. He gives me a wry look. I know perfectly well that he's just come from work, and is still dressed in his navy pinstriped suit and white fitted shirt. He starts to remove his blue tie.

"You don't like me in a suit?" he asks with a smirk. "Or do you prefer me in scrubs?"

"I didn't say that. You look very …" I blush. I'd been going to say hot or sexy. "Nice," I finish quickly.

"You're blushing, Abbie. Are you sure I only look nice?"

"Stop it!"

"Well, you look …" – he pauses suggestively – "very nice too. Hungry?"

"Yes, I'm starving."

"Good, because I'm ravenous!" He grins. "May I have a kiss?"

"Of course you can," I giggle. "As long as you don't want to eat me as well!"

"Now, that's a thought …" His voice is suddenly low and velvety. I look at him, confused. "I'd love to eat you, but a kiss will do for now."

"Have I missed a joke somewhere?" I ask.

He laughs aloud, and I feel stupid.

"Tell me!"

"Never mind, Abbie."

"No, tell me why you're laughing at me."

"It means to go down on you."

My face burns bright red, and I suddenly feel incredibly uncomfortable. He raises his eyebrows and laughs, his voice teasing. "Don't tell me you've never heard it called that before. Or never done it."

I stare at him, my cheeks flaming. I shake my head. He looks shocked by my response.

"Can you stop, please?" I don't want that image of Adam in my head, or the things he did to me. Edward walks over to me and puts his hand to the side of my face. I close my eyes.

"You're kidding, right? I'm just embarrassing you, aren't I?"

I shake my head.

"The answer is no … to both your questions." I hold my head down, embarrassed, and he lifts my chin and looks into my eyes.

Softly, he says, "Abbie … what happened to you? Tell me."

But I can't, not yet anyway. I don't think I'm strong enough to bear my soul.

"Can we please change the subject?"

"Of course. I'm sorry – I've upset you?"

"No, it's not you," I say, shaking my head.

He pulls me into his arms, kisses my forehead and breathes deeply. I know he wants me to tell him, but I can't. He studies my face.

"Are you okay?"

I hug him to me tightly. This is what I need – a hug and some tenderness. I smile.

"Are you sure you want to go for lunch?" he asks gently.

"Yes, let's go."

I need to stop thinking about Adam or I'm going to be miserable for the rest of my life. I smile at Edward, putting my ex as far to the back of my mind as I can, for now at least.

I want to enjoy myself today, so I fix a smile on my face. And this time it isn't a fake smile. It's real, just like the feelings I'm developing for Edward.

Chapter 3

We walk out into the car park and I notice the BMW. I smile, asking, "Not the Aston Martin?"

His grin is wide. "No, I use the BMW for work."

I raise my eyes. "Really? You have that much choice?"

"Yes." He smiles as he opens the door for me. I sit, waiting for him to get in and start the engine. We leave the car park.

"So, how many cars do you have?" I ask him, puzzled.

"Four. This one, the Aston, a classic, and a Range Rover."

"A classic?" I'm intrigued. "Which one?"

"E-type Jag."

"Really? Wow!"

"You like cars?" he enquires.

I shrug my shoulders.

"I don't know enough about them, but my grandad liked cars, Aston Martins and classic Jaguars. My gran would always say, 'Boys and their toys.'"

He laughs, and asks, "Have you managed to get your car started yet?"

"No," I say with a frown.

"Do you want me to sort it out for you? Although, frankly, I think it might be better going to the scrapyard."

"Hey, mine will be a classic soon! Although I have threatened it with the scrapyard quite a few times." I roll my eyes. "It never starts when I need it to."

"I'll sort it for you," he says with a wink.

"Thanks," I say, winking back at him.

We continue chatting as we drive. Edward tells me that his grandad is being discharged this week and going to stay with his mother. I'm pleased that he's well enough to leave. In fact, I'm so busy thinking what a relief it will be for Edward that I don't take much notice of where we're going. It's only when he indicates and turns into a small car park that I suddenly realise where we are. My eyes widen in shock.

No way – of all the places to come! I cringe as I read the sign. *Cob Wood Deli*, and in small writing underneath, *Part of the Baxter chain.* I hope he hasn't noticed.

I don't think anyone who works here now knows me, apart from Mrs Bracewell, but she retired a while back. I've been with my gran a few times to take care of some admin, but that was over a year ago. It's rather old-fashioned, though pretty inside, not contemporary like the town delis.

"Have you been here before?" I ask timidly.

"No, I spotted it on the way back on Wednesday morning. I thought the village looked quaint."

I smile at him.

"What?"

"Nothing. I'd just never have taken you for quaint."

"Really? Why not?"

"You strike me as more of a wine bar type of person. You know, the Drake or someplace like that?"

"Well, isn't this a good way to start then?"

"What do you mean?" I ask. "A good way to start what?"

"To get to know each other?"

I glance out of the car window at the deli. At this rate, he'll be getting to know me sooner than he thinks.

"Is that what we are doing? Getting to know each other?"

"Absolutely!" he says confidently. "Now, are you getting out of the car, or what?"

I giggle, uneasily.

"I thought lunch, then a walk."

Brilliant, I can give him a guided tour, since I know the village like the back of my hand. I grew up here and my gran still lives here.

He climbs out, walks round to the passenger door, and opens it for me. "Well, are you getting out?"

"Yes, sorry."

He puts his arm around me as I clamber out. As we walk through the car park towards the entrance, he looks at me.

"Are you feeling okay now?"

"Yes, thanks."

We walk in through the door to the aromas of fresh coffee and baked bread. I inhale deeply and smile. These smells always make me feel happy and safe. They remind me of the many times I spent here as a child with Gran and Grandad. This was the first deli they bought. Gran had fallen in love with its thatched roof, and the pretty picket-fenced garden at the front. Grandad bought it for her as a birthday present. She never changed the interior.

"It wouldn't be fitting for the village," she said, and of course Grandad agreed with her, as he always did.

It's still very quaint inside, with red-and-white checked tablecloths, mix-and-match chairs, and comfortable antique leather armchairs and sofas. Small posies of flowers are scattered around. Teapots and other knick-knacks sit on the shelves. It's become very trendy over the past few years, attracting not only regulars from the village but tourists as well, especially in the summer months when the gardens are open. I love this place.

"Do you like it here?" he asks, smiling.

I nod silently, feeling a little guilty that I'm not being honest with him. When the time is right, I'll explain, and I'm sure he'll understand.

A young waitress approaches us, blushing furiously.

"Table for two, sir?"

"Yes, please," Edward replies as I quickly scan the room.

I don't recognise anyone, so I think I'm okay. We're shown to our table by the young girl, who smiles prettily at Edward. Then much to my annoyance, wiggles her arse as she totters along.

"Menu, sir?"

Am I invisible? She smiles at Edward again, and I roll my eyes when he smirks at me. That's when I hear it, a loud voice, all excited. I close my eyes. Please, no!

"Good gracious me! What are you doing here, Abigail?" It's Mrs Bracewell. "I didn't know you were coming today; I've not seen you for months!"

Edward looks quizzically at me.

"Katie, I'll serve Abigail and ..." – she casts a questioning look at Edward – "and her friend. You run along."

"Mrs Bracewell," I say with a bright smile. "Hi! I thought you'd retired." I cringe as Edward coughs politely. "Sorry, Mrs Bracewell, this is Edward Scott, a friend of mine."

He holds out his hand to her and offers a charming smile.

"Pleased to meet you," she simpers as she shakes his hand.

"How do you know Abigail?" he asks her.

I make a stupid noise in my throat. Of all the people to ask! She loves my gran to bits, and is so proud of her. They're really good friends.

"Oh, I'm sure you haven't got time to waste chatting with us," I say quickly, gesturing around the deli. "You look very busy."

Edward realises I'm hiding something, and doesn't let it drop.

"Nonsense, Abbie," he says smoothly, pulling a chair out for Mrs Bracewell. "Please, Mrs Bracewell, take a seat and have a coffee with us." He gestures with his hand for her to sit. He smiles triumphantly, raising an eyebrow at me. The swine! She doesn't refuse, of course.

"Umm, I think ..." She pauses, then takes a seat. "I think I will, thank you. Three coffees," she calls to Wiggly Arse, who smiles back gleefully at Edward.

"Of course, Mrs Bracewell!" And off she jiggles.

Three cups arrive at the table within minutes. I cringe inwardly. Great, he's going to know my life history by the end of the first coffee. Well, I suppose he'd have found out eventually, but I'd hoped it would be later rather than sooner.

No chance of that, though, not with Mrs Bracewell telling a story. I've no choice but to sit there and listen as she begins.

"I've known Abigail since she was little, when she moved here to the village to live with her gran and grandad. She was only four ..." She pats my hand. "Those were sad times, dear." I nod reluctantly.

Edward takes my hand, smiling sympathetically at me, although he doesn't know the full story, or what the sad times were. He will soon enough though, the way Mrs Bracewell is talking. She's always loved the limelight.

"I've worked for Abigail's grandparents ever since, although they only had this place then, and not the Baxter chain."

Edward's eyes, full of intrigue, flick to mine. I bite my bottom lip, looking embarrassed.

"The chain ...?" he remarks sceptically, still looking at me, but now with wide eyes. "Really, Mrs Bracewell." He squeezes my hand, his voice now teasing. "My, my ... the things you learn about people when you're not expecting to!"

I move my hand and start fidgeting with my fingers, internally screaming, *Cheers, Mrs Bracewell.* She's falling for his charm, and I know she'll tell him everything he wants to know. He smirks at me, enjoying watching me squirm.

"And Mr Scott ..."

I roll my eyes. What's she going to say now?

He moves closer to her, as if he's fascinated by her. Oh, he's turning up the charm.

"Please, Mrs Bracewell, call me Edward."

I'm going to kill him. She's smiling at him like a schoolgirl with a crush. Oh Lord, she's hooked! Her voice grows soft and breathy.

"And, please, call me—"

"Mrs Bracewell, there's a telephone call for you. It's Mrs Baxter," says a member of staff interrupting her.

Holy shit, this just gets better and better. I put my hands to my face, shaking my head. Fantastic. She's going to tell my gran that I'm here, and with Edward.

"Oh, it's your grandmother, Abigail. Excuse me. I'll get your specials and have another drink brought over for you both."

I give up. I put my elbows on the table and my head in my hands. Edward laughs, seeing the confusion and dread on my face.

"Hey, it can't be that bad, can it? Me finding out a little bit about you?"

I sigh heavily.

"I'm sorry for not telling you. You know, about this." I sweep my eyes around the room. "Are you cross with me?"

"No, why would I be cross with you for not wanting me to know that you come from money? It doesn't change things in the slightest, especially how I feel about you."

I'm taken aback by this. Wow, he feels for me!

"You've never asked me about money, have you?"

I shake my head.

"Well, let's just forget it then, shall we? Although I'm still puzzled as to why you drive around in that old shed you call a car."

"I'll explain that to you, but not here, not now. Let's have our lunch and then go for that walk, eh?"

Katie returns, fluttering her eyelashes at Edward. He smirks at me, aware that I'm annoyed by her flirting.

"Thank you. You can leave the coffees, Katie. That is your name, isn't it?" I add sarcastically.

Edward sniggers, so I kick him gently under the table.

"Ouch!" he replies loudly. "That hurt." I stick my nose up at him, and Katie blushes and walks away. "Are you a little jealous, Abbie?"

"Not in the slightest. What on earth gave you that impression?"

"Oh, nothing …" He leans down, pretending to rub his leg and making a sad face at me. "Apart from the bruise forming on my tibia."

I'd laugh if I was certain that he meant his shin.

"There, there. Would you like me to kiss your tibia better for you?"

He sits back up quickly, grinning at me.

"Umm … yes, please!"

"Well, tough! You shouldn't flirt, and you're lucky it wasn't something else I kicked."

"Oh, Abbie, you are jealous! I can't help the way I look. It's not my fault if women find me irresistible."

I shake my head at him, laughing and rolling my eyes.

"You don't think I'm irresistible?" he asks with a smirk.

"Our food is here," I say, ignoring his comment.

Katie places the plates on the table, still disregarding me and practically slavering over Edward.

"Two specials, sir," she says with a beaming smile. She's really starting to get on my nerves. Is this what I have to put up with – women swooning and flirting in front of me? Edward nods his head confidentially at me.

"Confirmed, wouldn't you say?"

I glare at him and he grins and winks. The swine.

"Anything else, sir?" Katie asks, blushing. God, anymore forward and she'll be asking him for his number right in front of me.

"No, thank you," Edward remarks authoritatively. "I have everything I want right here. Do you want anything else, Abbie?"

I shake my head and smile. I get the message, and I know Miss Wiggly Arse Beamer has finally got it too, because the grin disappears from her face and she turns and walks away, defeated.

"Eat up, Abbie. It smells delicious."

"Yes, it's my favourite. Mrs Bracewell's asparagus and chicken pasta never fails."

"I'll have to remember that."

I pick up my fork and my mobile starts to ring. I don't get it out as I know who it is.

Edward glances at my bag. "Are you not going to answer that?"

"Oh, yes," I say reluctantly, trying to pretend I'd not heard it. I bend down and retrieve the phone. I see Gran's name on the screen as I swipe and press to answer.

"Hi," I say, blushing nervously.

"Abbie, are you at the deli in the village?"

"Yes." Oh, bugger.

"And with a friend?"

"Yes." Double bugger! My voice is a squeak, and I know what's coming next.

"Are you calling at the house?" Gran asks quizzically.

I knew it.

"Oh, um … yes."

"Good. I'll see you soon. Bye then, Abigail."

"Bye, Gran."

I'm going to kill that Mrs Bracewell. I'm so going to get the third degree from Gran about Edward. I've been totally taken off guard. I wanted her to meet him, but not yet. Bloody hell!

Edward raises his eyebrows at me.

"That was a lot of yeses!" he remarks.

"Hmm, yes, I suppose it was. That was my gran."

"I somehow gathered that."

He laughs as I look over at Mrs Bracewell. She smiles sheepishly at me, shrugging her shoulders in sympathy, as if to say, *it wasn't my fault*. I bet she couldn't wait to spill the beans. Nothing is secret – that's village life for you. Everyone knows everyone else's business.

Edward carries on pretending he hadn't heard the conversation.

"What did she want?"

"For us to call in on her."

"I take it we're going to visit then."

"Are you okay with that? Although, be warned, she'll give us both the third degree."

"I'm sure we'll be fine."

"I wouldn't count on that," I say dubiously. "You've not met my gran!"

"Are you not eating your lunch? I thought it was your favourite."

"It was."

"Are you nervous about me meeting your gran?"

I nod my head furiously, and he smiles.

"God, yes, of course I am!"

"I'll be on my best behaviour." He winks. "I promise."

"You'd better be," I mutter.

"Shall we go then?" I nod my head. "Do we need to take the car?"

"No, it's not far."

Edward walks to the counter and takes out his wallet, but Mrs Bracewell refuses him.

"Oh, no. Abigail's grandmother would never forgive me if I let you pay."

He smiles at her.

"Thank you, Mrs Bracewell."

She smiles at us both as she comes out from behind the counter.

"Please don't leave it so long again to visit," she says. Then she hugs me and whispers in my ear, "He seems very nice, and he's obviously smitten with you. I'm glad you're not with *him* anymore." She squeezes me, and then winks. I have to smile.

"I won't, Mrs Bracewell, and thank you."

We leave, and I sigh with relief. Well, it's my gran next. Edward takes my hand.

"It'll be okay! We can say we're just friends, if you'd prefer?"

"I thought we were friends."

"Well, everybody presumes we're more than friends!"

"That's the dating thing."

"The dating thing – what do you mean?"

"Nothing." I can't seem to keep my foot out of my mouth.

"Tell me. I'm intrigued to know."

Oh, why can't I just keep my big mouth shut?

"Are you sure?"

He nods.

"Well, rumour has it that you're a one-night stand type of guy, with a reputation to match," I say, pulling a face at him.

"Really? Says who?"

"Rumours, like I said."

"Well, maybe I've just not found anyone I fancy enough to take on a second date before."

I smile, because I'm a second date.

"What are you smiling at?"

"Nothing."

He squeezes my hand, understanding.

"Yes, the one-night stand thing, it's true. I'm busy, very busy, and my reputation …" he rolls his eyes before continuing with a grin. "Let's just say I work hard and play hard."

"Play hard?"

"I don't think I need to explain that, do I?" he says.

"No, I think I understand what you mean." I recall what I overheard Tom saying to Alison about him.

"So, the one-night stand thing – I'm a little puzzled."

"You are? Why?"

"Well, I'm a second date."

"That you are, and if you play your cards right, you might even get a third."

"Shut up!" I laugh, knocking his shoulder with mine. "Anyway, I might not want a third date Mr I'm Very Sure of Myself One-Night Stand Play Hard Bad Reputation.' Had you thought of that?"

"Be quiet! of course you do!"

I burst out laughing at his confidence, and think for a moment of how nice it is to banter with him like this.

"I wanted to ask you …" I hesitate. "I'm going to see Variety at the club on Saturday with Alison and Tom.

Do you want to come too? I know you don't do the dating thing at the hospital."

"My, my, someone has been feeding you, haven't they?" He sounds shocked.

"Well, yes, sort of, I suppose."

"I keep work and pleasure very separate," he explains.

"Is that why you don't date anyone from the hospital?" He shakes his head at me.

"They have been busy, the gossipmongers! But, yes, it's true."

"But I work at the hospital," I say, baffled.

"Really? You do?" he says sarcastically. "Which ward?"

"You're laughing at me again. Do I amuse you in some way?"

"Very much so."

I roll my eyes at him, shaking my head.

"I just can't seem to leave you alone, Abbie. You make me laugh, and the more I see you, the more I want you. I'm not sure what you're doing to me."

"Taming the tiger?" I growl.

He nods yes, but replies, "Maybe, just maybe, you are."

"So, the club on Saturday. It's fine. I know your position is very important at the hospital, and I fully understand why you don't mix work and pleasure." I pull a face as I speak.

"Are they giving you a hard time?"

"I'm okay. I'm tougher than I look."

"You go with Alison and Tom. Anyway, I was going to see my grandad on Saturday, and, what with me being away, I've a lot of work to catch up on."

"If you change your mind, I'd be more than pleased." I smile sweetly at him.

"Now stop it – don't tempt me!"

Wow, I can tempt him! I thought it was the other way round.

We stop and he kisses me on the forehead. I do like him. Then we continue walking.

"We're here, Edward. My gran's is just at the top of the lane."

I've butterflies in my stomach. He puts his arm around me, pulling me in close to him. I've got my fingers crossed that she'll like him, though why wouldn't she? He's charming, gorgeous, funny and intelligent. He makes me smile, and I've not laughed so much for years.

"What are you thinking?" he asks softly. "Are you okay?"

I nod a yes.

"I know things are going on in your life and you're not ready to say yet what they are, but I'm here for you, and I meant what I said. I wish you'd trust me."

I smile, nodding my head, knowing that he means what he says. I think I can trust him.

"I'm just coming to terms with things myself." I raise myself up on my tiptoes and kiss him on the mouth gently. "But thanks, and I do trust you. It's just going to take me a little time, that's all."

He kisses me back tenderly.

"Come on then. Let's go and meet your gran."

Chapter 4

We hold hands as we walk up the tree-lined lane, passing cottages and large brick houses. As we get closer, my tummy starts to turn over with nerves. The manor house stands grandly at the top of the lane, enclosed in an original walled garden. A huge pair of wrought-iron gates open onto an equally impressive laburnum-lined drive that sweeps around the garden and up to the front door. I smile, thinking that the house and gardens should be part of an historic tour. I can almost hear Alison's voice: *This is the manor house to your left.*

Edward looks impressed.

"What a beautiful building! It's architecture at its best, and the walled garden – stunning." He points to the walls. "See those?" He gestures to the top of the wall. I look up and he's pointing to the small stacks that pop up every so often along the top. "They're chimneys," he says, and I smile and nod. "Oh, you know that, do you?"

"Yes."

"And do you know what they were used for?"

I laugh, feeling like I'm on a school outing.

"They're to release the smoke."

He smiles at me as I continue.

"On the other side of the wall there are hollow cut-outs in the bricks. Fires would be lit in those hollows to warm the walls and release heat into the gardens, enabling the owners to grow fruit trees or flowers that wouldn't normally survive in our climate."

I smile inwardly, remembering Grandad explaining it to me when I was a little girl.

"Top of the class, Miss Baxter." He grins, giving me a nod of approval.

"Why, thank you, sir," I reply with a slight nod back at him.

"And how do you know all this?"

I squeeze his hand, knowing it's not far now at all, and since were not driving there's no point in pressing the buzzer to the electric gates on the main drive. We walk past the manor house. I hold Edward's hand, feeling nervy. It's just a little way around the corner and through the lodge-house gardens. I look up at him and wonder what his reaction will be.

"Come on," I say with a smile. "It's not far."

We stop at the old stone lodge at the side of the manor house. I giggle, pointing at the lodge, knowing I'm about to be a little facetious.

"And this, Edward, is the lodge where the gatekeeper lived."

He smiles at my cheek.

"We're here," I say, stopping at the little wooden gate.

"Is this where you grew up?" he asks, looking at the lodge.

"Umm, not quite here, no," I say as I release the latch, opening the gate onto a pebbled path.

He looks confused for a moment as he follows me through the gate, past the lodge, and along another path that leads to the main drive of the manor house. He throws me an astonished glance.

"You grew up here?"

"Yes, with my grandparents from the age of four."

"You're full of surprises, Miss Baxter!"

I smile weakly, and his tone changes as he sees my reaction.

"What happened to your parents?" he asks.

"They died," I say shortly.

"I'm sorry."

I can see that he's genuine, but he looks at me inquisitively.

"May I ask how?" he says softly.

I squeeze his hand and surprise myself by telling him.

"In a car crash," I say, lowering my head.

"I'm sorry," he says again, his voice full of sadness and concern.

I smile, thinking, *Me too*, and I hope he'll not continue asking me questions. Before he gets a chance, the front door suddenly flies open as we approach it.

"Abigail!" Grans stretched out her arms, beckoning me into them.

As I hug her she looks over my shoulder at Edward, and I grin nervously.

"And who's your friend?" she asks inquisitively.

I roll my eyes at her. As if Mrs Bracewell hasn't already told her. I step back and gesture towards Edward.

"Gran, this is Edward Scott, a friend from the hospital."

Edward holds out his hand to her.

"Very pleased to meet you, Mrs Baxter!"

Gran takes his hand and shakes it. Oh dear, it's all very formal and a little scary.

"Likewise. Please, do come in."

We follow her into the hallway, where I'm suddenly greeted with arms flying around me in a bear hug, and a squeal of delight from Glenda.

"Abigail! Oh, it's so nice to see you! How are you? Let me look at you. It's been too long, you know that, don't you?" She speaks in a stream, answering her own question.

"Gosh, Glenda, you're making me dizzy," I say, grinning back at her. She spots Edward and raises her eyebrows. A girlish grin appears on her face.

"And who's this handsome creature?" she says excitedly.

Gran shakes her head at her, and I giggle as I reply, "Mrs Campbell," I smile, "I mean Glenda, this is my friend Edward."

"Well, hello, Edward. Very pleased to meet you." She holds her hand out to him, and I can't stop giggling. She's so funny, and very flirty for her age. She's also married.

Edward tries to keep a straight face as he shakes her hand.

"Pleased to meet you, Mrs Campbell, or do I call you Glenda." I can hear the laughter in his voice, and his eyes widen as her hand continues to linger in his.

"Oh, my dear boy, the pleasure's all mine! And you can call me whatever you like."

Glenda is sixty-five, and she's worked for my gran ever since I arrived on the scene twenty-two years ago. You could say that she's the housekeeper, nanny and cook all rolled into one, but to me she's a friend, and to my gran, a very good friend, especially since my grandad died. She's a lovely, warm person. She has no children of her own, which is a pity as she and William, her husband, would have made fantastic parents. Instead she mothered me when I was growing up. William is just like her – kind and polite. It was like having two sets of grandparents. William still does all the gardening and odd jobs around the manor, and now he drives for my gran as well. They both live in the lodge house.

"Thank you, Glenda," Gran says, shaking her head and trying not to laugh at her. "I don't know what William will think of you behaving like this."

Glenda laughs out loud, winking at the two of us.

"Well, when the cat's away—"

"Coffee I think, Glenda?" says Gran. "Come on, I'll help you make it. Abigail, please show Edward into the sitting room."

They walk away down the long hallway towards the kitchen. Glenda nudges Gran, and we can still hear her clearly. She's not really very discreet.

"He's very good-looking, don't you think? But, of course, our Abigail is a stunner too. What a handsome couple they make."

I roll my eyes at Edward, who grins at me as I show him into the sitting room. Gran is keeping this formal: we usually sit in the kitchen.

"This way," I say, smiling at Edward.

The sitting room is cosy and warm from a roaring fire burning in the huge inglenook fireplace.

I smile wistfully, remembering sitting in front of it on the rug in winter, listening to Gran and Grandad telling me stories. I've missed being here, and missed Gran even more so.

Edward looks around, studying the walls.

"There's a lot of photos of you in here," he comments, walking around the room and inspecting them.

A lot of photos? There must be hundreds!

"Hmm, very cute, Abbie. And this one is even nicer." His mouth forms a wicked grin, and I see which picture he's staring at. I'm about sixteen, dressed in my running gear and holding a medal for coming second in the village run. "I like your pigtails! In fact, I'd like to see you in pigtails now."

I blush, and he grins suggestively at me.

"Stop it! You said you'd behave."

He pouts his lips.

"I am behaving."

I give him a warning look as the door opens and Gran walks in carrying a tray with a coffee pot, cups, saucers, cream and sugar.

Edward strides over to her, holding out his arms. "Please, let me take that for you, Mrs Baxter."

"Thank you, Edward. Please call me Elizabeth."

I let out a deep breath as I realise she likes him; she only allows people she likes to use her first name. Oh, thank God! I start to relax, because it matters to me what she thinks of my friends, especially after Adam. We each take a seat, all very polite and formal as we drink our coffee.

"So, Edward, what do you do at the hospital?"

"I'm a doctor, Elizabeth."

Gran raises her eyebrows.

"A doctor of what?"

"He's actually a surgeon, Gran," I jump in before she starts grilling him. I smile at him, and he gives me a modest look. It has the reverse effect, and makes me want to brag about how important and skilled his work is.

"A very accomplished surgeon at that, and an author of numerous educational books, too." I smile proudly at him. Gran also looks pleased, and she can see that he means a lot to me.

"You've accomplished a lot for your age, Edward. You must be very dedicated to your work."

I know Gran well enough to know what she's getting at. She's probably wondering what time he'll have left to spend with me.

"That's true. I suppose I have accomplished a lot for my age."

We both listen to him, and I wonder where this conversation is going.

"But when I set my mind to something, I work very hard until I've achieved my goal."

My eyes dart between them, and I know that they're actually having an extremely polite debate about me. I take a sip of my coffee, and nearly choke on it when Gran speaks.

"So, what are your intentions towards my granddaughter?"

God, I nearly fall off the bloody chair! I never thought she's ask a question like that, and certainly not while I was in the same room. I stare at her in disbelief, but Edward seems amused.

"They're honourable, Mrs Baxter."

I can't help but laugh. I feel like I'm in a film set from *Jane Eyre*. They both look at me, and I can see that Gran is trying not to laugh. She really does like him!

"I'm pleased to hear that, Edward," she replies drily.

I can't cope with anymore. Hell, next they'll be discussing what dowry I have. I put my coffee cup back on the tray and stand up.

"I'm just going to the bathroom."

Edward nods.

"Okay, dear," Gran says mildly.

I'm not going to the bathroom at all. I'm going to find Glenda, to ask her if Gran has been on the gin. It's the only explanation for what's she's saying to Edward.

I leave the room and find her at the sink in the kitchen. When I tell her what's happened she roars with laughter. Eventually she manages to calm down, wiping the tears away with a tissue. Then she grows serious.

"She's looking out for you this time, making sure that he's good enough for you. Because of ..." She sighs. "Well, you know who. She regrets so much that she didn't interfere, and didn't tell you what she thought of him. She was scared that you'd perhaps take it the wrong way and fall out with her."

I smile weakly back at her, and she takes hold of my hand. She's quite emotional as she continues, "Your gran used to pray you'd leave Adam. You wouldn't believe how many sleepless nights we've both had over you."

"I'm sorry, Glenda, truly I am."

"But I'm so pleased that you've left him at last!"

I nod. "I'd better go and rescue Edward from Gran," I say, and she gives me a watery smile as I leave the kitchen.

Edward and Gran are still talking to each other about this and that when I return. I don't pay much attention to their conversation. Instead I watch my gran, feeling worried and guilty now that I know what I've put her through.

I agree to go round for dinner on Sunday. Gran invites Edward too, but he tells her he's unable to. I guess he knows I want to talk to her alone, but I'm wondering now how much she really knows.

Later, Edward and I say our goodbyes and I'm sure that Gran is finally satisfied with the information she's plucked from us both. She surprises me once more by asking Edward to lunch with us on Wednesday. She obviously does like him, though I can't see any reason why I'd thought she might not. Edward tells her that he'll see what he can do. Then we leave the house and walk back to the car.

I'm pretty quiet, and Edward kindly leaves me to my thoughts.

We arrive back at the car park, and he smiles kindly as he parks. Then he takes off his seatbelt and turns to me.

"Are you okay? You're a little quiet."

We walk towards the doors.

"I'm fine," I say half-heartedly as I key in the code.

"Would you like to come in for a coffee and a chat?"

"Coffee and a chat would be nice."

I feel a little jittery, knowing that he'll probably ask about my parents. I look at his face, seeing that genuine look again, and think I'm ready to tell him, although I've not talked to anyone about my past for a long time. In fact, I've not really talked to anyone before about my parents, well apart from my grandparent's and Glenda. Edward will be the first.

We enter the flat and sit on the sofa, but I don't know how to start.

He leans forward.

"It's been nice today, meeting your gran. She's very, umm, forward …"

I cringe, wondering what she asked or told him once I'd left the room.

"Did she interrogate you?"

"Not quite. Well, she didn't get the spotlight out, if that's what you mean."

"I'm sorry," I say, laughing.

"Its fine. Don't worry about it. She's just looking after you."

"Yes, she is. She always has done."

"Always?"

I nod my head, closing my eyes briefly. If she'd known the real Adam, well, I can't imagine what she'd have done.

I know that Edward is wondering, if she's always looked after me, then why not with Adam? He knows about the abuse;

he must do – he would have seen the bruises on my body that night in the shower. They're fading, but you couldn't miss them. He's reaching a conclusion, adding two and two together, but is he getting four?

"Why are you finding it hard to tell me about any part of your past?"

"It's just how I am. I struggle to open up, and there's been so much in such in a short space of time. I don't want to sound all woe is me. Does that make sense at all?"

"Is that what you think? That I'd think you're some kind of drama queen?"

"I don't know, Edward. We didn't really meet in the conventional way, did we?"

He shakes his head.

"But that might be a good thing."

"Really, you think so?" I ask, puzzled.

"Yes, because it means that we're obviously very attracted to each other."

"We are?"

"Well, I'm very attracted to you. Maybe it's meant to be this way." He smiles, putting his head to one side and looking so cute that I can't help but smile back at him. "Aren't you attracted to me, Abbie?"

"I think you know the answer to that already," I say, blushing.

"Do I make you smile? Do I make you happy?"

"Yes, you do. You make me very happy, and, more importantly, you make me laugh, which I've not done for a long time. It feels so good to laugh."

"What's happened to you?" He traces a finger down the side of my face. "What's made you feel that you can't open up and tell me?"

I lean over and kiss him on the cheek.

"I will tell you, I promise, but not yet. Please don't pressure me."

"It's upsetting," he says slowly. "I saw the bruises, and you didn't want me to know you had money. Do you think my intentions towards you are shallow?"

I close my eyes, feeling trapped and confused, but I'm just not ready to tell him about Adam.

"No, it's me who has the hang-ups about money. I've always had them. I don't tell anyone about it. It's to do with my parents and how they died." I rub my hands over my face as I speak.

"You confuse me," he admits. "I feel like I'm just getting to know you, and then you close down."

"Okay, okay." I pause, and let out a deep sigh. "They died in a car crash, like I told you." He squeezes my knee. "I was four years old. We'd been to the beach for a picnic. It was a beautiful sunny day, really hot! I remember it so clearly: I was laughing and playing, my mum and dad were holding hands as they watched me, smiling at me, smiling at each other. I felt so loved, and they were so much in love. Then the journey home took us down the country lanes."

I pause, and my hands start to tremble as I recall what happened. But I push on. I want to tell him; I need to let him know that it's not him I have the problem with; that it's me.

"Dad was driving and we were all singing. Suddenly a stag darted out of nowhere and ran in front of the car. Dad swerved, slamming on the breaks to avoid hitting it …" I breathe deeply while Edward watches me silently. "The car skidded and went through a fence. A piece of the fence came through the windscreen, hitting my dad in the chest and killing him instantly. The car was out of control. My mum took off her seatbelt, and she was screaming and trying to steer the car. I was in the back, crying. My mum kept shouting to me – *It's okay, Abbie. Don't cry, darling. It's okay* … I know I was only four, but I knew she was lying, and that everything wasn't okay.

"I was terrified. I couldn't do anything to help her or my dad. The car was going faster and faster towards a steep part of the hill that was covered in trees. Then it suddenly stopped, and my mum screamed as the car had hit a huge oak tree."

Tears flow down my face as I share my memories.

"My mum was thrown out through the windscreen. I was screaming but I couldn't get to her or my dad. I was trapped by my seatbelt in the back of the car and couldn't get out. I don't remember any more. I woke up in hospital with Gran holding my hand and crying over me. She told me some time later that my mum had died instantly too."

Edward holds me in his arms, hugging me close to him and shaking his head. His voice is kind, but firm.

"You were trapped in the car; you were four years old. There was nothing you could've done."

"I know that now, I do. I know I couldn't have helped, but it still doesn't stop the guilt or the way I feel."

"You listen to me. Look at me ..." He wipes the tears from my eyes. "I'm sorry, I had no idea. I feel so privileged that you've trusted me enough to tell me."

"The money from my mum and dad's estate, I never wanted it. I don't want it. I would rather be penniless and have them here with me, instead of all this."

He nods at me.

"Of course you would, sweetheart."

"I feel guilty about spending money." I gaze into my lap, then look at him, frowning. "I do need to come to terms with it, but I've got so much other stuff to come to terms with as well that I don't know where to start. It's so hard. I've not told anyone before about my parents, although Alison guessed about the money after she met my gran at the deli in town. People's intentions towards you can change when they know you have money."

He nods in agreement.

"That's true. Can I ask you something? Adam's intentions, were they all about the money?"

I nod.

"Did he hurt you?"

I know I can't answer those questions, not yet.

"Sorry, I can't do this anymore. Please, trust me. I've told you more than I've ever told anyone. I will tell you the rest – I said I would, and I will – but, please, let me do it in my own time. Don't force me into a corner, Edward."

"Is that what you think I'm doing?" He sounds offended.

"Yes."

He looks shocked, and I rush on.

"No! I don't know anymore. It's upsetting, talking about my parents and ..." I stop, because it's like a rollercoaster – my parents, Adam and what he's done to me, and then my babies.

As soon as I think about them, my eyes fill with tears. "Can you please excuse me a minute?"

I stand and he rises with me. He goes to hug me but I shake my head, knowing that if he holds me now, I'll break down. I just need five minutes to compose myself.

"Please, I won't be a minute."

I go into the bathroom and sit on the side of the bath. I breathe deeply, running the cold tap and washing the tears from my eyes. I return to the lounge and Edward just looks at me. He breathes in deeply and speaks as he stands.

"I'm sorry," he says softly. "I'll not ask again, I promise. I'll wait until you're ready to tell me. I don't want to back you into a corner, or pressure you in any way. I just thought I might be able to help you, that's all."

I hug him tightly, really tightly, and smile into his chest.

"I know, and God, I want to tell you, but I'm not strong enough yet. I'm sorry."

He cups my face in his hands; my arms are still tight around him.

"Hey, come on. Chin up. Smile at me …" I do. "That's better." He kisses me, then puts his arms around me. "You tell me when you're ready."

"Thank you. I'll make that coffee."

"I'll make the coffee. You take a seat."

I sit on the sofa, twiddling my thumbs and wondering what he's thinking.

I can hear him moving about in the kitchen. His phone rings, and he answers while filling the kettle with water. I think it's Tom. I can hear fragments of the conversation about work, and then I hear him saying, "I'm here with her at the flat. I'm just going to make sure she's okay before I leave." He closes the door to the kitchen, but I can still hear him. "She won't say."

He comes back in with the coffees. We sit and drink them, and I start to yawn.

"Are you tired?"

"Yes, a little."

"Put your head here, then." He pats his chest, and I curl my feet up on the sofa, lie my head on his chest and wrap my arms around him. He strokes my hair, talking to me in a soothing voice. My eyes feel heavy and I quickly drift off to sleep.

Edward wakes me by kissing my forehead.

"Hi," I say sleepily. "You're still here?"

"Hmm … yes, but I need to leave. I need to go and see my grandad before he gets ready for bed or they won't let me onto the ward."

I grunt sceptically.

"I'm sure they will, with your charm and persuasion." He grins at me. "But I'm sorry – you should've woken me sooner."

"I was enjoying cuddling you and watching you sleep."

"My, my, a soft side!" I say as I get up and kiss him on the cheek.

He laughs. "Don't tell anyone. I've got a reputation to uphold, remember?"

"Your secret's safe with me," I say.

I squeal as he pulls me back down onto his knee. "Hey, I thought you were going."

"I am, after a kiss." He kisses me softly, three times. That's all. No open mouth, no tongues, and no suggestive remarks. I'm a little taken aback, but it was nice all the same.

He taps my bottom and growls, "Up, Abbie! Come on, I need to go."

"Yes, sir!" I shout, saluting him and laughing as I jump up.

He raises an amused eyebrow.

"Well, we'll get along mighty fine if you always do what you're told."

"Very funny!" I pause. "I'll not see you now until Monday?"

"No."

I grimace, and he continues, "You have a good time tomorrow, and on Sunday at your gran's. I'll ring you tomorrow."

"Please."

He kisses me again, then walks towards the door. "Bye then."

"Bye."

Then he leaves. I'm a little astounded that he's not tried anything on with me. We'd been alone, after all. I know I said I wanted time, but I feel disappointed now. He does baffle me, but then again I probably baffle him too. One minute I say no, the next I say yes, and then I don't know. I'm surprised he dared even kiss me. Poor Edward.

I change into my pyjamas, too worn out to shower or have a bath, and climb into bed. I'm out like a light as soon as my head hits the pillow.

I wake in the morning with a tummy ache. I go to the bathroom and notice that my period's started. They said it could happen like this, with heavy and irregular bleeding. I've been taking the pill for the past six months. Adam didn't know I'd started taking it, but I certainly didn't want to get pregnant by him again.

I get a bath running. While I'm waiting, I put my clothes in the washer, start it, and return to the bathroom.

Alison comes home.

"Hi, Abbie," she shouts from the hallway. "Do you want a coffee?"

"Please! I'm just in the bath. I won't be long."

I get out, dry myself off and put on my dressing gown. Alison's in the lounge as I walk past. "I won't be a minute. I'll just put on my pyjamas."

I return to the lounge and sit at the table with her.

"Are you okay, Abbie? You look a little pale."

"Time of the month. It's giving me a little jip."

"Here, try these. They're really good." She reaches into her bag and pulls out some painkillers. "Take two and go back to bed for a few hours."

"Thanks, I think I will."

"Are you all right for tonight still? And did you ask Edward if he was coming?"

"I did, but he said no. He's seeing his grandad, and he has a lot of work to catch up on. I know it's not just an excuse, but I also think it's because the club is at the hospital. I can't blame him, I suppose."

"What, you mean the dating thing?"

"Maybe. I was fine with it. He explained and I told him I understood. Which I do, especially since I got all that grief from Miss Fantastic Personality." I sigh heavily. "Do you think they'll be there?"

"More than likely," Alison says, pulling a face. "She always goes to the club. Trying to bag a doctor, no less, but the one she really wants never goes, and even if he did, he's with you."

"Yes, he is." I smile smugly. "She can keep her grubby little hands off him!"

"Fighting talk, Abigail Baxter. I like it!"

"I'm going back to bed for a bit," I say, laughing. "See you soon."

"Okay, hun. No worries."

I climb back into bed and fall asleep.

I wake up, yawn and stretch. My tummy ache's gone and I feel loads better. I decide to go for a run. I get up, use the bathroom to wash, and return to my room. Alison's nowhere to be seen. I dress in my running things, and then, as I'm leaving, I bump into her in the hallway.

"Morning again," I say, pulling a face at her. "Well, afternoon actually. I'm just going for a run."

"Do you want to borrow my iPod and earphones?" she asks.

"Please, if you don't mind."

"Of course not or I wouldn't have offered."

I laugh and she fetches it from her room.

"Just press there," she explains.

I press the play button and put one of the buds into my ear. "Like a Vi…" blasts out. I roll my eyes.

"There's all sorts on it, all proper feel-good songs." She continues.

"Thanks, that's just what I need right now." I answer smiling.

I leave the flat and step outside. Gosh, it's chilly!

Well, here we go then, I think as I plug in both earbuds.

I sing away in my head as I run. I must look simple with my head nodding away to the music. The track finishes, and when the next one starts I laugh out loud.

"Alison Bridge!" I exclaim.

It's very catchy, and has quite a bit of swearing in it, so I don't sing aloud to this one, just hum the tune as I pass people.

Soon I reach the park. I shake my head and think that maybe I should send this to Adam. The words fit him to a tee: *I think you're very distasteful.* The song is so apt that I can't stop laughing. I can even picture his face as he listens to it. I stop and sit down on a bench to get my breath back. It's hard, running and laughing at the same time. I pause the iPod as the song finishes. That's cheered me up no end.

I press play again and the intro to the next song comes on. I smile, thinking, *Has she made this for me?* I close my eyes, listening to the words. I'm completely caught up in the moment, miming with my eyes closed and swaying along to the music. I start to sing out loud with the earphones in. The song picks up its beat, and I'm there, I'm with her, and these words are mine. I start singing louder, really in the zone, when I suddenly sense people looking at me. I stop singing and open my eyes. I'm horrified to find a small crowd staring. I grin sheepishly, removing the bud from one ear.

"Was that a little loud?"

An old man with his dog nods yes.

"But don't stop," he continues cheerfully. "You were doing fine, love."

I grimace at him, laughing nervously and turning bright red. Inwardly, I'm screaming, *Oh, shit!*

"Fab tune!" I splutter with embarrassment, as I get up from the bench, my cheeks burning with shame, before making my way back to the flat.

God, I can't believe that just happened. How embarrassing, and me with the voice of an angel. I'm never going to listen to music again while running, or if I do then I'll only wear one earpiece.

I go back to the flat and give Alison her iPod back. Actually, I practically throw the damned thing at her, shaking my head.

"What?" she says, confused.

I tell her about what happened in the park, all those poor people with their bleeding ears, and she howls with laughter.

"Oh dear. I can't wait to tell Tom!"

She's only teasing, but I'm horrified at the thought.

"Don't you dare! He'll tell Edward."

"I'm sorry, but that is just a classic. I *have* to tell him."

"Alison Bridge, if you do, I swear I'll kill you."

"Sorry, Abbie!"

She goes running into her room, closing the door quickly behind her. Oh Lord, I'm going to be the brunt of everyone's jokes now – just what I need. I stalk to my room, shaking my head at myself and wondering why on earth I told her.

Chapter 5

Later, as we're leaving the flat to meet Tom at the club, Alison looks openly at my outfit.

I give her a strange look, asking, "What?"

"I can't believe you wore his jumper," she says observantly but with a giggle. "You've got it bad, girl. Although, I have to say, you pull it off well."

I grin at her. I'm wearing trousers and a blouse, and Edward's sweater is draped over my shoulders. It's silly, maybe, but I wanted to wear it because I can smell his clean scent on it. And as he can't come, this makes me feel closer to him. I wish, though, that he was coming. I miss him.

We arrive at the club and go straight to the bar, where we order ourselves a drink. We take the table where we sat last week, near to the dance floor. I watch the band tuning their instruments on stage. Alison looks at me and laughs.

"Are you going to give us a song tonight?"

I stick my tongue out at her.

"Very funny! I wish I'd never have told you now. Anyway, it wasn't that funny."

She coughs dryly, grinning at me, and I shake my head in response.

"Well, okay, I suppose it was," I admit reluctantly. "They must've thought I was barking mad!"

"Yes, I bet they did. I would've loved to have seen it."

I roll my eyes at her, changing the subject swiftly. There's something I want to tell her before Tom arrives.

"Alison." I pause for a moment to gain her full attention, then continue, "I'm going to move back home on Friday, after my shift. I'm going to phone a locksmith and meet him there before Adam gets home."

She looks a little shocked.

"Is that wise? I mean, won't that provoke him?"

I stare at her, wondering what she really knows.

She smiles somewhat sadly. "I've seen the bruises, Abbie. Sorry."

I sigh and close my eyes. "What did Edward say about you moving back?" she asks cautiously.

"We talked on the phone on Saturday, and he was lovely. He said he'd help me all the way."

"That was nice of him. Does he know about …?" She pauses. "You know, the bruising?"

I roll my eyes, nodding my head.

"Yes, he's seen the bruises. I haven't told him how they got there, but I think he knows. He asked me what had happened, but I wasn't ready to say. I know that sounds a little lame, but if I start thinking or talking about Adam and my past, it makes me feel weak. I know what I need to do, and I want to try to stay strong. I just need to focus on Friday and changing the locks. I'll deal with the rest as it comes along. And I'm damn sure that it *will* come along."

"He sounds like a nasty character."

I nod in agreement. Nobody knows the real Adam – what he's like and what he's capable of.

"I feel as though life has dealt me a shitty hand, and I want to change it. I want a new deck of cards, one without the jokers this time."

"Well, I'm going to stay with you on Friday night, and we'll shuffle that new deck of cards together. I'm here for you, and we will deal with him together."

I smile at her, as she confirms her statement with one sharp nod of her head.

"Thank you. You're a good friend. And I appreciate it, more than you'll ever know. I've not really had anyone who I could lean on, or who could help me make a stand against Adam, not like the way you and Edward are helping me now that I've finally left him. I knew this would be the hardest part."

I grow silent, apprehensive about what I'm doing and what I have to face.

Alison picks up on my vibes – she's very good at reading me. She pats my hand as if to say, *Don't worry.*

"Good, that's settled then. So chin up, girl! Let's forget about him and have a good time tonight."

"Okay," I say with a smile. "Another drink? Do you know, I can't believe how much alcohol I've drunk since I came here. I never drink as a rule. It goes straight to my head and then usually comes straight back up and down the loo!"

I can still hear Alison laughing at me as I make my way to the bar. I order another two gin and tonics and return to our table with them. I'm feeling a little tipsy now; the G&Ts are quite strong, and I've only eaten a banana and a yogurt with the painkillers.

Alison gestures towards the door with her head as I pass her drink over. I look over and see that Darcy's walked in with James. She's wearing yet another very short, classy dress. They see us and she throws me a dirty look and holds on very tight to James's hand as they walk past.

I let out a huff, rolling my eyes at Alison, and say quietly, "When is she going to get it through her thick head that I'm not remotely interested in him?"

James offers me one of his smarmy, slimy smiles as they pass, and Darcy flounces again as they make their way to the bar.

I want to pull a face at him and make a gagging noise, but I don't. I turn away instead, saying to Alison, "Urgh!"

She nods in agreement.

I take a large gulp of my drink, then shudder.

Alison grins at me as Tom arrives. She waves at him as he comes to join us.

"Would you like a drink, Tom?" I say, letting them have a few minutes to themselves.

"Please."

"Alison?"

"Go on then. Why not."

I finish what's left of my drink – it will be my third and, to be honest, I feel a little strange. I'm not sure if it's nerves, annoyance, or because I'm missing Edward.

Plus, I need some Dutch courage, as Darcy and James are both standing at the bar, gawping at me. I make my way to the opposite end of the bar and stand in the queue, waiting to be served. I can hear Darcy talking loudly to James, obviously for my benefit.

"Have you seen who's here?" she sneers.

Is she stupid? I think to myself. Of course he knows who's here. He's been watching me ever since he arrived. He doesn't answer her, but keeps looking at me. She's making snide remarks about me, but he doesn't seem to be paying attention to her.

I ignore them and wait in line. It's really busy, but I eventually order the drinks, another two G&Ts for Alison and myself and a pint of lager for Tom. As I make my way back to the table, I hear her still wittering on about me. I try my best to ignore her, but I'm struggling to hold my temper. The gin is once again getting the better of me. I fully understand now why Edward doesn't come to functions at the hospital. Tom and Alison thank me for their drinks as I sit down.

"I believe you might be singing tonight," Tom says, trying not to laugh.

I snap out of my thoughts and glare at Alison, shaking my head.

"I don't think so, Tom. Not tonight." I throw her another look. "Looks like I'm going to be the brunt of everyone's jokes for a while."

She laughs and shrugs.

I pick up my phone and check for messages. None.

Before I know it, I've finished yet another drink. My phone bleeps and I look at it; there's a message from Alison.

Give us a song.

I start to laugh. "No. Now stop it!" We both giggle, and Tom rolls his eyes, shaking his head at us.

"Okay, do you want to dance instead?" she asks with a smile.

"Oh, yes, let's dance!"

"Tom, what about you?" Alison asks him eagerly.

"No, thanks. You and Abbie dance. I'm fine watching you!" He winks at her, and she giggles coyly.

"You think I've got it bad?" I tease as we make our way onto the dance floor.

The band's just as good this time round. We dance to three songs before returning to our table. I check my phone again to see if there's a text from Edward. There isn't so I decide to text him.

You should have co

My phone is still in my hand, but before I can finish my text, I'm nearly spun off my chair and a voice I recognise hollers at me.

"My God, Abigail, you did it?"

I throw my phone onto the table as I turn around.

"Joe! It's so good to see you. I've been meaning to phone and tell you that I'd started." I look around expectantly. "Are you here alone?"

He nods as I jump off my chair. He throws his arms around me, and I hug him back. He's practically spinning me round, and suddenly, seeing him and hearing his voice, I realise that he's more than just someone from the running club. Maybe he's not the same sort of friend as Alison – he's more like a therapist – but he's always been a friend to me, and a good one at that.

Adam had put a stop to me going to the running club when he found out about me starting at the hospital, although he never knew about Joe and that we talked. God, the beatings were bad enough when he thought people were just talking to me at the club, influencing me. If he'd known I'd had an actual friend, and a man at that … I shudder at the thought of Adam and how controlling he was, and manage a smile for Joe.

I'm so pleased to see him again, but I feel the need to explain why I stopped going to the club, why I never called him. Because, unknowingly, he's changed my life. He couldn't have rung me; I wouldn't risk giving my number to anyone. It sounds selfish, I know, but I was dealing with far greater problems at the time.

"God, put me down," I say breathlessly. "You're making me dizzy."

He stops and then kisses me hard on the cheek.

"You look really well. What ward are you on?"

"ENT," I say with a smile.

He pulls a surly face in response.

"Under the direction of none other than Edward Scott, eh?"

"You know him?"

"Yes."

"Oh, of course, his grandad."

Joe nods – as he's now the registrar in Coronary Care.

He raises his eyebrows at me and asks curiously, "Do you know him well?"

I know what he's getting at, but I ignore his prying question and change the subject instead. We seem to take up just were we left off.

"Joe, these are my friends, Alison and Tom." I smile fondly at Alison, knowing that she's a true friend, my best friend.

"I know Tom already." He nods a greeting. "Tom."

Tom nods back.

Joe holds out his hand to Alison. "I'm Joe. Pleased to meet you, Alison."

She shakes his hand but throws me a confused look.

I smile reassuringly at her.

"Sorry, Alison. Joe is a friend of mine."

For some reason I suddenly feel compelled to explain to Alison how I know him, as I'd told her I'd had no friends when we first met.

"Well, to tell you the truth, he's the one who talked me into becoming a student nurse."

But I find myself unable to continue with my explanation, especially in front of Joe and Tom. "Are you going to join us, Joe?" I ask instead.

I see Alison look at Tom, and he shrugs his shoulders at her.

"I'll just get a drink first. Anyone else want one?" he asks.

Alison and Tom shake their heads, but I nod enthusiastically.

"A G&T for me please, Joe."

He walks off in the direction of the bar, and I notice a lot of women admiring him. I'm not surprised because he's extremely good-looking and has a great personality. He can sometimes be a little full on, though. I notice Darcy nudging James. God, is she just going to stare at me all night?

"What's going on?" Alison asks in a concerned voice.

"What do you mean?"

"With Joe, I mean."

"Nothing's going on. Trust me, I'm not his type."

"Well, I do hope you know what you're doing."

I nod, but really I have no idea what she means. Joe returns from the bar and sits down next to me.

"So Abs—"

I stop him before he continues.

"You can cut that out straight away. It's Abbie or Abigail." He knows perfectly well that I don't like Abs.

He laughs at me.

"Fancy a dance … Abs?"

I just shake my head at him as he continues to wind me up. Alison is watching me strangely. I smile at her.

"Do you want to dance?" I ask.

She shakes her head.

"No, I'm okay, thank you."

I'm a little puzzled that she seems off with me. Joe practically pulls me from my seat as the band start to sing a catchy Latin American tune.

He holds my hands, spinning me round the dance floor, and then he suddenly flings his arms around me, bringing me in close and holding me tightly against his body. He starts bending me backwards, then hurls me back up and straight into his arms. God, I think I'm going to be sick, but I can't stop laughing. He winks at me and spins me round again, then rolls his hips in time with the music. God, he can certainly move. By the time the song finishes, I'm shattered.

"Hell, Joe, I need to sit down."

"No stamina, Abs?" he says as we leave the dance floor.

Someone shouts to him, and he waves back at them.

"Be back in a minute," he says, winking at me before walking off.

I head back to the table to see Alison and Tom staring at me.

"He's a friend," I say, sitting down.

Alison smiles, but I don't think she believes me. She's looking at me oddly, but I suppose that's my fault if she's remembering that I'd told her about having no friends. Tom says something to her as he gets up from the table. Then he walks away in the direction of the men's room.

"Abbie, what are you doing?" she asks me, concerned.

"I don't know what you mean. I was only dancing with him. Honestly, Joe is just a friend. I can't say anymore."

She raises her eyebrows. I feel awkward, but I can't tell her. I promised I wouldn't. As for Joe behaving like he does, well, that's just him. He's full on, and if she knew him she'd understand.

I sit back in my chair and look towards the bar. Darcy is talking into James's ear with her phone in her hand, showing him something and pointing in my direction.

I turn away from them, and jump. Edward is standing beside me, glaring at me. He doesn't look happy. He's still in his suit, minus his jacket. I'm shocked that he's here.

"Hi! What are you doing here? Is everything okay?"

I go to stand, thinking it could be something to do with his grandad, as he looks like he's not been home yet. He frowns at me.

"A word, Abbie, outside," he asks in a flat voice.

"Sorry?"

"You heard. I want a word with you outside. Or would you prefer it if I say what I have to say in here, in front of everyone."

"Say what?"

He takes my wrist and starts pulling me in the direction of the doors. I'm confused.

"What's wrong?" I look towards Alison, who shrugs her shoulders at me. "Edward, what is going on?"

He ignores me and continues walking, still holding onto my wrist. Once we get outside he lets go of me and shakes his head. His voice is flat and cold.

"What are you playing at, Abbie?"

"What?" I'm baffled. I don't understand what he's talking about.

"The text, the photos."

"The text …" I smile at him but his expression is stern. "I didn't get to finish it. It must have sent anyway but you only received half of it."

"I received it, yes, and I also received some photos."

He's talking in riddles.

"Photos? What photos?"

He shakes his head in disbelief.

"I've no idea what you're going on about, Edward."

"Really?" he shouts, making me jump as he reaches into his pocket and takes out his phone.

"Don't shout at me," I snap at him.

He puts his phone in my hand.

"What's this?" There are photos of Joe and me: Joe kissing me on the cheek, us dancing together, him spinning me round.

I'm laughing in all of them and I look really happy. I'm momentarily confused as to who's been taking pictures of me, but then it dawns on me that it could only be one person. What a bitch! Will she stop at nothing to split us up? But I've nothing to hide, and I've done nothing wrong.

"That's Joe. He's a friend," I say, relieved.

"I know who he is," Edward replies curtly.

"Don't you believe me?"

"I trusted you. I thought you were special. How fucking wrong was I?"

"Don't swear at me! He's a friend, that's all ..." I close my eyes briefly. "I know how it looks, and I'm sorry, but I've done nothing wrong. Trust me."

He looks cross, and I can tell he's holding his temper in check.

"Trust you? He looks like more than friend to me."

"Edward, please ..."

Joe suddenly comes running outside, shouting, "Abbie, are you okay? What's going on?"

"I don't know. Someone's been taking photos of us dancing."

He looks at me, then at Edward, then back at me. I shake my head.

"Joe, don't."

Joe walks over to Edward, who looks furious and starts shouting at him.

"I'm warning you, Joe, back off! This has nothing to do with you. This is between me and Abbie. We're just talking, all right?"

"I was talking to Abbie, Edward, not you."

They're squaring up to each other.

I put my hands to my face, shouting at them, "Stop it, please. Both of you, just stop."

Joe looks at me.

"Are you seeing him, Abbie?"

I nod.

"Then tell him, because those photos don't look good."

"Tell me what?" Edward asks, almost shouting and looking frustrated.

I shake my head at Joe.

"I can't, Joe. I promised you."

"Come on, just tell him. It's not worth this, is it?"

I shake my head. I'm nearly in tears.

"Then just tell him."

I put my hands to my eyes to stop the tears. Edward sees and stares at me, confused. He looks hurt, but I promised Joe. God, I feel so torn.

"Abbie, tell him, or I will."

Joe rolls his eyes and walks back inside. I look at Edward.

"I'm sorry, I can't. I promised Joe. But he's just a friend, honestly. Please trust me."

"A friend?" he asks disdainfully. I nod, but he shakes his head at me and I know he doesn't believe me. I can't blame him, but what he says next floors me. "A friend that wants in your pants, or has he ..."

I put my hand up to stop him. He glares at me as I shake my head. I'm hurt that he would think that of me, and my voice shakes.

"Don't you dare finish that sentence!"

"Is there any point in me continuing?" he huffs.

God, I've really hurt him, I can see it in his eyes. I'm torn, so torn. It looks bad – the text, the photos. I exhale sharply and Edward shrugs his shoulders and starts to walk away.

"Edward! God, don't. Please don't walk off."

He turns to look at me.

"I'm sorry. Yes, it looks bad I know, but he's …"

"He's what?" he demands.

"He's gay," I say quietly.

He looks taken aback, then confused. He tips his head to one side.

"Joe's gay?"

I nod. "He a friend, a good friend, that's all. He helped me when I was at rock bottom, and I'll always be thankful to him for that. I helped him too. He has a partner that he's been with for six months, so you could say we helped each other."

I tell Edward how Joe and I met at the running club and how he persuaded me to become a student nurse. I don't tell him why I left the club or why we lost contact because I can already see the anger in his face deflating.

He walks quickly back towards me.

"God, Abbie, I'm sorry," he says genuinely. "Can I give you a hug?"

I nod, relieved that he believes me.

"Yes, please. And I'm sorry too. I know what those photos looked like, and I couldn't bear it if you thought of me like that."

"I should have trusted my instincts. I know deep down that you'd never do anything like that – you're too sweet – but the text confused me. *You should have co.* And then, of course, the photos followed. I thought you were punishing me for not coming out with you tonight."

I'm shocked that he'd also think that of me.

"God, no, I would never do that."

"I know, but I was jealous …" He laughs shortly, and raises his eyes as though he's going to continue to say, *Yes, me, jealous.*

I'm stunned by his admission.

"Someone else dancing with you, holding you, when I wanted it to be me, and I thought you wanted it to be me too."

And he nods his head, answering his own question. "Didn't you?"

"Of course I wanted it to be you."

He smiles and seems satisfied by my reaction.

"How were you planning to end the text?"

"Can I tell you later, please?"

He nods.

"Do you want to go back inside?"

"Not really, but I need to tell Joe it's sorted."

He smiles.

"And I need to get my bag and tell Alison I'm going home."

"Do you want me to come in with you?"

"If you want to."

He winks and wipes the tears from my eyes. Then he hugs me tightly against him and nuzzles his face into the side of my neck. "I'm sorry," he whispers.

And I know he is. I'm not scared of Edward, not in the way I was scared of Adam, but I am scared of how I just felt at the thought of losing him. That scared me more than anything. I turn and hold his face in my hands.

"I'm sorry too."

We kiss tenderly.

"Let's get your things and I'll walk you home," he says contentedly.

I smile as we walk inside. Alison, Tom and Joe are standing together talking. Alison sees me and comes over. She hugs me.

"I'm sorry, Abbie. Joe's told us."

I look at Joe, shaking my head, muttering quietly to him, "You didn't have to do that."

He shrugs his shoulders, takes hold of me and speaks quietly into my ear: "Yes I did. You've been through enough hard times."

"Thanks, Joe. And I want to explain why I've not contacted you."

"You owe me no explanation whatsoever, Abbie. I'm just glad that you've finally left Adam. Have you sorted it with Edward?"

I nod.

"Who sent the photos?"

I give him a look.

"You know?"

I nod again, looking in the direction of the bar, towards Darcy.

"Yes, and I'm going to sort that too!"

Edward interrupts me, wanting to speak to Joe. I smile, knowing he wants to apologise. I watch them talking to each other for a minute, then I see Joe look towards the bar area and gesture with his eyes in Darcy's direction. Edward looks furious and starts towards the bar. Joe grabs his arm, shaking his head at him, and says something quietly. Edward looks again in Darcy's direction, and then back at me. I know that Joe has just told him who's taken the photos, and why she did it. He speaks again to Edward, but this time I catch what he says.

"Trust me, Edward. Let her deal with this."

Edward looks doubtfully at Joe, and then turns to me, nodding his head.

"I won't be a minute," I say firmly. "I'm just going to the ladies' before we leave."

He raises his eyebrows, because he knows exactly where I'm going, but he doesn't try to stop me this time. I smile as he looks at me protectively. Alison says she's coming with me, but I'm not going to the ladies', I'm going to the bar. I walk off, with Alison following some way behind me, and walk straight past the toilets.

"Abbie, Abbie!" Alison calls as she realises where I'm going. She starts running to catch me up.

I walk straight over to Darcy. She shakes her head and pulls a mocking sad face. I stay calm. How, I don't know, because I want to kill her. I see her phone in her hand, and I'm nearly shaking with adrenalin as she smirks at me.

"Dear me, he didn't like that, did he?"

I want to knock her head off, but I won't lower myself to her level, although it's taking all my willpower not to. I look at her phone instead. James watches as she goads me, wiggling her phone in front of my face.

"Every picture tells a story, Abbie. What's yours then, eh? See a good-looking doctor and can't resist batting your eyelashes at them?"

I close my eyes briefly, telling myself keep calm.

"You tart," she sneers.

I grab for her phone and prise it out of her hand.

"Give it back, you little bitch!" she screeches.

I stare at her and step backwards as she reaches for it.

"Don't you fucking dare!" she spits, seeing what I'm about to do.

I hold her phone over James's pint and wiggle it, savouring the moment. I don't take my eyes off her. Then I pull a startled look.

"Whoops, butter fingers!" I say smugly, as I drop the phone into the beer.

She's livid. "You'll pay for that, you bitch," she screams. Then turns to James and scowls. "Are you going to let her get away with that?"

"I think she already has," he sniggers.

She raises her hand to my face but I grab her wrist, shaking my head.

"I'd put that down if I were you!"

"Well, I'm not fucking you, am I? I'll k-kill—"

The look on my face must say it all, because she stutters to a halt.

When I speak, I'm surprised by how calm I sound, although I must be radiating anger.

"Don't you ever cross me again, Darcy."

I walk calmly away.

Alison is practically clapping her hands.

Revenge is a dish best served cold, and that, my friends, was practically frozen, I think. Darcy's screeching all sorts of things, but do I care? Not in the slightest. People start to laugh as she tries to fish her phone out of James's pint glass.

I walk back to Edward, my eyes locked onto his. He's grinning and shaking his head at me.

As I reach him, he remarks proudly, "My, my, Abbie, that was classy!" He winks. "Would you like me to walk you home, my lady?"

I giggle. "Yes please."

Alison goes to get her bag, but Tom shakes his head at her, whispering something into her ear. She smiles at him, then at me, and puts her bag back on the table.

"We're just going to have …" – she raises her eyebrows – "umm, another drink with Joe."

I smile, hugging her, knowing that they're giving us time to talk.

"Okay, see you later then." I hug Tom and then Joe.

Joe hugs me back, whispering, "He's a good one is Edward," and I smile, nodding my head in agreement.

Edward coughs to attract my attention.

"Is there anyone else you want to hug before we leave?" he asks, amused.

I nod. "Yes, sorry. You!" And I squeeze him hard, until he laughs.

He puts his arm around me as we're leaving and I can't resist turning as we walk through the doors. I can see Darcy getting the third degree from James as she dries her phone. She looks away from him and sees me leaving with Edward. I smile at her with an air of satisfaction, thinking how pleased I am that everything is working out so nicely for her. Then I squeeze Edward tightly and we leave the club and walk back to the flat.

We arrive at the doors of the nursing block. I smile at him, blushing. I try to calm my nerves by reminding myself that he's kind, that he cares and respects me.

"Do you want to come in?" I ask softly.

He doesn't speak but nods his head. His look says it all. My hand is shaking as I punch in the key code, and even though he must see this, he still doesn't say anything. We walk down the corridor in silence. I open the door to the flat and we go inside.

The chemistry is raging between us.

I drop my bag on the floor and he lunges towards me, grabbing me quickly and pulling me into his strong, safe arms. We're face to face, staring at each other with an intensity that makes my heart race. His eyes smoulder with that come-to-bed look and his breathing is erratic. He's inviting me to give myself to him. God, he looks edible and I want to accept that invitation.

I throw my arms around his neck and wrap my legs around his waist while he holds onto my bottom. A husky moan of anticipation comes from my throat as he starts walking me towards the table. I pant, biting my bottom lip.

He sits me down on the table and stands between my legs, still holding them tightly around him. I think I'm going to faint. I've goosebumps everywhere and I'm tingling from head to toe. I gulp hard as he takes my mouth with his and moves his fingers through my hair and holds onto the back of my head so I don't move. He thrusts my lips open impatiently with his tongue and groans.

I pull him closer and trace my fingertips slowly over his strong back. I increase the pressure and feel his toned muscles tense then relax at my touch.

He runs his hands over my shoulders and his jumper falls away. His fingers move towards my blouse and he gently undoes the top button and slides a finger over my skin.

He's driving me crazy, but I know we have to stop. I gaze into his eyes, and God, they're sexy. My face is flushed, and my heart is racing but I place my hand on his and shaking my head. He looks confused.

"You're saying no?"

I want to cry. My voice is a whimper.

"I'm sorry, but we can't."

"We can't?" he exclaims. "Why? Because of Adam?"

I shake my head. "No, not because of him!" I say firmly.

"Then why?"

"Edward, don't make me say it."

"Say what? I don't understand. You want to and, God knows, I want to."

"I know, I'm sorry. It's a woman thing."

"What, playing hard to get?" he says, his voice sharp.

I want to laugh. "God, are you really that thick around women?"

He's taken aback, although he can hear the amusement in my voice.

"Excuse me?"

"I mean …" Oh, God, I can't believe I'm going to have to spell it out to him. "It's the time of the month."

He raises an eyebrow at me, then smirks.

"I've never had a girlfriend before, remember?"

I raise an eyebrow, blushing.

"I'd not noticed. God, that was awkward."

"So how long do we have to wait?" he asks with a grin. I try my best not to laugh at him.

"A month!" I joke.

"What?" His eyes are like saucers.

I can't help it – I burst out laughing.

"You're kidding, right?" He's nodding his head, answering his own question again.

"Yes, I'm kidding. About five days."

He's still shaking his head at me, but he's grinning now.

"I should spank you for that!"

"Really? I don't think so, Edward Scott."

He holds his head to one side and tuts.

"It was worth a try!"

"Hmm, yes, I can't take that away from you. You're a trier, all right."

"Well, you know what they say," he says.

"And what's that, in the world of bachelors and one-night stands?"

He laughs.

"If at first you don't succeed, try, try, again!"

I giggle.

"That's nice. I love it when you laugh." He squeezes me tightly to him, nuzzling the side of my neck and kissing it gently.

I squirm with pleasure.

"Do you like that?"

I do, but I don't say so.

"No, it tickles."

"What about this?" His voice is velvety as he kisses my neck again.

He runs his tongue slowly over my skin, tracing a line from my ear and down towards my shoulder. It sends shivers down my spine and I wriggle again, pushing my neck towards his mouth.

"I think you like that very much," he purrs.

"Hmm … I think I do too, but you're going to have to stop."

"What if I can't?"

"Please, you have to."

"God, this is so hard. I've never wanted anything so much in my whole life as I want you right now."

"Me too," I say quietly.

He makes a growling noise in his throat; it's comes of frustration, and I feel it too. He lifts me off the table, shaking his head at me.

I pull in my lip and whisper, "Sorry."

He looks puzzled.

"Two things."

He pauses to ensure I'm listening.

"First, what was the end of the message?"

"You want to know?" I reply, still breathy from his kiss. He nods.

"You should have come; I wanted to dance with you."

He nods, liking my answer.

"Okay, and secondly, were you wearing my jumper tonight?"

I blush. Damn, what do I say? I feel silly, but I nod and he smirks.

"Why were you wearing it?"

I close my eyes tight.

"Tell me."

"Stop it – you're embarrassing me!"

"I know, but I want to know."

"You mean you want me to say it. You already know why."

He pretends he doesn't know, shaking his head and shrugging his shoulders. He looks so cute. His eyes are sparkling, and I can't resist him when he's playful like this.

"I'm thick around women, remember?" he says in a silly voice, batting my words back at me.

I give him a stunned look, because I'm damned sure he's not.

He pushes out his bottom lip and holds out his arms to me.

"Please tell me," he asks, giving me puppy-dog eyes and making me feel sorry for him, although I'm trying my best not to laugh at him.

I answer as best I can, without giggling.

"You're not going to stop until I tell you, are you?" I sigh, and he shakes his head to confirm it.

"I wore it because I felt ..."

His raises his eyebrows and grins at me, waiting for me to say it.

"Close to you. And I could smell you on it." My face is bright red as I finish. "Are you happy now that you've made me say it and embarrassed me again?"

He grabs me tightly and squeezes me.

"I knew it. You are sweet! Do you fancy that dance now?"

I nod and he starts to spin me round the lounge. And, boy, can he dance! I thought Joe could dance, but he's not a patch on Edward. I giggle as he twirls me round and round, and I feel happy and carefree, as though I've known him for years. He kisses me deeply and I don't refuse him.

The door to the flat opens suddenly. Tom and Alison walk in. They start to laugh.

I feel daft, but I'm still smiling.

Edward whispers into my ear, "This is torture. I don't think I can wait five days."

My heart beats faster, and I blush. He knows the effect he has on me.

He takes me by surprise again, slapping me on my bum. Then he calmly turns to face Alison and Tom. "Little minx wanted to dance."

I shake my head in disbelief at his cheek, but he just winks at me.

"I really do need to leave now. I've still a lot of things to sort out."

He kisses me on the cheek and says goodbye to Alison and Tom.

"I'll see you on Monday at work, Abbie. Have a good day with your gran tomorrow, and say hi to her from me."

Then he leaves me with my jaw nearly on the floor.
My God, what just happened?

Chapter 6

I wake before the alarm goes off. It's still dark outside. I squint, focusing on the clock, trying to see the time. I yawn and stretch out my arms and legs. It's only 5 a.m. and I'm tempted to go back to sleep, but I've still got a lot of packing to finish. I throw the duvet back, climb sleepily out of bed, head to the kitchen, and make myself a coffee.

I can't believe it's Friday already. I haven't seen Edward since Monday, and that was only briefly. He's very busy and works so hard; he's really dedicated to his job and patients. I'd never have thought he could be so caring, not after our first encounter, but he seems to be one surprise after another.

He's called me every day after work, and we've chatted for at least an hour. I'm surprised by how easy it is to talk to him. He's asked what I've been doing at work and whether I'm enjoying myself. I've told him that Sister's keeping me busy, but that I really like working with her. I've wondered whether he finds it mundane, listening to me going on, but he seems genuinely interested, and I could listen to him for hours and hours talking about surgery. I find it fascinating.

We've quite a few things in common too. Books are one. He laughed when I told him that I only read books, that I'm not clever enough to actually write one. His reply was sweet.

"Nonsense, Abbie. Everyone has a book in them."

"Maybe," was my response, "but I'm sure no one would want to read mine."

He'd been as modest as ever when I asked how many books he's sold. "A few."

I do love that about him, because at first I'd thought he was pompous and arrogant, but that couldn't be further from the truth. Now that I'm getting to know him, I know that he's kind and considerate, and, well, I'm falling for him. I smile as I remember one particular conversation.

He'd said that he liked to run, and did so with his dog on the beach every morning. If I wanted to, then when I stayed over I could join him. My eyes nearly popped out of my head – he was asking me to stay over with him! I told him I'd think about it, and he roared with laughter when I said I didn't think a run with him was a good idea because I'd whip his butt, and that wouldn't be very good for his self-esteem. The thought of Edward with a dog made me grin.

"What kind is it? A handbag one?" I asked with a giggle.

He'd sniggered before coughing dryly. "Actually, it's a German shepherd called Shadow, an ex-police dog, highly trained and obedient."

"I couldn't imagine it being anything other than obedient!"

"Meaning?"

"Nothing," I said, changing the subject quickly. I hadn't wanted to get into a debate with him.

I feel so happy with Edward, and I'm glad we're taking it slowly. I smile to myself, thinking about Saturday night and knowing that if Mother Nature hadn't intervened, well, I'd be telling a different story right now. I can't believe how I behaved, or the passion I felt towards him. It was more than exciting. I didn't sleep that night; I kept tossing and turning, my heart racing, though I put it down to my hormones. I've missed him, but I've also loved this week of not seeing him, of flirting on the phone, of laughing with him. Best of all, I've loved getting to know him.

I take my coffee back to my room and finish packing. Then I shower, put on my uniform and write Alison a note.

Thank you so much for letting me stay with you. I cannot put into words how much I appreciate it. I'll see you at my house tonight.

Love Abigail xxxx

I grab my bags and make my way out through the door. I've left my key on the coffee table along with the note.

As I close the door I smile, thinking, *Wow! This has been an eventful stay.* I've made two really good friends, Alison and Tom, got back in contact with Joe, and made one very special new friend that I'm hoping to get to know much better. I'm so grateful for it all.

I walk down the corridor and out of the building. It's chilly outside, and there's a slight frost on the ground. December. Winter has definitely set in and it will soon be Christmas. I wonder what it'll be like this year. No Adam controlling me, telling me what to do or where I'm allowed to go. No having to watch Margo and her lecherous boyfriends get drunk. I huff, remembering the previous Christmas and how her latest beau had made a pass at me in the kitchen. Adam had come in and caught him, though, of course, it was my fault not his. He called me a slag in front of everyone. Then later that night he beat me said I deserved everything I got. I woke on Boxing Day with a black eye. His mother and boyfriend's response? *I needed it, to keep me in check.* I was a slave, imprisoned in my own house.

I shake my head in contempt. Well not this year. I can see whoever I bloody choose to. My gran, Glenda, William. Even Edward. And if I want a Christmas micro meal for one, I'll damn well have one!

I smile warmly as I walk to the car. I can go to the carol service at church by candlelight this year with Gran, like I used to do before I met Adam, then afterwards to the deli in the village for hot mince pies, roasted chestnuts and mulled wine, all put on for free by Gran for the villagers. I can make snowmen if it snows. For years I've had to lie and make up excuses about why I couldn't go with her. I knew it really upset her, but she never pushed me. A wide grin creeps across my face. I know what I'm going to do – I'll go, but it'll be a surprise.

I shiver and pull up the collar on my jacket. I breathe in deeply to fill my lungs with the cold air.

I suddenly feel uplifted, though I'm not sure why because I have an extremely arduous task ahead of me. Maybe that's why I'm feeling happy, because I'm finally closing this chapter on Adam and starting a new phase in my life, one that doesn't include him.

I've sorted things out with my gran. We talked for hours, and it turns out that she didn't know about Adam hitting me or controlling so much of my life. I'm relieved about that, though I still feel guilty about keeping so much from her. I just didn't want to hurt her with the truth.

I arrive at my car and throw the bags in the boot. Between them, Edward and Tom managed to get it started and moved for me on Sunday morning.

I walk onto the ward through the main doors. I turn off my phone and put it into my bag, then go to the handover. Sister is now my mentor, and she's an excellent teacher. I've learnt loads and I'm really enjoying myself.

Darcy is on shift today, but we've not spoken to each other since Saturday night, and that suits me just fine. I heard through Alison that James has dumped her. I want to say, *What-goes-around-comes-around*, but I've managed to hold my tongue. Emily's not speaking to her either. Darcy is finally reaping what she's sown.

I get my jobs from Sister. We start with a medicine round, which is interesting, though there's a lot to take in. She tells me to write down the drugs that I've given and to research them – what they're for, their side effects, and whether they're safe to use with other medications. Homework, she calls it.

I can't seem to put my finger on my mood now. The time is ticking on; it's nearly 2 p.m. and I'm not sure if I'm nervous, scared, happy or content. Probably all four. Nervous about going home. Scared about changing the locks and Adam's reaction, which I know isn't going to be a good one.

Happy that I'm finally doing it. Apprehensive, maybe. Content? I'm not sure about content. Content with my decision, or content with Edward? I feel very mixed up. I've support now, from my gran and Alison, even Tom. Edward? Well, he's just great. He wanted to come to the house with me tonight, but I said no, that I'd be fine. I know that Adam will be twenty times worse if Edward's there, or if he knows that I'm seeing him. Edward wasn't happy about my decision, but I convinced him in the end, telling him it was something I needed to do by myself.

It's 2.30 p.m. and Sister has said I can go. She shouts goodbye to me as I'm leaving the ward. I walk past Edward's office and hear him on the phone, talking about work. I smile at the sound of his voice. I don't want to disturb him; he's too busy, and I know he'll stop what he's doing if I go in. I'm tempted though, really tempted, because I've not seen him properly all week.

I leave the ward, feeling a little jittery at the thought of what I'm about to do. I sigh, telling myself that I can do this.

I arrive at the car park, take out my keys, unlock my car and climb in. I put the key in the ignition and turn it. Nothing.

"Come on," I mutter. "Don't do this to me, not now."

I try again, but still nothing happens. I lose my temper.

"Start, or I swear to God I'll scrap you!"

It doesn't start. I get out and slam the door shut, muttering under my breath.

"Bloody car! You started the other day when you didn't have to go anywhere, didn't you? That's it. You're going. You're always letting me down, you shit."

I kick the wheel as a man walks past, raising an eyebrow at me.

I'm so angry that I shout, "What?"

"Nothing, love," he replies with a startled look on his face.

I'm really not in the mood now, because I need to get home to meet the locksmith. I can't afford to miss him. I've been dreading this all week, and if I don't do it now then I'm not sure I'll be able to do it again.

I've had weeks to psych myself up, and I'm not changing my mind now. I get my phone out and order a taxi.

"I'll meet the driver at the main entrance of the hospital."

He tells me it will be there in five minutes. I run around to the boot of the car and grab my three large, heavy bags. Why didn't I tell him to come here to pick me up? I slam the boot, give my car a dirty look, and start running hell for leather towards the main corridor. Inside the hospital, I keep my pace up, shouting excuse me to people who are sauntering down the corridors with all the time in the world.

I see my taxi pull up at the kerb just as I head through the main doors. It's now 2.45 p.m. I'm shattered and my bags are really heavy.

I walk over, relieved that I'll make it home on time.

A man in his forties gets up from a bench and shouts, "Hey! That's my taxi."

"No, it's mine!"

The taxi driver lets down his window.

"Where to?" he asks. He's looking at us both, and I'm fuming.

"Elizabeth Drive!" I say, annoyed.

"Claire Street!" says the man, clearly not amused.

I need to win this one, and I'm not in the mood to give in. I shout loudly at the taxi driver, "I'll tip you!"

The taxi driver shrugs his shoulders.

"Elizabeth Drive it is, then."

"That taxi was mine."

"Not unless you've moved, mate!" I reply sarcastically.

He shouts all kinds of obscenities at me from the roadside as I get into the car.

"I thought nurses were meant to be helpful."

"Nah, that's just a myth," I call back, thinking of Darcy. "Sorry!"

I close the door and he starts banging on the window. The taxi driver looks at me with a half-smile.

"It was his taxi to Claire Street."

I roll my eyes. Great, but I'm in now, and I'm certainly not getting out. I need to get home.

The man bangs aggressively on the window. He's not giving up, but neither am I. I pull down the window, shouting at him as the taxi drives off, "First up, best dressed!" Then I close it and watch the man as he shouts and swears at me from the roadside.

I sit back and let out a huge sigh.

"Bad day, love?"

"You could say that."

I don't say much for the rest of the journey. Why is it that the thought of Adam makes me behave the way I do to people? Always defensive and with my guard up. The taxi driver chats away, but I just nod. I've too much to think about, so I stare out of the window.

We arrive at my house and the taxi pulls up to the kerb.

"Nice place, love. Is it yours?"

"Thank you," I reply, not answering his question. I get my bags out and give him a twenty-pound note, telling him to keep the change.

"Cheers, love. You have a nice day!" he shouts as he's driving off.

I stand on the drive, looking at my house and wondering, Am I ready to do this? I take a deep breath as I walk towards the door. Then I reach into my bag for my keys. I open the front door, step into the hallway and lock the door behind me. I continue to breathe deeply as I put my bags down on the floor. I nod my head at myself, speaking aloud.

"I'm home. This is *my* home, and it will be my home for as long as I live."

I look at the grandfather clock in the hall. It's 3 p.m. The locksmith is due at any moment. I go down the hall, passing the lounge and the dining room on the right. The morning room is opposite on the left. My mum called it the morning room because it's always sunny in there. Next to it is what used to be my playroom, but now it houses my bookcases and plants.

There are two huge, old brown leather chairs next to the old wood fire surround. French doors lead out into the garden. I love this room; it has many happy memories for me. It's been redecorated, but the cupboards in the alcoves still have the old wallpaper inside. Every time I go in them, I smile and think of my dad. The room used to be decorated in Danger Mouse wallpaper. It was my dad's favourite cartoon. Mum wanted fairies and princesses, but Dad won as always.

"Charlotte, don't fill her head with all that nonsense and make-believe. You'll have her going soft!"

He was very practical, my dad, a very good businessman. He'd made a lot of money. He didn't want my head filled with fantasy but, then again, was Danger Mouse any different? Funnier, yes, but still fantasy. My mum was loving, beautiful, and indulged me far too much. She could wrap my dad around her little finger just by smiling at him. They were perfect for each other. Those were happy days, the short time I had with them. I miss them so much. However, it's still my room. I've spent hours in here alone with my thoughts and books. Adam never came in.

I continue down the hall towards the back of the house and the kitchen. On the way past, I close the cellar and downstairs cloakroom doors. He never bloody shuts them. After the flat, this old Georgian detached house feels enormous – it has four large rooms downstairs and five bedrooms on the upper floor – although it's smaller than the house I grew up in with Gran and Grandad. The gardens wrap around and I have the same gardener my parents had. I don't know for how long though, because he keeps threatening to retire, does Mr Green.

I walk into the kitchen, which spans the full width of the house at the back; a conservatory has been knocked through into it.

Adam was always pestering me to sell the house and get something smaller. He wanted the money. I know it's worth a lot, and it's in a very desirable area, but I refused.

I wouldn't have cared if it were a two-up, two-down with a toilet in the yard. It was my parents' house, and it holds too many fond memories of them. That's worth more than any amount of money. Over the years, before I moved in, it was rented out to families. That's nice. It's a family house and should be filled with lots and lots of children. I would never sell it; I just wish I could fill it with lots and lots of children.

I walk over to the sink and notice two cups in the bowl. One has lipstick on it, and it's not mine. I close my eyes. I pick up the cups and throw them both in the bin. I'm furious: she's been here, in my house.

The doorbell rings and I run to open it, shouting, "I'm coming."

I look through the spy-hole first, just in case. It's the locksmith. He looks about sixty years old.

I open the door as he greets me. "Afternoon love. Three locks to change?"

I nod.

He walks in and wipes his feet. "I'll start here, shall I?"

"That's fine. Thank you for coming at such short notice."

He smiles at me.

"Would you like a tea or coffee?"

"Tea, please."

"Sugar?"

"Four, please, and don't stir it." He grins at me. "It's an old joke, love."

I smile at him, remembering my grandad. He used to say things like that to my gran.

"Four?"

He nods.

"Four it is then."

He gets to work changing the locks.

"Do you mind if I get on with something?" I ask.

"Not at all, love. You crack on. Which are next? The back door, then the French doors?"

"Yes, and if you get stuck, just give me a shout."

"No problem, love. I will."

He really does remind me of Grandad. *Crack on. No problems.* I smile as I walk upstairs with my bags.

They were very wealthy, my grandparents, although if you met them away from their house you'd never know that they had money. They had no airs or graces, always worked hard, and never forgot their roots. They ensured my feet were planted firmly on the ground. I never lost my accent. I went to the local schools, and they brought me up to know the true value of things. They taught me that life is precious. They were down to earth, and so funny with the things they'd say, especially to each other. I adored Grandad; I miss him greatly. And my gran, well, I just love her to bits.

I enter my bedroom at the front of the house and my face drops. The bed hasn't been made, and both pillows are out of place. She's slept here, he's had her here, in my bed.

I throw my bags down and start ripping the sheets, then the duvet cover, off the bed. I pick up the pillows and throw them into a heap on the floor. Then I run downstairs to the kitchen, open a drawer and get out the bin liners. Back upstairs, I ram the sheets and covers into one of the bags. Then I get another and stuff the pillows in. The duvet goes into a third. I take all three bags out of the bedroom and head downstairs. The locksmith moves to one side as I take them to the bin.

He doesn't speak, but smiles gingerly at me as I make my way back into the house. I go back to the bedroom and look at the bed in disgust. It has to go.

I get out my phone and Google *beds for sale.*

I find one place close by, ring the number and order a new bed, paying extra so they'll deliver it today and remove the old one. The man is kind, saying he'll come on his way home from the shop tonight, around six thirty. It's costing me the best part of eight hundred pounds for that privilege, but I'd have paid double.

I walk over to the dressing table and see an earring that's not mine. I go to the bathroom: makeup, really? Has she moved in? I grab the towels, makeup, Adam's stuff and the contents of the linen basket, and empty the whole lot into the bin liner. The bag goes outside with the other trash.

The locksmith is just finishing the front door.

"I've done this one, love."

I smile quickly at him.

"I'll start at the back now, shall I? I've left the key in the lock, and locked it for you."

He nods sympathetically at me. I know what he's referring to. He can tell what's going on; he's not stupid.

I show him the other doors.

"Thank you."

"It won't take long now, love. I'll soon be out of your hair."

I go back upstairs and take another deep breath before starting on Adam's wardrobes. They're chock-a-block with clothes – new stuff, designer stuff, ten, twenty, thirty different suits, plus shoes and coats. I start to remove the clothes, folding them neatly into the bin liners. Then I step back. What am I doing? I screw them up tightly, just to ensure I'll get extra creases in them, knowing how much this will annoy him. I rip out the other things, stuffing them into the bin liners. The locksmith shouts up to me.

"All done, Ms!"

I head down the stairs, shouting back, "I'm coming. How much do I owe you?"

"One hundred and eighty pounds, love. Sorry, it's sixty pounds a lock."

"That's fine." I smile, relieved they've been changed. "Thank you for coming at such short notice."

I pay him his money, but then something occurs to me. Damn, I've forgotten about the conservatory doors. He sees the look on my face.

"Are you okay?"

"I was just thinking about the conservatory."

"I've no locks left. I only brought three with me. If you're worried at all, then just leave the key in the lock and he won't be able to get in. I can come back and change the other lock for you, if you want. But I'm not free until next week."

"Oh, right. Can I telephone you next week to arrange a date then, please?" I pause. "If I leave the key in the lock, you're sure … it can't be opened?"

"I'm sure."

I nod, smiling at him. I offer him a tip of twenty pounds, but he refuses. "You keep it, love, and I hope it all works out for you."

"Thank you, Mr – oh, I don't know your name."

"Smith," he says with a grin.

"No! Really?"

"Really!"

"Well … thank you again, Mr Smith, and I'll see you next week."

"All the keys to the new locks are in the doors. If you have any problems with them, please don't hesitate to give me a ring."

He leaves, and I feel a little more secure now. I lock the door behind him, check the others to make sure they're all locked, and then put the key in the conservatory door.

It's grown quite chilly now. I shiver and switch on the heating to warm the house. I glance at the clock. It's 5 p.m. and it's dark outside. Where's the afternoon gone?

I return to the bedroom. I see all the full bin bags and shake my head; I've only emptied one wardrobe. I start gathering them up and taking them outside onto the drive.

It's started raining hard. I giggle aloud and don't fasten the bags. There's a smirk on my face as I go back inside, knowing that will really annoy him.

I make my way back upstairs and start on wardrobe number two.

I'm half way through when I hear a car pulling up onto the drive. I look out of the window. At first I think its Alison's Mercedes, so I head for the stairs to let her in. Then I hear a key going into the lock. I stop on the stairs, half way down. I hear the key being taken out and then reinserted.

I'm confused.

There's a knock at the door. The letter box opens and a woman's voice calls through.

"Adam, are you in? My key won't work."

I sit back on the step. I'm well and truly dumbfounded. It's Nicky, and she has a key to my house.

How dare she?

How dare he?

I go back upstairs to my bedroom and look out of the window. She's standing on the drive, looking round. She notices the bin liners and peers into one, then looks up at the window and sees me. She shakes her head, shouting at me.

"Open the door now or I'll ring Adam."

I just shake my head at her. *The bloody cheek!*

I hear her on her phone. "Adam, I can't get in your house. She's inside, and she's changed the locks. I don't know, but you better come quickly."

She screams at me from the drive, "He's on his way. You're going to be so sorry. He's really mad!"

I bet he is! His house, eh? She has no idea, the stupid cow, and I'm well aware of his temper since I've been on the receiving end of it more than once. I open the window in the bedroom and tell her to move, but she snipes, "Piss off!"

I continue to bag his things. Then I throw them out of the window. I did warn her.

"You can't do that, you crazy bitch!"

She's on her phone again. "Adam, she's throwing all your stuff onto the drive from the window." She hangs up. "He said you have to stop or you'll be sorry."

Really? Well, he's got to get in first. Ten, fifteen, twenty minutes pass. I continue throwing out his things. I'm past caring. He can do what he wants. I'm not scared of him anymore. He's nothing but a bully.

His car pulls up onto the drive next to Nicky's, and she runs to him. He shoves her to one side, shouting up at the window to me instead.

"Abbie, please stop. Let me come in, and I'll explain everything to you."

Nicky screeches at Adam, "You pushed me!"

He grabs her by her face, shouting at her, "Shut the fuck up! Get back in your car! This is your fault, you stupid little tart! I warned you this would happen, but you couldn't resist, could you? Now get in the car and shut up!"

"Adam, please!" She's shocked that he raised a hand to her. She cowers and gets into her car. He hasn't changed.

"Abbie, please! Let's talk. If you never want me to see her again, then I won't."

"Leave, Adam, or I'll ring the police."

"I mean it, Abbie! Open the fucking door!"

I shake my head. "Just leave!"

I see Alison's car coming up the road. I ring her immediately; I don't want her walking into this. She answers straight away.

"Alison, drive past and pull in up the road. Adam's here, outside on the drive with Nicky, and he's going mad. He's threatened her and she's in her car."

"Oh my God! Are you all right?"

"I'm fine. He can't get in; the locks have been changed. If he doesn't leave soon, I'll ring the police. You just sit tight and wait for me to ring you, okay?"

"Okay, if you're sure."

"I'm sure he'll get fed up and leave soon, once he knows I'm not backing down."

I hang up and close the window.

Adam paces up and down the drive, muttering to himself. He starts picking up the bin liners and walking towards his car with them. He opens the boot and throws them inside. I watch him from the window, hoping he'll get his things and then leave. He goes to Nicky's window and bangs on it, saying something to her that I can't hear. He takes her mobile phone from her hand. My phone starts ringing repeatedly but I ignore it, not bothering to check the number because I know it's him using Nicky's phone. I put mine on silent, placing it down on the cabinet next to the bed. I'm desperate for him to leave.

I look up the road. I can still see Alison in her car, talking on her phone. I can see the light on. Five, ten, fifteen minutes pass, but Adam's still on the drive. Nicky gets out of her car a few times, only for Adam to order her back into it.

Another car drives past slowly. The headlights flash as it pulls in behind Alison's. The driver gets out. Great, it's Tom; she must've called him. She gets out of her car, and I ring her immediately. Tom shakes his head at her, saying something. Alison doesn't answer my call. They both start walking towards the house. I'll have to go downstairs and let them in. I run down to the door and unlock it. I open it just as Alison and Tom are walking up the drive. I stand in the doorway.

When Adam sees me, he starts shouting again.

"Abbie! Let me talk to you, please."

I shake my head. Alison and Tom walk straight past him and he doesn't bat an eyelid at them. He's just focusing on me and the open door.

"Please, Abbie." He holds out his arms to me.

Is he for real! Like I'm going to walk into those arms. I shake my head at him as Nicky gets out of her car. I ask Alison and Tom to go inside. I know Adam's temper, and their being here will only make the situation worse.

"Please, for me, just go inside let me sort this out. If he turns nasty, I promise I'll shout for you both."

They go inside but they're not happy with me. Tom looks down the street before entering the house. He removes his mobile from his jeans pocket and rings someone. I can't quite catch what he's saying because Nicky is shouting so bloody loudly.

"Where are you?" He nods. "Good."

Alison looks at him.

"Well?"

"Five minutes," he says cryptically.

They both walk into the hall. I'm sure Tom might have just called the police. My head feels like it's going to explode.

Nicky is screaming and yelling, and Adam is just standing there staring at me. Nicky keeps grabbing Adam's arm, but he's really sharp and nasty towards her.

"Stop fucking grabbing me, Nicky! Did I tell you to get out of your car?"

She goes silent, and I look at him in disgust. She's pregnant, but he doesn't care. He never has before, so why should he change now?

"Just leave, Adam. Take your things and leave. I want a divorce."

"Never."

"You don't have much of a choice, really, do you?"

He walks over to me and I back away from him. Nicky is screeching again, but he's focusing on me. I look at him with contempt. This is becoming unbearable. I wish he would leave, and I wish to God that she would shut her mouth.

His voice is calculating. "Give me a new key to the house and I might leave."

"I don't think so. This is my house, and you're never stepping foot over this threshold again."

"Give me a fucking key!"

"No."

"What does she mean, it's her house?"

She has no idea, no idea at all. But then he's very good at hiding things. Hiding the truth, being manipulative. Let's face it, he's had a very good teacher – his mother and her devious ways. A chip off the old block, you might say. She married for money, but that soon fell through. He divorced her, leaving her penniless, to bring up Adam on her own.

"This is my house, Nicky. My money. The car he drives? That I paid for. Or did he forget to tell you? That's why he's so desperate to make up with me. I'm guessing you have money too." I point towards her car. "That's why he's with you. Am I right in thinking that, Adam?"

He stares at me. Nicky watches him quietly.

The look on his face is a warning – that I should shut up. I know that look all too well, but I don't shut up. I continue to caution her, although I don't know why, since I owe her nothing. But I despise him with all my heart. He knows that if I divorce him then he won't get a penny without a fight. I continue, nervous, but still angry.

"Or did you think he loved you, Nicky?" I shake my head in disapproval. He's not capable of love. "He loves your money, maybe. Looks like you've found another sucker, Adam. What are you doing, tapping into clients' details now?"

He looks spitefully at me, his eyes narrowed as I continue, "Have I hit a nerve, touched on the truth?"

His face changes, and I know what's coming next.

"I said give me a fucking key, you frigid, barren little bitch. It's no wonder I only fucked you!"

"Frigid? Barren?" I scream back. "Fucked me?" I'm disgusted with him. "You never fucked me, you practically raped me from day one!"

I move out of his way as he lunges for me, trying to grab the keys from my hand. He catches the side of my face with his knuckles.

I shout again. "Leave, before I call the police!"

He raises his hand again; I think to hit me properly this time.

Nicky looks bewildered and moves her hands protectively over her belly.

I jerk backwards, closing my eyes and waiting for the blow.

Suddenly Adam screeches loudly, "Take your fucking hands off me!"

I open my eyes to see what's happening. Edward has Adam by his jacket.

"I think the lady asked you to leave!"

Adam squares up to Edward, shouting, "Fuck off. This has nothing to do with you."

Edward pushes Adam hard, and he falls backwards on to the bonnet of Nicky's car. I feel dazed as I watch what's happening. Edward is on top of him in a split second. He's got him by the throat with two fingers, that's all, but Adam is almost paralysed. He doesn't move and he looks scared to death. I suddenly feel pleased that he's on the receiving end of someone else's temper for once, that he's experiencing some of his own medicine. He looks utterly shocked.

"She said, leave," Edward says, loudly but calmly. "What fucking part of that do you not understand?"

Adam stares at him for a long moment, and then throws his hands into the air in defeat. He looks scared.

Edward lets go of him cautiously.

"Okay, okay, I'm going!" says Adam, coughing and spluttering.

Nicky gets into her car, a look of dismay etched across her face. I'm hoping she's seen and heard enough. Adam gets quickly into his, shouting something before he drives off. I don't catch what he says but, to be perfectly honest, I'm not interested. I'm just glad they've both left.

Chapter 7

I look at the empty drive as Edward approaches me, holding out him arms. I stare blankly, stunned by everything that's just happened. He pulls me tightly into his arms and strokes my hair.

"Has he hurt you?"

I don't know what to say.

He takes my face in his hands, studying my reaction. "Are you okay?"

I'm in a daze. I don't know how I feel.

"Hey, come on, Abbie. Speak to me."

But I can't. I just want to go to my room, close my eyes and pretend the past four years never happened. I shrug my shoulders and start to walk inside.

Edward watches me, puzzled. Alison appears beside me.

"Abbie, are you okay?"

I feel numb. When I finally speak, my voice is quiet.

"I'm just going to the bathroom."

She smiles at me, knowing I want time on my own. Edward starts to follow me, but Alison grabs his hand and shakes her head.

"Leave her, Edward," she whispers. "Let her calm down. Please, just let her have five minutes to herself."

He sighs and rolls his eyes, then smiles at me sadly. I gaze back at him, feeling desperate inside, desperate to be alone. I turn. I feel him watching me walk up the stairs.

I head into the bathroom, wanting to scream until I have no breath left in my lungs. I put my hand to my cheek and it hurts, then, looking in the mirror, I notice a red mark on my cheekbone, and I'm instantly reminded of my past with Adam – the abuse, the mind games. I recall all his nasty words and threats.

The doorbell rings and I jump. I automatically throw my hand to my heart, as if I might stop it from leaving. I close my eyes tightly.

My hands are shaking. It's Adam; he's come back. I just want him to leave me alone, but I know he won't, not until he gets what he wants. I've said too much tonight, and in front of Nicky. I've provoked him, and he's going to take his revenge. I take deep breaths as those old, familiar feelings of panic and anxiety rise up – bad memories and visions of how cruel he can be.

Alison runs up the stairs, calling me and knocking on the bathroom door.

"Abbie, you have a delivery."

I open the door to the bathroom. I can hear Edward and Tom talking to some men downstairs.

She smiles kindly at me. "A bed?"

I sigh, lifting my head up and thanking God.

"I'd forgotten."

I'm so relieved that it's not Adam.

"If you want, just tell me which room it goes in and I'll sort it out for you. You come down in your own time."

"They need to remove the other bed first."

"Okay, I'll tell them." She points down the landing. "Is it the room at the front?"

I nod my head, mouthing "Thank you" as I watch her running back down the stairs.

I go back into the bathroom and sit on the stool, still in a daze, still confused, angry, upset and scared. Edward's downstairs. Tom must have phoned him, not the police, as I'd first imagined, and he came to my rescue.

He must have heard what Adam shouted at me, and what I shouted back at him. I'm so ashamed of my past with Adam and what he did to me, how he made me feel so weak. And, now, I'm too embarrassed to speak or even look at Edward. I don't want him to quiz me about my past – I'm not ready to speak to him about any of it – though I'm sure he will.

I think back to how I felt before I came home today. I felt a little stronger, but now I'm wondering whether that was just because I'd been away from Adam for so long.

I've experienced freedom, and meeting Edward made me forget about him for a while. I knew what would happen tonight, but I'd not anticipated everyone being here, listening to my private life being screamed about on the drive. I feel as though I'm struggling once again to come to terms with everything, and I know Adam will up his game now. At least I did kind of stick up for myself this time. I didn't give in or give him a key. I stood my ground, answered him back, but this won't be the end of it. No, he only left because Edward turned up and threatened him, and he fled like the bully he is.

I look towards the door as I hear men coming up the stairs, followed by Alison. She's giving them directions, telling them which room to remove the bed from.

"Nice gaff, Missus!" one of them remarks. She doesn't answer them.

I hear them moving the old bed out and the new one in. Alison lets them out and thanks them. Then she closes the door and locks it.

"Is she okay?" I hear Edward ask. "Will you please ask her if I can see her, if I can talk to her?"

I close my eyes. I want to hug him close to me, because he makes me feel safe and wanted, but I don't want him to ask me questions right now.

"I won't be a minute." Alison runs back upstairs. "I'll just make sure she's okay. I'll ask her for you."

"Thank you." He sounds so apprehensive.

I hear Tom speaking to him. "Are you all right, mate?"

Edward doesn't respond, and I know he wants to come and comfort me. But I need to clear my head first, because at this moment in time I know that if he asks me any questions then

I'll tell him everything. I feel so vulnerable and weak, but I'm not ready to be judged on why I stayed, or how stupid I was. I already know that for myself, and I don't want someone else telling me the bloody obvious. It's easy to judge someone else's mistakes in hindsight.

Alison knocks on the bathroom door.

"I'll be down shortly," I say, not opening the door. "I'm just going to have a quick shower."

"Okay. Edward's asked if he can talk to you."

"I know, I heard him, but can you please just say that I'll be down shortly?" I'm sure she can hear the pleading in my voice.

"Okay, I will." Her voice is soft, and she's trying to comfort me. "I'll make the bed up for you if you want me to. Where's your bedding?"

"In the cupboard on the landing."

I feel bad for not opening the door to her, and not speaking to Edward. I don't want to hurt his feelings, but I know I'm breaking, and I'm fighting to keep everything together. I just want to be left alone. I'm not coping with my emotions anymore. I feel sick with stress and worry, although I don't want to be here in the house on my own. I play Adam's words over repeatedly in my mind. I wish to God I could blank out the things he's done to me, said to me, and the threats he's made about what he'd do to me if I ever left him.

I run the shower, hoping to wash everything away. When I'm done, I get out and reach for a towel. Then remember that I binned them. I pop my head around the bathroom door to see if the coast is clear. I run down the landing and grab a towel from the cupboard and my dressing gown. I put it on and make my way back to my bedroom. I pass the room on the landing that would've been the nursery. I take a deep breath, trying hard, really hard, not to go in. But my hand is on the door handle, turning it. This is what I do to myself when I'm at rock bottom. I know I shouldn't go in while I'm in this frame of mind, but I can't help myself. It's like I have to punish myself for what I allowed him to do to me. I remember what he shouted at me on the driveway. *Barren.* But I'm not barren. I've been pregnant.

I walk inside the room and a lump immediately hits the back of my throat, so hard that it takes my breath away. I stroke my hand down the side of the wall, my lip quivering. My heart feels so empty.

I walk over to the half-built cot and touch it with a shaking hand. I close my eyes, feeling so alone. I wrap my arms tightly around myself in the hope that it'll give me some comfort.

Everything is getting too much, piling on top of me. I want to run away and hide, where nobody can find me or hurt me anymore. I want these feelings to stop. I want my brain to stop working, and banish every sad memory.

I want my mum and dad. I miss them so much, and I want to ask them what I should do. But I can't have them. I talk to them sometimes, but they never answer me. It's always been the same, for as long as I can remember. No parting of the clouds, no wise or wonderful words of wisdom from them. Just a one-sided conversation, me talking, and silence from them. My heart feels heavy in my chest, like it's been replaced by a rock.

I place my hand back on the cot and see the bunny mobile and the toy chest. I can't cope. I cry out, the tears stinging my eyes.

"I want my babies!"

I stamp my feet, hitting my hand on the cot so hard that it falls over with a crash. I scream and stamp like a spoilt child.

"I want my babies!"

I look out of the window and up to heaven, shouting, "Why? Why did you take them? They were mine, not yours! Don't you have enough people to love you already? Wasn't it enough to take my mum and dad away from me? Answer me, goddamn you, why?"

Tears fall hard down my face. My nose is streaming and I can't get my breath. I'm sad, frustrated, and so bloody angry.

I hear someone come into the room. I turn slowly. It's Edward. He switches on the light. I close my eyes. I don't want anyone to see me like this; this is private.

"Turn it off!" I snap.

He flips the light switch, but not before he's seen the room. I look back out of the window. I'm still crying and shaking; I can't stop.

He walks over and slips his arms around me from behind.

"Let go of me. How long have you been there?"

"Shush, it's okay, Abbie."

"I asked you how long?" I push him away. I'm trembling. I can't control what I'm saying. I'm so angry – at the world, at God, at Adam, at my parents for leaving me, at my miserable life and my inability to stand up to my husband.

"I heard what you said … I'm so sorry."

"I don't want your pity," I sniff. "I want my babies. I want my mum and dad. I want my life back. I want this pain to end."

My legs go from under me. I'm drained, exhausted of having an argument with a god who never answers me, never tells me why.

Edward steadies me with his arms and turns me towards him. I try to push him away, but he looks sadly at me, shaking his head.

"I can't do this anymore." I shrug my shoulders. "Now you know, since you heard everything. I'm damaged, cursed even. Look at me. I'm a mess. I'm fucked up. I've no one, and nobody cares. You should leave me, walk out of that door and never look back. All I'll bring you is misery."

He squeezes me tightly to him.

"Don't, Abbie. Don't say that. You're not damaged, fucked up or cursed. You're hurting. Grief is hard." He pauses, looking at me. "And I care."

I can't answer him. I've no words left. I just whimper softly.

"It's not fair. Why mine? Why me?"

"Shush, it's okay. You cry if you need to." He holds me, rocking me, stroking my hair, comforting me and whispering into my ear, "Shush, it's okay." He kisses the top of my head very gently. I nuzzle into him. I need him to hold me, to tell me that everything is going to be all right. He takes my hand and smiles at me affectionately.

"Come on. Let me take you to your room."

He leads me from the nursery, closing the door behind us.

"Which one is it?"

I point. He walks me down the landing towards my room and opens the door. I see the newly arrived bed that Alison has made up for me. I breathe out and try to smile, but I feel so alone, and pathetically sad and sorry for myself.

"Hold me, please," I whisper.

He takes me again in his arms, and I suddenly feel warm. His arms are strong, and the feeling of loneliness is subsiding. He looks at me with an expression that's both thoughtful and sensitive, and I suddenly start to feel things that I shouldn't, not right now. I need him to comfort me, to kiss me. My heart starts beating faster. What's happening to me, and why am I thinking this? I want to kiss him. I shouldn't, but he's here and I need someone.

I pull away from his arms, lifting myself onto my tiptoes and kissing his cheek. I move to his lips, but he doesn't return the kiss. I move my lips slowly down his chin, across his jaw line, on to his neck, then working my way back towards his lips. Still he doesn't move. He looks confused, as if he wants me to stop, but I can't. Why is he not kissing me back? I move to his ear and kiss softly around it. I need this. I need him. I need some connection.

Without any thought at all, I speak softly, pleadingly into his ear.

"Please. I need you to take all this hurt, pain and pity from my body. I'm ready to say yes."

Edward closes his eyes briefly, then opens them. He traces a line gently down the side of my face with his finger, wiping my tears and shaking his head.

"Abbie, this isn't right, sweetheart."

I'm confused. This is what he wanted, to have all of me. Now he's rejecting me.

"No, don't say that. I need you now."

"I can't, not while you're like this. It's not right."

"It is."

"It's not, trust me."

"I thought this is what you wanted." He looks into my eyes. "I'm ready. I'm saying yes, Edward. This is what you've wanted from the start, isn't it? To fuck me?"

He looks shocked.

"Abbie, no! God, please stop. Don't talk like that. This isn't you."

"I don't want to stop … I need you to take this hurt away, and I need you to want me. I want to forget," I shout out in frustration. "Edward, take me."

"Stop this, please."

I put my hands onto his chest and pummel him. He takes them gently in his.

"Stop. Come on, stop." He lets go of my hands and pulls me so tightly to him that I can almost feel his heart racing. I sob into his chest.

"Hey, come on."

"Edward, please. I couldn't bear it if you rejected me now."

He looks perplexed. "Stop, Abbie!"

"I'm confused," I whisper.

He smiles gently at me. He moves me to sit on the bed, and then he kneels in front of me. He looks frustrated but also sad. His body is tense.

"Edward, I don't understand. I thought—"

He places a finger to my lips. Then he takes my hands in his.

"Abbie, listen to me."

"But why?"

"I said listen to me! Please." He's getting cross. "There is nothing more I'd rather do at this moment. To take all that hurt and anger from you. To love your body until you can't walk. I've wanted that from the moment I saw you. I've never wanted anything as much in my life. I can't stop thinking about you. I'm desperate for you. I like things my way. I've always got what I wanted, when I wanted it." He closes his eyes and inhales sharply.

"You're lucky," I say sadly. "I've wanted all my life but never got it."

He smiles softly at me.

"I know, I can tell. That's why this isn't right." He rubs his face with his hands. "Believe me, it's taken all my willpower and strength to stop myself just now, and it did back at the flat too. I'd never reject you. I want you, I want you desperately, but I'm trying to help you. This isn't what you need right now. I'm not a total bastard, Abbie. Though I have been in the past. I've treated women badly, got what I wanted from them and then left. I never cared for any of them, or cared what they thought of me." He breathes in sharply, continuing, "But you, Abbie, God, I care for you. This is very new to me, these feelings I have for you, and I cannot or will not treat you as I treated the others. You're changing me – the way I think and feel. You're far too vulnerable and you need time. Like you said, we need to move slowly, and I am more than happy to wait for you."

"Time?"

"Yes, time. For you and for the loss of your babies. For everything that has happened to you. This pain you're feeling? You're still grieving, and I won't take advantage of you. I like you and respect you too much."

I know that my feelings are still very raw. I close my eyes, trying my best not to cry again, but his words are so full of meaning and hope. I've never let anyone in before. I've always hidden behind the safety of the wall I built. But Edward, I can't seem to stop him from entering my life, and I don't want to.

I answer quietly. "You do?"

"I do." He nods.

"Then just hold me, please. I need you to hold me."

He puts his arms around me and holds me tight to him. I can feel his heart beating fast in his chest. I cry and pull him closer. I let out all the sadness and emptiness I feel inside, everything I've stored up inside me over the years. I've never had anyone to hold me who cares as he does, and it feels right.

"Shush. Don't cry, Abbie."

But I can't stop, because I've not cried like this before, and I think this is what I need, to let it all out. I cry until I have no tears left, and all the while he just holds me, rocking me, comforting me, taking all the hurt and pain away. I know everything he says is right. It's not the right time – I would have regretted it in the morning – but I still want to love him, and for him to love me. Is that so wrong?

Edward gets up off the floor.

"Come on. You need to get some rest." He pulls back the duvet. "Get in."

"Please stay with me, Edward."

"I don't think I can, Abbie. I'm not sure if I could stay in the same bed as you right now."

"Please, I can't bear to be alone, not tonight."

"Abbie, I can't."

"Please."

"Stop, Abbie. Please stop. Don't look at me like that, with those sad eyes." He runs his hands through his hair. He seems frustrated.

I'm afraid he doesn't want me, and I'm so confused. He wants me, but can't stay with me. I don't understand him.

"Edward, do you think I'm a tart?"

"No, why are you saying that?"

I shrug my shoulders.

"Is it because of what you said to me, asking me to fuck you?"

He's blunt, but I did say that and I feel embarrassed now. I can't believe I said it – that wasn't me at all. I nod my head.

"No, I don't think you're a tart. Far from it. At any other time, I would've been flattered, honestly, but I don't want you to do something you'll regret, and I certainly don't want you to hate me for taking advantage of you. I know you're naive, shy, very inexperienced ..."

I blush.

"I knew a little about what had happened from Tom, but I didn't understand how bad you were actually feeling, not to this extent. Then you asked me to take all the hurt away from your body. I knew I couldn't; it wasn't right. I think you're beautiful, and intelligent, but you have a poorly heart. A poorly heart that needs mending by a surgeon." He smiles at me and raises an eyebrow. "And he's very willing to help you mend it, if you'll let him."

I smile back at him.

"That's better. Are we friends again?"

I nod, and he squeezes me tighter, kissing the top of my head.

"Do you want me to help you?"

I can't believe what he's just said to me, but I smile and reply truthfully, "What have I done to deserve you? I can't bog you down with my problems."

"Why not?"

"Because it's not fair on you."

"But I'm happy to help you, plus when you're all mended, I get to keep you! You're my prize, and I know you're worth mending."

"Thank you. That was a nice thing to say."

"I meant it," he says, kissing me firmly on the cheek.
I wince.

"What's wrong?"

He takes my chin and looks at my face. His expression
darkens.

"Did he hit you?"

I don't answer.

"Abbie, did he hit you? Answer me! When did he hit you?"

I shrug my shoulders.

"Abbie?"

"Just leave it, please. It's over with."

"Like hell it is!" He looks furious. "He's hit you before?"

I close my eyes. I need to forget what Adam's done to me.
I need to bury the past. I sigh.

"Leave it be, please. I've not got the strength anymore."

He nods curtly, but I know that's not the end of it.

"I'll go and make you a drink."

He leaves the room and a few minutes later, Alison pops
her head around the door, smiling at me.

"Can I come in?"

I nod, and she sits on the bed next to me. She looks at my
face.

"Adam. He's hit you, hasn't he?" She shakes her head.
"And he's done it before?"

I pull my lip in tight and nod.

"Don't tell Edward."

"He knows already. I heard him telling Tom while he was
getting you a drink. He asked me to come and sit with you."

"Why? Where's he going?"

"I don't know. He didn't say."

I jump off the bed just as Edward is coming through the
door.

"Edward, please don't."

He knows that I know something's going on. He glares at
Alison, but she ignores him and smiles at me.

"I'll leave you two alone. Do you still want me to stay?"

"Please. If Tom wants to stay, too, he can. He's very welcome. The other front bedroom is the guest room."

Alison smiles, then kisses the top of my forehead before leaving.

"I'll ask him. I'll see you in the morning."

She nods at Edward as she leaves the room.

Edward passes me my drink. "Drink it. It'll help you sleep."

I take a sip and cringe. Its brandy and it's warm. I hold my nose and drink it straight down, wincing at the taste.

Edward looks at me with a raised eyebrow.

"I didn't mean down in one!"

He smiles, shaking his head. Then he sits down next to me and takes my hand.

"The next time you want to go in there, ask me to come in with you. We can talk together if you like. We can both shout at God."

I let out a moan. "I don't mean to shout at God; it's just I've no one else to blame. So he gets the brunt of my temper every now and again. I suppose we all do it when we don't understand something, or when bad things happen. We pray to God to help us, but when it fails, well, we blame him. It's sometimes a little easier, having someone to blame."

He smiles at me, and I feel a little silly.

"Come on. Get into bed. You look shattered."

I get in and he pulls the duvet up over me and kisses the top of my forehead gently. I look at him and hold out my hand for him to take.

"Stay with me, please."

He shakes his head and I can tell he's torn.

"I don't think I should."

"Please, I really don't want to be alone."

"I've wanted you so much, Abbie." He sighs. "I'm not sure if I can trust myself around you."

"Please?" I smile at him.

He grins ruefully back at me.

"We're a bit of a mess, aren't we?" I say.

He laughs lightly. "It seems that way, but fate keeps bringing us back together."

I smile at him. That's something my gran would say.

I nod. "It does. Maybe it's meant to be that way."

"Maybe. Come on ..." He's still smiling. "I'll stay with you until you fall asleep. Is that okay?"

I nod my head. "Thank you."

He removes his jacket and shoes and lies next to me. He pats his chest with his hand, gesturing for me to put my head there, so I do, and listen to his heart beating.

It sounds like a lullaby, comforting and soothing. I place my arm around him, squeezing him tight as a way of saying thank you.

He puts his arms around me, cradling me tightly to his chest, and I feel wanted.

He kisses the top of my head and whispers gently to me, "You sleep, angel. Close your eyes and sleep. I'm here, and you're safe, and nobody is ever going to hurt you again."

I smile into his chest, knowing that I'm falling fast. These feelings I have for him, they scare me, and they're like nothing I've ever experienced before. I start to close my eyes and drift off. I know he's only staying with me until I fall asleep, but that's a start, and a very big step for us both.

Chapter 8

I wake, yawn and stretching out my arms across the bed. There's an empty space beside me. My heart sinks. He's gone home. I sigh. He meant what he said.

I knew deep down he wouldn't be here this morning, but I'd hoped he would be all the same. He always sounds so confident, saying what he means and knowing exactly what he wants. It must be nice to be so self-assured and in control of your life and the choices you make.

Whereas I'm the total opposite. I say one thing but, more often than not, I mean something else. I smile to myself, remembering the kind words Edward spoke to me last night. I'm glad he didn't take advantage of me last night. I would've regretted it this morning, just like he said. Though I was a little surprised at his reaction, turning me down the way he did. I wasn't expecting that from him, given his reputation. Maybe the gossipmongers have been adding two plus two and getting five, or judging a book by its cover, as my gran would say.

I sit up in bed and look at the alarm clock. It's 9.30 a.m. I look to see if there's maybe a note from him, but there isn't. I'm sure he'll ring me, but if he doesn't, I'm going to ring him, if only to say thank you. I want to take it slowly with Edward, but I do want us to try. There's something there, a connection between us, one that I've never felt before with anyone else.

I get out of bed, still wearing my dressing gown, and make my way to the bathroom. I can hear the radio on downstairs. Alison and Tom must still be here. I shower quickly and wrap a large towel around myself. Then I hurry back to my room.

I open the door and jump. It's Edward!

"Hi! You stayed!"

He smiles and nods his head, surprised, I think, by my reaction.

"I thought you'd gone home."

"No. I thought I heard you get up. Coffee?" He holds out the cup.

"Thank you, and thank you for staying with me." I smile nervously. "And for not taking …" I pause, blushing. He raises his eyebrows at me. "You know."

He nods his head, smiling.

"Where did you sleep?"

"On the sofa. I was struggling!"

"You were?"

"Yes, you kept moaning in your sleep and then you wrapped your arms and legs around me."

"I did?"

"Urm … you did, and you only had that silk robe on." He closes his eyes for a moment, as though he's trying to wipe the thought from his mind. "So I thought it best to leave."

I grin and marvel at how sweet he can be, though he still confuses the hell out of me.

"So, then, Mr Scott, your reputation precedes you?"

"My reputation? And, pray tell, what might that be?"

"I can't say. I'm sorry." I giggle as I take my coffee, poking out my tongue.

He ignores me, trying not laugh.

"How are you this morning?" he asks.

"Better now that you're still here, thank you."

"Good. I'll leave you to dress, then."

"Are Alison and Tom still here?"

"No, they left early this morning, around seven o'clock. Tom's working."

"You're not working today?"

He shakes his head.

"Although I have to leave in about ten minutes. I've a lot of things to sort out."

I push out my lip. "Oh … okay … right." I feel a little disappointed. I really wanted us to talk, now that he's here and we're alone. I frown at him.

"I don't want you to get cross with me," he says, and I roll my eyes, wondering what he's going to say next.

"But I've asked Alison to come back at 10.30 a.m. to take you out. I've booked you both into the Blue Spa."

I frown again. "You have?"

"Yes, I thought, after yesterday, you needed some time out to yourself, and I can't put off what I need to do today ..."

He looks worried that I'm annoyed with him for planning my day, but that couldn't be further from the truth. It's so thoughtful of him.

"Are you cross with me?" he asks, and I shake my head. "Then why the frown and the sad eyes?"

I shrug my shoulders, biting on my lip and feeling emotional yet again at the kind gesture. I'm not used to this.

"Abbie, have I upset you?"

I need to tell him the truth.

"No, it's just that I've never had anyone like you, looking after me the way you do."

He smiles, tilting his head to one side and giving me a cheeky look.

"And is that so wrong? Me wanting to take care of you, or spoil you and look after you?"

"No, it's lovely! I'm just a little overwhelmed, that's all. Why couldn't I have met you years ago?"

He's still smiling at me, and then he winks.

"Good. I'm glad I've not upset you." He's back to being cocky. "And I'll pick you up at seven on the dot. I'm taking you to dinner!"

I giggle.

"And what's funny?"

"You are! You're so sure of yourself, in everything you do and say. Do people always do what you tell them to do?"

He winks at me again.

"Oh, I can think of one person, not so far away from me, who doesn't do what she's told."

"You can?" I laugh, batting my eyelashes.

He nods.

"So, are you going to answer my question? Dinner at seven?"

I want to throw my arms around him and scream, *Are you kidding? I'll be ready and waiting on the dot.* But that seems a little desperate, so I reply as calmly as I can while I twirl my hair.

"I'm not sure. I think I might be washing my hair."

He coughs dryly, trying not to laugh at me, knowing exactly what I'm doing.

"What, again?"

I giggle. "Nothing gets past you, Edward Scott, you Sherlock Holmes, you!"

He winks and grins at me.

"Hum ... and I deduced that all by myself from your hair being wet."

We both laugh and I take a small bow.

"Elementary, my dear Mr Scott. So you're not just a pretty face, then. You have a little intelligence as well."

"Careful, Baxter. I think you might be getting out of your depth."

I stop laughing, noticing his face has suddenly changed. His eyes have narrowed and he doesn't look amused anymore. I stick my tongue out at him and change the subject quickly.

"What time did you say you'd pick me up tonight?"

He smirks, knowing I've given in.

"About seven o'clock. I think there's a lot we need to talk about."

'Hmm," I say, nodding my head in agreement, "I think so too. But do you have to leave right now?"

He shakes his head, grinning again.

"No, not just right now. So get dressed. I'll meet you downstairs."

He turns and leaves the room. I dry myself off and grab some underwear from my drawers. He's such a gentleman, I think as I head to my wardrobe and pick out a skirt that falls to just above my knee.

It's navy blue with little white daisies on. I choose a white T-shirt to match and get dressed. I tie back my still-wet hair and make my way downstairs, grinning from ear to ear.

He makes me feel so happy, and like a woman, one who's flirting with someone she likes. It's not something I've ever done before, but I'm enjoying it.

I walk into the kitchen and take a deep breath, smiling inwardly as I look at him sitting at the kitchen table. He looks so handsome; his hair is tussled over to one side, and the light stubble on his chin makes him look rugged and sexy. He looks up at me as I enter. His eyes sparkle and dance in the sunlight shining through the window. He blinks, his eyes adjusting to the brightness, and suddenly they have a hooded look, mysterious and sexy. I smile at him, and my heart starts to race.

"Hello again," he says, smiling at me as his eyes wander mischievously over my body. I suddenly feel naked, and I can feel the creep of my blush deepening on my face again. He grins as he stands up and walks over to me with his arms outstretched. "I like what you're wearing! May I have a morning kiss from you? And why are you blushing?"

He knows exactly why. I wish I didn't blush so much around him, but I can't help it. I walk into his outstretched arms without replying and hug him to me. I feel so relaxed around him. He hugs me back tightly. I smile into his chest, and it feels so right. He leans back and points to his cheek with his finger, raising an eyebrow.

"One kiss just there; that will do for now," he says confidently.

I giggle, knocking his shoulder.

"Like I said, Mr Scott, you're very sure of yourself!"

"That I am, and I'm also still waiting!"

I kiss him on the cheek. I love it when he's like this, and I love that I can be like this with him, especially after last night.

He grins at me. "Thank you." Then moves away and picks up his jacket. "Is seven o'clock okay?"

I nod, and he kisses me firmly on the mouth.

"Good, seven it is then."

I nod again and he smiles and puts on his jacket.

"Where are we going?" I ask. "Then I'll know what to wear this time."

He looks at me wickedly. "Just wear a skirt," he says suggestively.

"Just a skirt?"

His eyes narrow, and he gestures at the one I'm wearing. "That skirt, if you like."

"What, no top?"

"I'll leave that up to you."

"You are bad!" I say, shaking my head.

"Always! I can't help myself around you. You're so bloody irresistible."

"You're forgiven, but before you go, may I have a kiss please." I put my finger to my lips and mimic him. "Just one here, please, for now."

"Now who's being bad?" he growls.

I simply raise my eyebrows. He walks over to me and kisses me again. He pulls away quickly, shaking his head and looking frustrated.

"I'm sorry, Abbie. I need to leave now before … I'll pick you up at seven o'clock on the dot. Don't keep me waiting, or you'll be sorry." He winks, and I bat my eyelashes at him.

"Oh really?"

"Really!" He walks back to me, taking me in his arms and kissing me hard on the lips. Then he slaps my bum really hard.

"I can't believe you just did that!" I squeal.

He laughs and winks, looking pleased with himself. He walks out and down the hallway, and I hear him shout back to me.

"It's better for you if you don't play those sort of games with me, because you'll never win, my girl." I make a choking noise. "Bye, Abbie! See you at seven o'clock."

The door shuts.

Bloody hell! I moan as I rub my bottom to soothe the sting. I walk to the front door and open it just as Edward is driving past. He sees me and slows while letting down the window on the passenger side.

"Is it smarting yet?" he shouts. Then he pips the horn, waves and drives off.

I wave back in a daze. I'm still standing at the door as Alison pulls onto the drive.

My God, I think, he's a ball of pure frustration just waiting to explode.

I gulp, wondering now what this evening will bring. Alison climbs out of her car, and I look at her, still feeling a little flustered.

"Hi, Abbie. Are you okay? You look a little preoccupied."

"Hi! No, I'm fine. I'll just get my things."

"It's very kind of Edward to do this for us both," she says as she's locking the car.

"Yes, it's lovely of him, isn't it? Come in. I won't be a minute. What do we need to take?"

"I presume just a swimsuit; that's all I've got in the car."

"I'll just get mine. What time are we booked in?"

"Eleven o'clock."

I run up the stairs and get my swimsuit. Then I grab my denim jacket and meet Alison in the hallway.

"Ready?"

"Ready," she giggles. "This is going to be so much fun."

"To be honest, I've never done this before, been to a spa, but a day of pampering is just what the doctor ordered." Then I laugh.

Alison rolls her eyes and groans at the pun.

"Oh dear, are you going to be like this all day?"

I giggle back at her, unable to contain my happiness any longer.

"More than likely, Alison. I can't help it."

"Good! It's so nice to see you happy. And, yes, this is just what the doctor ordered. A day of happiness, laughing, liquid lunches and a catch-up with some hot juicy gossip."

"Oh, what gossip do you know?" I ask innocently, because I know she's referring to me and Edward.

She pokes her tongue out at me.

"Abbie, don't be mean! I'm dying to know how you two are getting on. You're so right for each other."

I lock the door behind us, and we get into her car. "I'll just have to ply you with alcohol all day to loosen your tongue."

"Really?" I say with a laugh.

We arrive at the Blue Spa. It's very posh, yet another five-star establishment. I smile to myself. You've done it again, I think. Flimsy skirt, white T-shirt, a worn denim jacket and slightly scuffed pumps. I'm seriously going to have to re-think my wardrobe.

We enter the reception area. It's bright and clean, with posters advertising the latest in body wraps:

Lose those unwanted pounds for Christmas.

There's a picture of a woman lying on a table, smiling and wrapped up like a mummy. I wouldn't be smiling at the price – four hundred and fifty pounds! They saw her coming.

As we walk towards the desk, a woman with a fake posh accent looks up and smiles.

"Oh, good morning! How may I help you?"

I smile at her. "We have a reservation."

She goes to the computer.

"Name, please?"

"Abigail Baxter."

"Aha, Miss Baxter, yes, and your friend. Hmm ... somebody is having a treat. Is it a birthday or special occasion?"

I shake my head, and she smiles.

"Oh, just being spoilt then for the day."

I look at her, puzzled.

"You're in for the full day, on our platinum package."

I smile again at her, and then look at Alison. She grins at me.

"You knew?" I mouth, and she nods.

That's Edward, I think – all or nothing. Five stars. Only the best will do. I wonder if he comes here too. I smile inwardly knowing what he's doing, he's helping me to forget Adam. And that is what I'll try to do. I can't keep overthinking everything.

So I'm not going to do! well not today anyway. The lady continues,

"Please be seated, ladies" – she points to a seating area – "and I'll call through to Fabio and tell him you've both arrived."

We take a seat and I glare at Alison.

"Fabio?"

God, where has he sent me? We're both trying our best not to laugh as a door swings open. I presume this is Fabio, swinging his arms as he marches towards us, grinning at us both with teeth so white and dazzling they could stop traffic. As he approaches, I think that he looks shocked, and I automatically assume that it's because of how I'm dressed. It's only as he gets closer that I realise he's overdone it a little, well a lot, with the Botox. He looks like he's just been electrocuted, and I can't stop staring at him. He flaps his arms around in the air, shouting at us in an accent that's neither Italian, English nor French.

"Ladies, ladies, welcome to the Blue Spa! This is your first visit, I see."

I struggle to keep a straight face.

"Your guests of Mr Scott? Well, pamper he said, so pampered is what you shall be." He gestures with his hands for us to stand. "Come, come. You must be Abigail," he says to me with a smile, and I nod. "He was right, as always, Mr Scott."

"Sorry, Mr Scott was right about what?" I enquire.

"Follow me, please. Walk and talk. We've a lot to get through on our platinum package today."

We follow Fabio up a corridor. As he walks, his bum wiggles in time to the swing of his arms. He's as camp as Christmas, but funny.

"He said I'd know you as soon as you smiled, since you have the ability to light up a room. I thought, no! I don't think so. But now I've met you, I see his description was right."

Fabio claps his hands imperiously, suddenly reminding me of someone I know, and I laugh silently to myself.

Fabio continues, "Stacy, come on. No time to waste! Our platinum girls are here. Show them through to their suite. Chop, chop! I'll be back with you ladies in ten," he says with a cheesy grin. Then he walks into an office and closes the door behind him.

I look at Alison and we both burst out laughing.

"Follow me please, ladies."

Stacy leads us to our room and opens the door. It's dazzling inside. Everything is white and looks sterile, like Fabio's teeth. There are two sofas, a coffee table with glasses on a silver tray, mineral water and fresh flowers. There are also two tables with fluffy white towels, slippers and dressing gowns. Lit candles are scattered around the room, and soft music plays quietly in the background. It's not to my taste, but it's relaxing enough for the time being.

"Please, ladies, if you'd like to change into your swimwear and put on your robes and slippers, Fabio will be with you shortly. Your itinerary is on the table; your bathrooms are there." She points at two separate doors with her manicured finger.

"Thank you," we say in unison as she's leaving the room. The door closes and we both laugh again.

"Come on, Abbie. Let's get changed before Fabio arrives." We take our bags into the bathrooms. They're huge. Mine has a round Jacuzzi that's simply enormous.

I do believe I could take a swim in it. Two sinks are set into cabinets, a separate shower cubical stands to one side, and umpteen fluffy white towels and unlit candles in glass jars sit on the shelves. Wow, it's the perfect pamper room, and romantic as well. I briefly wish that Edward was here with me, but then I feel a little jealous at the thought of another woman massaging him. I bite my lip. Hmm … I might just have to take a course in massage so I can do it myself. I smile to myself as I imagine running my hands over his olive skin, kneading that toned body while I sit on his bottom. I start to fan my face, feeling quite flushed at the thought.

I change into my swimsuit, a plain black one, nothing fancy. I can still see the bruises on the top of my legs, but they're fading. I wrap the large robe around me and leave the bathroom. While I wait for Alison on one of the sofas, I check my phone.

There's a text from Edward, sent at 10.45 a.m. *Hi gorgeous, how's your arse? I can't stop thinking about you!*

I laugh as I reply at 11.02 a.m. *Hi, I've arrived and it's beautiful. My arse has now stopped stinging, and thank you for your concern. I'm sat waiting for Fabio who, I have to say, is hilarious. He's hugely overdone the Botox and fake tan, and what's with his fake accent? Anyway, I wanted to say thank you so much for this; it's so kind and thoughtful. I might not be able to text or ring until later, as Fabio is very strict, and he told me what you said. I can't wait to see you tonight. I'm missing you already! xxxx.*

Edward: 11.05 a.m. *I'm glad you're enjoying yourself, and you're very welcome. I thought you'd like Fabio. I knew he'd make you laugh. Has your package arrived yet?*

I smile as I text back. 11.06 a.m. *Package? No, no package, Edward. xxx.*

Edward: 11.07 a.m. *Okay, no worries, sweetheart. It'll probably come this afternoon. I'm looking forward to tonight too. 7 p.m. remember, on the dot.*

I laugh out loud. 11.08 a.m. *Oh, I'll be ready, my little ball of frustration. 7 p.m. on the dot, as requested xxx.*

I cringe. I'm not sure I should have sent that, but what the heck!

Edward: 11.09 a.m. *I'm your what? Little ball of frustration? REALLY! Are you being brave because you're on the phone? I should spank you for that comment!*

I giggle. He's joking, I hope. I think I've hit a nerve, as I'm a little frustrated myself. I love these flirtatious little texts.

Reply: 11.12 a.m. *Are you shouting at me Edward? xxx.*

Edward: 11.13 a.m. *I was shouting, but I'm now curious. Do you like playing, Abbie?*

I laugh and reply: 11.14 a.m. *I'd love to play with you, Edward! And please don't shout at me, I was only teasing you. Don't get all moody on me! xxx.*

Edward: 11.15 a.m. *Sorry, but I'm a little jealous. I wish I was there massaging that warm oil into your beautiful, soft, toned body, making you moan. Hmm ... the thought!*

Reply: 11.16 a.m. *Edward Scott, my face is as red as a beetroot. You're very naughty, and can even make me blush in a text message. I should've known better than to play with you, you bad boy! xxx.*

Edward: 11.17 a.m. *Ha, ha. I can picture you now, sitting with your phone, smiling that beautiful smile, rosy cheeks. What a picture! And as for playing games, I think I've already warned you on several occasions not to play those sorts of games with me, as you'll never win!*

The cheeky bugger. He'll always win, will he? Well, we'll see about that.

Reply: 11.19 a.m. *Like I said, darling, my little ball of frustration. Now, what did you say? Oh yes, as you put it so eloquently: 'massaging that warm oil into your beautiful, soft, toned body, making you moan.' Hmm, I can't wait! But I'm sorry, I have to go now. Alison's ready, and Fabio is knocking at the door. I'm sure you'll agree that it would be rude of me to keep him waiting. Ciao for now, darling! See you tonight. xxx.*

My phone starts ringing just as Alison comes out of the bathroom. I look at the number and let it ring. I don't know why I checked, since I know exactly who it is.

"Aren't you going to answer?" Alison asks, puzzled.

I roll my eyes, thinking, *No I bloody daren't.*

"Nah, I'm sure it will keep till later."

"You're leaving him in limbo?"

I don't reply. Instead I just grin and put my phone into my bag, feeling giddy, knowing how badly I've just affected him.

Chapter 9

There's a knock. I get up to answer it, but Fabio walks in before I reach the door.

"Hi ladies! You're ready then, I see."

He grins as he looks at us, and once again I have to suck my lips in tight and try my best not to laugh. I know I'm being childish, but I seem to have the giggles, and they won't stop. I cough nervously, trying to pull myself together.

Fabio ignores me and continues, "This way. Come, come. Let me show you through to your rooms."

A squeak leaves my throat, as Alison glares and Fabio stares trying to raise his eyebrows, but they don't move. He has that same startled expression on his face, and it's making me even worse. I try to apologise.

"I'm sorry, I just feel a little—"

He doesn't let me finish, and I think I've offended him.

"This way."

He leads us out of the room and down a corridor.

"Ms Bridge, this is your room. Beth will be taking care of you today."

Beth smiles at Alison, and they both enter the room.

He glares at me. "And Ms Baxter, this is your room. Karla will be looking after you today." His voice is strict. "And Miss Baxter, I hope your giggles soon rectify themselves."

He walks off down the corridor, leaving me to enter the room, and I feel well and truly told off. I pull a face as I enter. Karla smiles at me and holds out her hand.

"Hi, I'm Karla. Pleased to meet you, Ms Baxter."

We shake hands formally, though she seems very friendly. She's slim and pretty, wearing a black dress with pink piping and a badge that reads *Senior Beautician, Blue Spa*. She has long dark hair tied in a ponytail.

"Please, call me Abbie."

"Okay, Abbie. Please take off your robe and slippers and lie on the table for me, face down, and pop your head through the hole." She points. "See?" I do as she asks. "I'm just going to roll your swimsuit top down – is that okay?"

I nod. I remove my straps, and she rolls the top of my swimsuit down to my bottom. I lie on the table, feeling a little embarrassed and exposed. She places a warm towel over my legs and starts telling me what she's going to do. As she finishes explaining, background music fades in quietly. It sounds like whales talking to each other, and I'm not sure whether it's relaxing or annoying. Karla starts to apply warm scented oil to the back of my neck and onto my shoulders. I'm a little tense, and I jerk slightly.

"Sorry," she says. "Does that hurt?"

"A little."

"You have some faded bruises. Are they still tender?"

"Mmm …"

She doesn't ask how I got them, which I'm glad about, as I don't want to think of Adam, or be reminded of how they got there.

She continues massaging my shoulders and neck, then moves onto my back. Surprisingly, I begin to relax as she places another warm towel over me, then starts on my legs, gently at first. She must see the bruises, but doesn't mention them.

I yawn.

"Good, it's working, Abbie. You're relaxing," she comments.

"Yes, very much so. Thank you," I reply sleepily.

"Well, it's fine if you want to close your eyes. Mr Scott did say to pamper you."

I smile inwardly, thinking of Edward. I close my eyes and allow myself to be hypnotised by the whales.

Startled, I'm woken by Karla.

"Abbie, if you'd like to take five minutes, then you can sit up, and put your things back on."

"Oh, sorry. Did I fall asleep?" I ask, embarrassed.

"It's fine. It just means my job is done and you're all relaxed."

"I certainly am relaxed. Thank you."

She smiles. "You're having lunch now, back in your suite, and then back to me for a waxing and manicure."

"Oh!" I stare at her and repeat myself. "Oh ... waxing?"

She nods. I raise my eyebrows, a little surprised.

She sees my look and continues, "You've not had a waxing before?"

"No. Does it hurt? I usually just shave."

"Not really ... well, not after the first strip."

She smiles reassuringly at me. I smile back, knowing I'm a coward when it comes to voluntary pain. Karla leaves me in the room, saying she'll meet me back here at 2 p.m. I stay on the bed for five minutes, as she instructed, then replace my swimsuit. My skin feels so soft! I put my dressing gown back on, yawning and feeling sleepy. I walk back to the suite in a trance-like state, although I'm not sure whether it's because I'm so sleepy, or the hypnotic effect of the whale music.

Alison's already back and waiting for me.

"Hi. You look shattered!" she says as I walk in.

"I fell asleep," I admit with a giggle. "Did you?"

"No!"

"Oh."

"Your phone keeps bleeping, by the way. I think a certain person has been trying to get hold of you."

I screw my face up.

"What have you done?"

I giggle again, remembering the last text I sent him.

"You're behaving like a schoolgirl." She teases.

I nod, because I know I am, and I'm enjoying the feeling. It's not one I've experienced before and I know that I'm falling so very fast for him. I pick my phone up, still grinning, and I'm shocked to see I have five missed calls from Edward. I press the first.

11.21 a.m. "Oh dear, Abbie. Answer your phone." He sounds amused.

11.25 a.m. "Abbie, Abbie, Abbie." He still sounds amused. I giggle again as Alison watches me.

11.45 a.m. "Abbie, answer your phone or you'll be sorry, girl." His tone is playful, and I smile.

11.55 a.m. "Tut, tut, Abbie, it seems we're playing games. Well, if it's games you want then games you shall have. I can't wait for tonight now." I can hear laughter in his voice.

I giggle but I'm nervous as I listen to the next message.

12.25 a.m. "Umm, Abbie, I'm sitting here on my own, trying my best to focus on the work I need to finish, but somehow my concentration span isn't lasting longer than a few seconds before it returns to you and the last message you sent me. Therefore, seeing as you won't answer my calls, I'm going to tell you what I'm going to do. Firstly, I am going to release that ball of frustration upon you tonight. Secondly, you said you liked to play, and, my little beauty, I want to play with you, so play we will! So relax for now while you have the time, because at seven o'clock tonight, you're mine. Ciao for now."

I gulp down hard and a flustered squeal leaves my throat. Shit, what have I done? He's going to devour me. His voice was very firm. My face flushes and my eyes are like saucers. My heart beats fast as I begin to feel excited, very excited. Alison's still watching me with a raised eyebrow, and it's pretty obvious she can tell how flummoxed I am.

"Do you need a glass of iced water?" She laughs out loud. "Or a cold shower?"

I smile nervously, but just as I'm about to answer her, there's a knock at the door. Alison opens it and a young man enters, pushing a trolley. He greets us both politely.

"Ladies, your lunch has arrived." He turns and leaves the room.

I watch as Alison takes the lids off the plates. There's fresh chicken, sandwiches, salads, two bottles of champagne on ice with crystal glasses, and a full plate of desserts.

"Wow! There's enough to feed an army."

"Hmm ..." She takes the champagne from the ice bucket "For you, Abbie?" I nod. She pops the cork and pours us both a glass.

It's delicious and fruity, very light. I drink mine a little too fast, burping as I feel the bubbles tickling my nose.

"Excuse me! Sorry." I hold my glass out to Alison, smiling. "Can I have another please?"

"Slow down. It's quite strong stuff!"

"Hmm, I know!" But I need it to settle my nerves.

She pours me another glass, but I sip it this time and say, "This is very nice."

"I think you should eat something if you're going to be drinking champagne at this rate."

I pick up a sandwich from the plate.

"Happy now?"

She rolls her eyes as I finish another glass of the delicious champagne, getting a bit of a head rush. Whoa!

There's another knock at the door. This time, I walk over and open the door.

"Ms Baxter?" I nod. "These are for you." He hands me the largest bouquet of red roses I've ever seen.

"Thank you," I say with a smile.

I read the card. *Please keep me!* I giggle as I shut the door.

"Wow, Abbie, someone else has it bad too! They're beautiful." Alison says, sounding pleased.

"Yes, aren't they?" I say with a wide grin, taking out my phone again – no more calls from Edward. I ring his number but there's no answer. I wonder if he's playing me at my own game so, not to be outwitted by him, I decide to text instead.

1.45 p.m. *Hi Edward, your flowers have arrived and they're beautiful. Thank you so much! I will be keeping these. I can't wait to see you tonight. xxx.*

I let out a sigh of contentment and smile at Alison. She grins at me as I place my phone in my bag.

I finish yet another drink, and I seem to have acquired a perpetual smile on my face. I can't believe how happy I feel.

"Are you ready, Abbie? We need to be heading back to our rooms for the waxing."

I roll my eyes. I don't fancy it, and I nod my head reluctantly.

I sit on the bed, waiting for Karla to begin on my legs. She applies the first strip, smooths it down and then rips it off. I let out an involuntary scream.

"Sugar Ray Leonard!" My hand shoots to my smarting leg where the strip has just been ripped off with half my bloody skin.

Karla giggles, then apologies immediately.

"Don't worry – I'll be quick."

She repeats the process several times.

I squirm, tears stinging my eyes.

"Next leg, Abbie."

I nod, nearly ripping the towel to pieces. This is definitely not relaxing.

She finishes my legs and moves onto my underarms.

"Now, this might sting a bit," she says, applying the warm wax and the strip under my armpit. "Ready?"

I nod very reluctantly, screwing my eyes tight shut, waiting for the sting.

"Holy shit!" I scream. "Sting a bit?"

"Sorry. I've nearly finished," she says, working quickly, "Okay, Abbie. I'm done. If you'd like to lie down, I'll do your bikini line."

"My what?" I practically shout at her, thinking, *That's a little too intimate.*

"It's not that bad," she says, holding back her laughter.

I sigh, knowing that I've been defeated by a tiny tub of hot wax, so I lie back down on the bed, muttering silently to myself.

God, I hadn't realised this beauty malarkey would be so bloody painful. I close my eyes. Well, here goes – no pain, no gain.

She applies the hot wax, and I feel my face blush. Then she applies the strip.

"Deep breath. Ready?" She rips off the strip, and I swear like I've never sworn before.

"Bloody hell, shit me, my God, shit! You bitch! Oh, hell, I'm sorry, I didn't mean that. Shit, that hurt."

Karla looks at me, astounded, and I'm sure she's trying not to laugh.

"Sorry, did that hurt?" she asks as tears well in my eyes.

"Did that hurt? Oh my God, are you kidding me?"

She grimaces, chewing her bottom lip, nervous now.

"Do you want me to carry on?"

"No bloody way!"

"It might look a little odd – there's a patch missing."

"I don't bloody care if there's a patch missing or a smiley face. I'm not having that done ever again in my life!"

She can't stop the smile creeping across her face from my last remark, and we both burst out laughing. God, I need a drink. It's smarting like no tomorrow.

"So, Abbie, just your hair and makeup left to do."

I look at her nervously.

"Oh, right … I think I can live with that, but no more waxing."

"No, no more waxing."

I hardly recognised myself when Wendy, the stylist, had finished my hair and makeup. I stare at myself in the mirror, admiring her talent. My hair is done beautifully. She's put my hair up; soft curls gently fall around my face.

The cut on my head has nearly healed, so I've removed the Steri-Strips. I smile to myself, knowing that Edward will probably tell me off for that, but it makes me feel all warm inside, knowing that he'll fuss because he cares.

Wendy's covered over the red mark that was still visible on my cheek and I momentarily forget about Adam and where he hit me. I must confess, she's done a fantastic job. I'm not at all sure it's me looking back at myself, what with the changes to the outside, and those I'm feeling inside, I like who's staring back at me from the mirror.

I'm very pleased with the new Abbie. I breathe deeply, smiling internally.

We're finished. Fabio comes in to say goodbye to us both. He screams and jumps about, saying we look like models and wanting to take photos of us both for the salon and beauty rooms. We laugh at him and he hugs us both, saying that we have to return very soon. We promise we will.

We head outside and I place my flowers carefully in Alison's car, smiling at her.

"You look lovely," I say honestly.

"So do you."

As we drive back to my house, Alison is still taking the mickey out of me about the waxing. She says she could hear me screaming and swearing in her room. I tell her I'm sure all of Lytham must have heard me, and we both laugh until we pull up at my house.

I pick up my flowers, smiling as I see the note again. I hug and kiss her goodbye. She makes me promise to ring her tomorrow, and I ask why. She doesn't reply, but sticks her tongue out at me, warning me to call her.

I stand in the hallway with the stupidest grin on my face. My heart feels like a feather, I'm so happy. It's like I'm floating, and the most comforting thing is that I've barely thought about Adam or about what happened yesterday.

He's not called or texted me, and I wonder if he's finally got the message. Because it's not just me anymore – someone else stuck up for me, and he fled like the bully he is.

I am, though, a little apprehensive about the fact that he left as he did; I know Adam well, although I've never met any of his so-called friends. I've heard him on the telephone when he thought I wasn't around, but I put those calls down to Adam being Adam. Nasty and horrible. I never listened in – I didn't want to know what he was saying or discussing and I'd enough things to worry about, like not getting another beating. I did once overhear something about money, and him shouting on the phone.

"Right, I'll get the money. Fucking soon, okay?"

I'd walked away, not interested, like a zombie doing what I was told.

I shrug my shoulders. Huh! Mind games.

I bet he wants me to think he's backed down, but has he? I'm not sure now, but then again, I'm not sure if I really care anymore.

I place the roses in the lounge, still smiling. I seem to be smiling a lot today, especially when I think of Edward. This is the first time I've had flowers like this. Well, apart from the ones I'd presumed were from Adam and accidently threw away.

I pull a face again at the thought of him, then I realise what I've just done. If I can dismiss him like that then maybe, I am finally ready for this. Edward is good for me. I screw my nose up affectionately, thinking about him, noticing the time on the grandfather clock. It's 5.30 p.m. I squeal, and my heart skips a beat. I suddenly feel jittery.

I make my way into my bedroom and start rummaging around in my drawers. I find a pair of brand-new lace-top stockings and a new black lace thong buried right at the bottom. I giggle to myself. Why not indulge him with stockings and a thong? Hmm, let the games begin! I'm not sure why I'm thinking like this, but I feel brave after the champagne. I lay them out onto the bed and make my way into the bathroom to clean my teeth.

I've butterflies flapping around in my tummy again as I notice the time – 5.55 p.m. I need some Dutch courage, especially if I'm going to take on the master of seduction. I return to my bedroom, undress and put on my dressing gown. I then head downstairs to the kitchen. I open the fridge, take out a bottle of white wine and pour myself a glass. I drink half, then top it up and make my way back upstairs to my room with the wine.

I remove my dressing gown and put on my thong and lace-top stockings. Then I finish the glass of wine and a head rush hits. I sit back on the bed, taking in deep breaths. I'm not used to drinking so much.

I've taken my dress out of the wardrobe. It's never been worn and still has the label on. Adam made me buy it along with the underwear. Five hundred and ninety pounds. It was for an important dinner with business clients. He'd insisted I go as all the other wives were attending with the partners, and if they closed the deal it would bring thousands of pounds to the firm. It's short and tight in all the right places. Adam said I'd be a distraction if the conversation ran dry. The back of the dress falls open to the bottom of my back. I didn't want to wear it, especially not for him or his business clients, and I said as much to him that night. It provoked another argument, because I wasn't doing what I was told. I breathe in deeply, remembering how the evening ended. I didn't go to the dinner. I couldn't, not with a black eye and a bruised cheekbone.

That would certainly have been a distraction, but definitely not one that would have done Adam any favours, especially not with his business clients.

I run my hand over my face and scowl at myself in the mirror. I breathe out to free my brain of the memory. Then I think of Edward, how caring and thoughtful he is, and it makes me smile.

I pick up the dress, remove the label and wriggle into it. I turn to look at the back in the mirror.

It's very revealing, so low you can almost see the top of my bottom. I can't wear a bra. I feel quite exposed. I turn back around and check the front. I don't know if I should! It's very fitted and really shows off my figure. I don't want to give Edward the wrong impression, but I've nothing else decent to wear and I don't want to feel like I did when we went to the Drake. Am I asking for trouble?

I check the time. 6.40 p.m. I suddenly feel giddy again. God, my mind is all over the place. I've no time to change now. I giggle again, knowing I'm a little tipsy. What the hell. I get out my black shoes, the ones with the killer heels, and put them on. I look tall and very slim. Oh well, in for a penny, in for a pound. He'll either love it or hate it, but I feel very sexy in it. Was that my intention all along?

I sit at the dressing table and spray on my favourite perfume. I love No. 5 – it reminds me of my mum; she always wore it. I grab a bag, putting in my lipstick, perfume, a couple of tissues and my phone. Then I make my way downstairs, holding onto the banister for dear life with one hand, and the empty glass and my bag with the other. I make my way into the kitchen and pour another large wine from the fridge. I cringe a little when I see there's not much left. I need to slow down but I need this drink to calm my nerves.

It's 6.55 p.m. The palms of my hands have started sweating. I can feel my face flushing. My heart is racing. Oh, I shouldn't have worn this dress. I start to fan my face. I'm really warm. Shit, I think I'm drunk.

The doorbell rings. I jump and nearly drop my glass. Whoops! I neck the wine before I answer the door. Whoa! I sway and giggle as I walk to the front door and open it. I'm greeted by the most handsome man I've ever seen. I want to growl at him; he looks so bloody sexy and he smells divine. I blush as I remember what he said he was going to do to me. He's going to spank me, he said. Well, that's what he thinks! I might spank him instead – that would shock him. Or would it? I start to laugh at the thought.

"Well, hello you!" I say. "Come in, beautiful."

He raises his eyebrows. I turn and gesture with my hand for him to enter the house, but I nearly fall over in the process. I grab the door quickly to steady myself. I let out a giggle and continue. "I'm not used to these heels ..." I hiccup. "Sorry, ex … cuse me!" Edward looks at me in surprise, a smirk on his face.

"Abbie, have you been drinking?" he asks casually but observantly.

I pause, studying his face before replying.

"I may have had a little one ..." I pause, then continue cheekily, "Sherlock …"

He lets out a laugh as I make my way to the kitchen, holding onto the wall and thinking it's probably best to sit down before I fall down. I sit at the table and sigh heavily while Edward shakes his head at me, grinning.

"I'll make you a coffee."

I roll my eyes and pout my lips. I perch carefully on the chair and stare at him. He is stunning! He's wearing grey trousers that fit tight around his bottom, and what a lovely bottom it is. Mmm, I want to squeeze it. He's also wearing a white shirt through which I can see his strong arms and muscular back. I'm nearly panting.

Has he done this on purpose? God, I shouldn't have drunk so much wine.

I want to pounce on him, but I control myself and sit, watching him make my coffee. He brings it over to me, and he looks dee-lish-us! I want to bite him. He smiles and puts the black coffee in front of me on the table.

"Drink it, Abbie. And have you eaten today?"

I nod.

"What have you had?"

"A sandwich."

He's trying not to laugh at me.

I hiccup again, and then frown. "Why?"

"How much have you had to drink?" he asks, picking up the nearly empty wine bottle. I shrug my shoulders.

"Just a teeny-weeny one! Why, does it show?"

He bursts out laughing.

"No, not at all," he says sarcastically. "Now, please drink your coffee, and then let's get you something to eat before you collapse on me."

He notices that I've removed the strips on my head. "Can I take a look at your head?"

I nod. He reaches out, and I grab his hand and kiss it. He raises an eyebrow.

"You have beautiful hands, Edward."

I kiss them again, but he ignores me.

"I think this has healed." He cradles my face, holding it still.

I smile at him. I want to kiss him so badly. I lean forward but nearly fall off my chair in the process.

He sniggers, sitting me back on the chair. "Sit still before you fall, and drink your coffee."

I do as he says, but I pull a face at him.

He smirks back at me. "Are you okay?"

I nod my head. I really want to kiss him. I can't contain myself any longer and move to his lips.

"Kiss me, please."

He moves his mouth over mine and our lips touch. I lean into him and he groans, kissing me back. Then he pulls away.

"Come on. Let's get you something to eat."

I sit and sulk.

"Come on, Abbie."

He passes me my bag. I poke my tongue out, and he laughs.

"Finish your coffee."

I drink it, and he takes my hand, helping me stand.

"Do you have your coat? It's cold outside."

I shake my head.

"Well, you look stunning!" he comments. "Extremely sexy."

I giggle as we walk down the hall and out through the front door. Edward locks it for me, putting my keys in his pocket. "You don't want to lose them, do you?"

I shake my head.

He opens the car door, but I turn my head sharply. I can hear a noise in the garden, a rustling coming from behind the large fir tree near to the door.

"Are you getting in?" he asks, and I nod slowly. "Are you okay?"

I nod again, looking in the direction of the noise. "Yes, I thought I heard something, that's all."

"It's probably a cat," he says as he helps me into the car. I feel a flicker of relief.

"Ah yes, it's probably Marmalade from next door. She's always in the garden, or trying her best to get into the house."

We sit in the car and Edward grins at me.

"What?" I ask, grinning back.

"Belt up."

I put on my seatbelt, although I'm not sure that's what he meant. He chuckles quietly to himself, shaking his head.

"Where are we going?"

"The Manor House."

I laugh.

"What's funny?"

"You are."

"Me? Why?"

"Do you ever go anywhere that hasn't got at least five stars?"

He winks at me.

"They have beautiful rooms there."

I raise my eyebrows at him, and he winks again. He's as forward as ever! I wonder how many girls he's taken there.

"Really?" I reply harshly, annoyed by the thought.

"Mmm … really …" He pauses, and I'm about to make a snide remark when he continues, almost laughing, "The dining room dates back to the 1600s; it's very impressive. And the food is fantastic as well. You need to eat something and sober up."

I fell for that one. I deserved it, especially after the assumptions I made when we went to the Drake. I stick my tongue out again before replying, "Very funny!"

He laughs, but then grows serious.

"I want you sober tonight, Abbie. I don't want you to be drunk the first time I have you."

I don't answer him. I can't. I think I've just sobered up pretty damn quick. He doesn't say anything else, but then he doesn't need to. He concentrates on driving, looking straight ahead with no facial expression at all that I can read. Oh Lord! I watch him carefully. Does he mean tonight? My tummy is in knots again. I don't ask him. He's just floored me with that comment. God, I wish I could read his mind. I'm not sure if I'm ready to unleash that ball of frustration after all. I gulp down hard and decide it's best to keep my mouth shut before I get myself into any more trouble.

Chapter 10

Edward still hasn't spoken or looked at me. I observe him, trying to read any signs that might indicate what he's thinking, but there's nothing. He just concentrates on driving, looking stubbornly ahead. The longer the silence stretches on between us, the more my heart is racing. I look out of the window, trying to distract myself, but it's dark and I can't see anything. I look back at him; he's biting his bottom lip. It looks like he's trying not to laugh. My heart is beating so fast now that I think I can see it pounding in my chest. My tummy is still in knots, and the butterflies are dancing the tango. I can't take my eyes off him, and I can't stop thinking about what he's just said. *I don't want you to be drunk the first time I have you!* My face flushes at the thought. Edward turns to me with a smile, breaking the silence.

"Are you warm, Abbie? You look a little flushed." Then he grins.

I smile at him, but don't answer. I can't, I've no voice. There's too much whizzing around in my head.

"Do you want some music?"

I nod my head, still unable to reply, thinking the music will distract me.

He presses a button and a song comes on, one I know all too well. I close my eyes as he starts to sing. Oh God, has he done this on purpose? This certainly isn't helping, or distracting me.

"Do you know the words?" he asks with laughter in his voice.

I want to scream, *God, yes, I know the words. Bloody hell turn it off,* but all that comes out is a stupid noise.

"Hu … uhhh."

I close my eyes again as he sniggers. Oh, the swine! He's playing me so damned bad and I have no defence, none at all. My wall has totally gone.

It crashed down in front of my very eyes, and I'm left exposed, ready for him to devour me. All I can think about is my dream – Edward swaggering towards me, singing in my ear, waiting desperately for me to agree that he can take me. The song tortures me: "Let's Make Love!"

My face has lit up like the Christmas tree in Times Square. My brain is telling me to stop thinking like this, and quickly, as my pulse has just reached red at two hundred beats per minute. My head is spinning and my stomach is doing the tango, cha-cha and salsa all at the same bloody time. My hands have started to shake so much that I have to sit on them. I can't take much more. Bloody hell, stop the song, stop the car, stop the world – I need to get off before I self-combust. Edward looks at me again with a raised eyebrow.

"Do you want the air con on? You still look flushed."

That's it. That remark sends me over the edge.

"Stop. God, stop this!" I shout, and he laughs.

"What's wrong? Don't you feel well? Do you want me to stop the car?"

Oh my God, is he serious?

"Stop it. You're driving me insane with this. I can't take anymore."

"With what?"

"Please, Edward, just stop!"

I'm nearly crying with frustration. He gives me a slow grin.

"Now you know how I feel. Every time I look at you, every time you speak to me, every time you smile at me and every time you kiss me. I just want to take you, hold you, have you. I don't think I can take much more either."

I want him so badly. I shake my head at him and make yet another pathetic noise.

"Let's go back to mine then," I say quietly.

"Really, are you desperate for me?"

I stare at him in silence, because there's no denying it any longer. I *am* desperate for him.

My body is sending him all the right signals. I might as well be wearing a neon sign around my neck saying: Stop the car, bend me over the bonnet, and take me, you delicious bad boy!

"What are you thinking?" he asks softly.

I watch him as he indicates and turns onto the drive of the Manor House. I'm thinking, let's skip dinner and get a room. I need to calm myself down. It's the wine; I don't normally behave like this or think like this. All my inhibitions have been thrown to the wind. God, he affects me so much.

Edward pulls up to the entrance and parks the Aston Martin. He turns off the engine and looks calmly at me. I'm a bag of nerves now, but so in awe of him. I'm so desperate to kiss him, for him to kiss me. He removes his seatbelt and looks at me. I smile, blushing. He moves over in his seat so he's closer to me, still smiling his beautiful smile. I inhale as his scent rolls over me. He smells divine. I want him.

He breathes in deeply, whispering, "Mmm, No. 5," and his breath catches the side of my face. I've goosebumps in their millions rippling over my body. He puts his lips to my ear and nips it with his teeth. "Good things come to those who wait," he murmurs.

I'm almost panting. He sits back in his seat, opens his door and gets out. Then he walks around to my side of the car. I don't think I can move or stand in these heels. He opens my door and holds out his hand. I take it, gazing at him, and the cold night air hits me, bringing me quickly out of my daze. I shiver.

"Are you coming?" he says thickly. He grins, tilting his head to one side.

I can't miss the insinuation, and I don't take my eyes off his as I reply, "Are we playing games?"

"Do you like playing games?"

"I don't know; I've never played before."

"Really, Abbie? You should, because they're fun."

"I'll think about it over dinner."

He laughs at me, and I smile back.

"Well, then, let's go and get you some dinner, my little beauty," he says, pulling me tightly into his arms and kissing me on the cheek.

I giggle. "Flattery will get you everywhere!"

"I already know that," he says, running his finger down my bare back, making me shiver and wriggle in his arms. "Do you like that?" He groans, pushing his hips hard into me, holding me firmly so I can feel his manhood pushing into my belly.

"Mmm … but not as much as you seem to like it," I tease. He growls, squeezing my bottom tightly.

"Come on. Let's get you fed and sobered up."

I laugh as he takes my hand and walks us to the entrance of the Manor House. It's all very grand, and very much in keeping with its name – polished oak floorboards with deep, thick rugs scattered around; an enormous open fire burning logs in a huge inglenook fireplace with stone seats at either end; large pictures, hanging on chains, of dukes, earls and barons, all grandly dressed in doublets and hose with ruffles at their necks.

"I couldn't see you wearing that," I remark, turning to Edward with a smile. He laughs, then squeezes my hand as we continue to walk down the long galleried hallway towards the dining room. He stops, then squeezes my hand again, gesturing with his head to a large portrait on the wall. His eyes narrow alluringly and his voice is low and husky, stopping me in my tracks.

"Mmm … but I could picture you wearing that tight corset and petticoat!"

I shake my head, blushing. "Do you think of nothing else, Edward Scott?" I don't know what else to say as he's managed to take me off guard once again.

"No. Well, not around you, Abigail Baxter." He nods his head, as though it's common knowledge.

We arrive at the dining room and a waiter greets us.

"Names, please?"

"Scott." I suddenly wonder if his name would be better suited to Mr Blunt. I grin. *Mr Blunt.* Hmm … I might start calling him that from now on.

"Ah, yes, Scott," the waiter replies as he casts his eyes over the reservation list. "Table for two, sir?"

He beckons us to follow him. Edward keeps a tight hold of my hand, which I'm glad of as the floor is a little slippery in these heels. We follow the waiter into the dining area and arrive at a table next to the window that overlooks the gardens. There are spotlights on outside, and I can see beautifully manicured topiary bushes of all shapes and sizes. A maze of small laurel hedges play host to flowers and shrubs. I smile.

"You like the gardens, madam?"

"Yes, they look very pretty."

Edward smiles as he pulls out my chair for me.

"Why thank you, sir," I say, grinning at him, and he winks at me.

"Menu, sir? Madam?"

Edward nods as he sits down.

"Wine menu, sir?"

Edward raises an eyebrow at me.

I shake my head. "No, thank you. A glass of iced water, please."

"And the same for me, please," he says with a laugh.

"You have wine if you like."

"I'm driving, remember, and I need a clear head." He winks, then continues. "For later."

The waiter removes the wine menus, leaving us to look over the food menu. I can feel my face flush again at his suggestive remarks.

"What do you recommend?" I ask.

"On the menu?"

"What else?"

"The wild-boar steak is very good," he replies with a smirk.

"The wild-boar steak it is then."

"You're easily pleased."

"Yes, aren't I?" I snigger as the waiter puts down two glasses of iced water on the table.

Edward orders our food. "Two wild-boar steaks, medium, thank you."

The waiter nods and walks off.

"Well, Abbie, where do we go from here?"

That takes me by surprise, and I shrug my shoulders.

Edward looks at me quizzically. "Do we take it to the next level?"

God, why on earth can't I seem to answer him when he's so direct?

"You're blushing again. Do I embarrass you?" He's so bloody cocky. "Well, are you going to answer me?"

"I think you like embarrassing me and making me blush," I answer.

He nods. "You blush a lot!"

"I know. I can't seem to help it, for some reason. I wonder why that is." I frown at him. "Have you any thoughts on the matter?"

He laughs at me, which makes me cross, which in turn makes him laugh harder.

"I can't help blushing, Edward. It's an involuntary reaction, especially to remarks that are so suggestive and blunt, but I expect you know that already, don't you?"

He tilts his head to one side, smiling at me.

"I do, and that's the turn-on."

I blush even more as he studies my face. He doesn't care what he says or where he says it – he just blurts it out for anyone and everyone to hear. He holds his hand out to me over the table. I pout as I take it. "It's also a very endearing quality, and one that I like very much. It suggests innocence and purity. I think you're beautiful, Abbie, with lots of beautiful qualities."

"That's a very good chat-up line," I reply sceptically.

He laughs out loud. "I thought so too. Is it working?"

"Yes, I think it might be."

The waiter arrives with our food. He places the plates down in front of us. The steaks are huge, practically hanging off the plates, and they smell delicious. We thank the waiter, and I stare at Edward.

"Eat up – you'll need your strength for later." He winks at me, grinning.

I giggle and start eating my food.

"Abbie?" he asks quietly.

"Yes."

"I'm sorry, but I need to ask. What have you decided to do about—"

I put my hand up, shaking my head at him.

"Don't, please, not tonight. Don't spoil it, please."

"You don't want to talk about him?"

"No, not tonight. I know we were going to talk, to sort things out, and I promise I'll tell you soon."

He can see that I mean it. I don't want to ruin this evening by talking about Adam, though I'm thinking about him now anyway, even though I don't want to. Why did he have to say that? I don't feel hungry anymore, and I start picking at my food. Suddenly I need a moment alone. I stand abruptly.

"I'm just going to the ladies'."

I need five minutes to clear my thoughts. I leave the dining room, following a sign for the ladies' toilets. I go inside and use the loo, wash my hands, then sit on the chair at the side of the mirrors and take a few deep breaths. Is this all happening too quickly? I'm not at all sure of myself now. I like Edward. I like him a lot, but am I ready for this? I feel ready when I'm with him, but the question he just asked made me feel sick to my stomach. Am I ever going to be free of Adam? I blow out a deep breath, nod my head yes I can do this.? Edward's out there, and I'm in here. Why, when we both want the same thing? We want each other.

Come on, girl, pull yourself together. Get your courage back, march out there, back to the dining room, and plant a huge kiss on those delicious lips of his.

So that's what I do. I march determinedly out of the ladies' and head straight back to the table. I see Edward. He's standing up and shouting at someone on his phone. Everyone's looking at him.

"For God's sake, I'm not even on call tonight … Fine!" He's angry and pushes his phone down into his pocket. He sees me, puts his hands in the air and shakes his head with annoyance. "Sorry."

The waiter comes over.

"Can I pay the bill, please?" Edward snaps, handing him his card. He turns to look at me, and continues in the same frustrated tone. "We have to go," he sighs. "I'm sorry, Abbie. There's been an emergency at the hospital."

I feel so let down. I was ready! Why did this have to happen? He looks annoyed as he studies my face. I take his hand, knowing that it's not his fault. I try to make him feel better.

"Hey, it's fine. It's work. I understand."

"You're so sweet," he says.

"It's okay, honestly. Come on, let's go …" I roll my eyes at him. "I suppose this is what happens when you date Doctor Kildare!"

"You're funny *and* sweet."

"I try my best, although I can't say that I'm not gutted as well."

"You are?"

What the hell! I'm just going to tell him how I feel.

"Of course I am. I like you a lot, Edward. An awful lot."

"That's a good answer, because I like you an awful lot too, and I so wanted to have you tonight. I know you wanted it too." He stares at me as we're getting into the car. "Answer me – you wanted it too?"

"Yes!"

He breathes out deeply, nodding at me.

"Fasten your seatbelt."

I stare again at him, wondering what he's thinking, His eyes are boring into my soul, and my heart is racing, knowing how desperately I want him. He starts the car, and we drive back to my house. We don't talk on the way. We're silent, each with our own thoughts.

We arrive and he pulls up on the drive. We sit for a moment looking at each other, each knowing what the other is thinking. I remove my seatbelt as he gets out of the car and walks round to my side to help me out.

"I'm sorry."

"Me too," I say, going to kiss him but he takes my face in his hands, cupping it gently. He closes his eyes and breathes deeply, and when he opens them he speaks softly.

"Look at me."

His eyes are wild with passion. He moves his lips over mine and kisses me deeply, opening my lips with his tongue and moving it gently inside my mouth. Every hair on my body stands on edge. I start to lose myself in this erotic embrace. I really don't want him to stop. My mouth follows his, and my hands glide softly over his back, drawing him closer to me. He runs his hands down my bare back, and I whisper and moan in agreement. He breathes deep, moving away from my lips and onto my neck. It's sending me wild! I start moving myself against him, pushing myself forward, panting and moaning as I feel his erection against me, and he makes a groaning noise in his throat.

"I want you so badly."

"Stop, please, or I'll not let you leave. Trust me."

"Shit timing!" he says, pulling away from me.

I nod.

"I'll call you tomorrow. It will probably be an all-nighter."

I nod again reluctantly.

"Okay, tomorrow," I whisper.

I walk towards the door, and he shouts after me, "Abbie, your keys!"

"Thank you." I take them and kiss him hard on the lips one last time. "Call me tomorrow?"

"Yes, I'll ring you. Now go inside and lock the door. Then I can go." He kisses me gently. "Until tomorrow, Miss Baxter," he says with a sigh. I smile at him.

"Tomorrow, Mr Scott, and thank you for a lovely night."

I close the door and lock it, leaving the keys inside. I hear him get into his car, start up the engine and reverse off the drive, and I smile ruefully as the sound of his car fades away.

"Life is so bloody unfair," I mutter resentfully as I kick my shoes off, hurling them down the hallway.

I was so ready to say yes, and that's not the wine talking, because I feel stone-cold sober now.

I wander down the hallway and into the kitchen. I throw my bag on the table and put the kettle on, still huffing away to myself.

I make myself a coffee and sit at the kitchen table drinking it, daydreaming about tonight. It's been a funny night. I was drunk at the start and sober at the end. I'm sure it's meant to be the other way round. I laugh out loud, thinking, yes, that's me, I'm always doing things arse about face. Edward was as blunt as ever, saying exactly what he meant. No matter what he says or where he says it, he always takes me by surprise and makes me blush. But is that part of the attraction? Then again, there are so many attractions when it comes to Edward Scott.

I finish my coffee and my tummy starts to rumble; I only ate a quarter of my meal tonight. I go to the fridge and get out some cheese and crackers. I make another coffee, then pick up my bag and wander into the lounge. I put on the telly and flick through the channels. A film has just started. It's funny and sad. I remember watching it with my gran and Glenda at the cinema. I curl my feet up on the sofa and watch, laughing out loud in places.

Well, if you can't bake it, just cheat.

I sit with the tissues on my knee; the film's really sad and emotional, and I cry. I can't help it – it happens every time I watch it.

My phone rings. I look at the time – 11.45 p.m. It's Edward.

"Hi," I say, sniffing loudly as I answer.

"Abbie, are you okay? Are you crying?"

"Yes."

"Why, what's wrong?"

"I'm okay. I'm just watching a film."

"Ah, I see. Which film?"

"*Calendar Girls*. It gets me every time."

"You're a big softy, then?" he asks, chuckling to himself.

"I am. I'm a sucker for a sad film."

"Anyway, I'm ringing to tell you that the emergency has been cancelled. We had no ICU beds and they've had to divert the patient to another hospital. They managed to get hold of Howard in the end. He was supposed to be on call, the bastard … Sorry, but I'm going to kill him on Monday. He's gone to meet the patient at the Beaumont. So the question is, my little sad friend, do you want me to come over, or are you too sad and tired now?"

"God, yes!" I blurt out, giggling. "I want you to come over, please." I pause, trying to sound sexy. "And Edward … bring your toothbrush."

He bursts out laughing.

"Oh, my little beauty! I'm on my way, and I've already packed my toothbrush."

"Oh dear," I reply nervously.

"I'm coming for you, Abbie." He says, his voice rough and seductive.

He hangs up. My phone's still in my hand, my eyes wide, and my mind is screaming at me, *Bloody hell, game back on!*

Chapter 11

I drop my phone and it falls to the floor. Holy mother of God, what have I just done? He sounded so sexy. A shiver runs over me. He's coming for me. I squeal with delight. He's going to devour me! I'm flapping and shaking like a sheet in the wind. My heart beats so fast in my chest that I think it's going to leap straight out of my mouth. My pulse accelerates quicker than a Formula One car. I start giggling nervously. He's on his way and, boy, am I ready for him.

I jump off the sofa and run to the mirror in a panic. I remove the clips and shake my head, letting my hair fall around my face. Wow, that is a sexy look! I take my lipstick from my bag, but I struggle to get the lid off because my hands won't stop shaking. I manage after the fourth attempt. Then I pucker up my lips, apply the lipstick, and finish off by smacking them together and smiling. Hmm, these lips will soon be on his ... and then I wonder if Edward will suit this shade of pale pink.

I look at the clock. Its 11.47 p.m. I can't keep still. I'm walking around in a tizzy, and I can't stop thinking about what he said to me, and how he said it. *I'm coming for you.* I grin, feeling giddy, nervous, excited and anxious, all at the same time. I glare at the clock again; it's only 11.48 p.m. Bloody hell, has time stopped? What if I can't do it? What if I let him down? What if I disappoint him because I'm not experienced? I'm doubting myself. I frown, confused and frustrated by these sudden mixed emotions. I let out a deep sigh and start pacing around the room again like a caged animal. The anticipation is killing me.

I go back to the mirror and check my face. It's almost scarlet. I've got panda eyes from crying at the film – I didn't see before, and it's not an attractive look. I run my fingers under my eyes to remove the mascara. I could do with a drink, but then I instantly think better of it.

I look at the clock again: 11.49 p.m. I stand staring at the second hand going round and round – 11.50 p.m., 11.51 p.m., 11.52 p.m. This is torture! Three minutes have passed. Is that all? Everything seems to be in slow motion. I'm not going to be able to wait much longer. I don't think my body can carry on like this, and then I wonder if you can overdose on adrenalin.

My palms have started sweating, and my heart starts jumping around in my chest again. I'm working myself into frenzy. God, I think I'm going to have a heart attack. I keep checking the time. Oh, Lordy, Lordy, Lordy! I shake my hands, then my arms, breathing deeply, like I'm psyching myself up to start a marathon. I'm almost panting. I tell myself off: *Come on, Abbie. Get a bloody grip! At this rate you'll be comatose before he arrives.* 11.55 p.m. This has literally been the longest ten minutes of my life.

The doorbell rings, and I squeal, clap my hands and jump up like the starting gun's just fired for a race. "What am I doing? I'm behaving like a child," I mutter breathlessly, but I can't physically control myself.

Wow, he must have broken every speed limit known to man to get here so quickly.

I'm panting, trying to control my breathing as I run out of the lounge and down the hall towards the front door. I trip over fresh air, momentarily losing the use of my limbs. I steady myself and then run to the door with a wide grin on my face. My heart's pounding like a foundry mill hard at work. My hands are shaking so much I struggle to turn the key in the door. I need to calm down. God, he's going to think I'm desperate. Breathe, Abbie, breathe. I turn the key again, and this time it unlocks. I fling it open with a smile.

"Hi ..."

I stop, transfixed by the sight of Adam standing there on the doorstep. Panic sets in immediately.

I put my hand to my mouth as vomit rises in my throat, and I think I'm going to be sick. I try to scream and slam the door shut, but he's stepped over the threshold. I push hard, using my shoulder to try desperately to close it, but it bounces back on to me.

He's pushing it, laughing, and I notice he's wedged his foot in the doorway. I stamp hard on it, but make no impression and he doesn't move. I feel a hard punch to my shoulder, and I fall backwards to the floor, hitting it hard. He steps into the hall.

"Get out!" I scream.

He's on top of me in a split second, shouting and screaming in my face. I can smell whisky on his breath. I punch and kick out at him as he tries to grab me. I start shuffling backwards on my bottom, trying to move away from him, but he follows me, still grabbing at me. He reaches for my hair and pulls it hard, yanking my head upwards.

"Get off me!"

He pulls so tight on my hair that I'm forced to stand. I slap him hard in the chest, but he just shrugs his shoulders and sniggers.

"Is that the best you can fucking do? This is going to be easier than I thought."

Oh God, what does he mean? I stare at him, and he has that slimy look on his face, the one I remember so well from before when he used to … I shake my head, knowing I cannot let him do that. I'm scared, petrified, but I can't let him see it or he'll use it against me. His eyes are shadowed and evil. I'm trying desperately to think of what to do. I need to be firm and stand up to him.

"Get out of my house!" But I can hear my own voice, and it sounds weak and scared. He looks at me with a shallow expression.

"Fuck you, Abbie," he snarls. "Your fucking house? I don't think so. Don't you mean our house?"

His eyes bore into me, and I feel them burning my soul. The stench of whisky on his breath is overpowering. I close my eyes. I know his temper all too well, especially when he's been drinking, and I know what he's going to do to me, as he's always done. Fear hits me hard.

He's never going to rape me again, not ever! A surge of energy hits me. I can't and won't back down. I twist my body frantically, trying to get him to let go of my hair.

It hurts, really hurts, but I'm not going to let him touch me ever again. I manage to break free, and he laughs nastily.

"I'll let you have that one, Abbie." He nods his head at me. "This is new, you fighting back. I'm quite turned on now. I like it." He walks closer towards me, and I step backwards. His look is complacent. He knows he has the upper hand, he's far stronger than me. "Lover boy's gone now," he sneers. "You're all alone now. I saw him leave."

He's been watching us. Watching me, watching the house. Fear freezes in my veins as I remember the noise I heard earlier. It must have been Adam hiding outside, watching and waiting. He nods his head at me, playing games, revealing in how much I fear him.

"You've been on the phone though, haven't you?" He goes silent, waiting for me to answer. "Fucking answer me!" he screeches when I say nothing.

I feel dazed. How long has he been watching me?

"You're not talking to me, but you like talking to him?" He starts to laugh, and pretends to sulk. "Oh dear, Abbie. Did you think it was him at the door? Is that what the lipstick's for?"

His expression changes quickly. He's really scaring me now. He lunges at me again and grabs my hair, harder this time. I try to push him away, but he just laughs.

"Hmm, you were never this energetic before. I like it, you know, I like it hard and nasty."

I close my eyes. What's he going to do? I'm so scared. Why isn't Edward here yet?

Adam starts to push himself into me. I try to move backwards, away from him, but the wall's behind me and I can't go any further. He pins me against it and my head hits it hard.

He pulls and grabs at my hair, then whips his hand across my lips and onto my cheek, screaming in my face, "Is this lipstick for him? I always preferred you to wear red when I fuck you!"

I'm going to be sick.

I try to push him away and scream at the top of my voice, "No! No! No! Get out!"

"Hmm …" He jerks his hips forward, pushing hard.

I can feel him against me. My eyes blur with tears. He can't, not again. I want to die.

He runs his tongue up the side of my face and whispers through his teeth, "I like this fighting back, what a turn-on. Fuck, I'm so hard."

He grabs my hand and forces it on to him, shouting, "Feel it!"

I screw my eyes tight shut, and try to pull my hand away. "I said, fucking feel it, you bitch."

"NO!" I scream in his face.

He seizes me by the throat. I choke and splutter. He moves his hand from my throat and down to my breast. I try to slap him away but he grabs my breast and squeezes it hard. I cry out in pain, and he pants with pleasure.

"Lover boy's not here to help you, Abbie, so what are you going to do? Submit or fight?"

My breathing is erratic. I have no choice. I pull in a deep breath, knowing I will not submit any more to him.

"Fight!" I scream. I want to hurt him, kill him, but he's too strong. I try hard to push him off me, but the more I resist, the more he enjoys it. He keeps banging me against the wall. My head is hurting and I feel dizzy.

"Edward is on his way," I manage to gasp.

"Really? Or are you just saying that?" He grabs my face with his other hand and squeezes my cheeks together. He's almost spitting in my face with anger. "Not in the mood? Got another headache? I'm still your husband, Abbie."

He pushes me hard against the wall once more. He moves his hand between my legs and I scream in his face and lash out with my hands. He's strong, angry and drunk, but I'm determined now. If he lays one finger on me, as God is my witness, I'll kill him.

Adam looks towards the front door. "I think you might be telling the truth, so I'll make this quick."

I'm terrified, but adrenalin has kicked in, and kicked in big time. He's never, ever going to touch me again. It's fight or flight. I take all my strength and push him so hard that I shock myself. I swing my foot up and kick out, catching him right between the legs.

"Get out of my fucking house, Adam. NOW!"

He grabs at his crotch, shrieking, "You little slag! You're going to regret that. You've asked for this. I'm really going to enjoy this. I'm going to fucking hurt you so much while I fuck you!"

My heart is racing so fast that I'm struggling to breathe. He can't, he can't do that to me again. Think, Abbie. Get him out of the house. Tears stream down my face. I'm scared, scared to death.

"Edward is on his way," I blurt out.

"So you said." He grins. "Maybe he'd like to watch."

"Do you really want to risk running into him again?" I shout back with such determination that he has no choice but to listen. He stops and sneers at me, remembering what Edward did to him. He's a coward and a bully. He only hits women, not men.

"Well, just think about this as I'm leaving."

Oh, thank God! He's leaving.

He grabs at me again. I dodge out of his way, but his voice is cold and spiteful. "He won't always be around to protect you. Until death us do part, Abbie. You'd be wise to remember that, you little bitch!"

He slaps me hard across the face, then turns and stumbles towards the door. He stops suddenly and turns back to me. I want to cry because he's not going. "As for him, if you see him again, I'll fucking kill him! Do you hear me, Abbie? I'll kill him, and I'll make you watch."

I just nod, desperate for him to leave.

"Fine, I'll leave him," I say desperately. I need to tell him whatever he wants to hear, anything to get him to leave. He walks out of the door, muttering angrily to himself, leaving me frozen to the spot.

I've never heard him sound so calculating and cold. His eyes were hollow and dark; I could almost see into his soul, and it was black and empty. Did he mean it when he threatened to kill Edward and make me watch? My throat fills with bile at the thought of it. I turn, run to the cloakroom and vomit into the toilet.

I'm overwhelmed by fear and a terrible need to lock the front door. I fly out of the cloakroom and run down the hall, panicking as I see the door begin to open. It's Adam, he's come back!

Edward walks in.

"Bloody hell, Abbie. I didn't realise you were that desperate for me, leaving the front door open like that," he says as I fly at him and fling my arms around him.

I burst into tears.

"Shit, you're trembling!" He pulls away from me, studying my face. "What on earth's the matter? Why are you crying? And why is the door open? Abbie, tell me what's happened. Are you okay?" He cups my face with his hands, confused. "What's wrong?"

I put my arms around him again and squeeze him hard. I can't stop crying and I'm terrified.

"Don't let go of me, Edward, please."

"Tell me what's wrong! Has someone been in the house?"

I nod mutely, my head still buried in his chest.

"Who? Who's been here?" He starts to shout. "Was it Adam?"

I nod again.

"Has he hurt you?"

I don't know what to say. I'm scared to tell him the truth about what Adam said and did. It's not just what he did to me, it's what he said, and the way he said it. The thought of what he *could* have done to me, what he implied ... And worst of all, he threatened to kill Edward. I feel sick, knowing that Adam has no remorse – how can he when he killed his own babies?

Because that's what he did when he beat me, played those dreadful mind games with me, controlled me until I was like a robot, causing me to miscarry.

I feel a sudden wave of nausea and pull away from Edward with my hand over my mouth. I run back to the cloakroom.

Edward shouts after me as I throw up into the toilet. He bursts in to the cloakroom, his voice cold with fury.

"I'm ringing the police."

I shake my head – no.

He moves my hair away and wipes my face with his hand. "Has he touched you?"

I shake my head again and he pulls me to his chest, holding me tightly, kissing the top of my head.

"Hey, come on. It's all right. I'm here. I've got you."

I can feel his chest moving fast, his breathing quick and shallow. He's really upset.

He takes my hand. "Come on, tell me what happened."

I nod shakily, as he walks me to the lounge and guides me to the sofa.

"Sit down."

He pulls a throw from the chair, covers me with it and kisses me on the cheek.

"I'll go and make you a drink."

He walks out of the lounge. I hear him close the front door and lock it, then walk swiftly down the hall. He's talking quietly to someone on his phone, but I can't hear what he's saying.

He goes into the cloakroom, flushing the chain then washing his hands. I wipe my eyes with a tissue as I hear him moving around in the kitchen.

I turn to look at him as he comes back into the room. He smiles, holding out his hand with a drink in it.

"Here, drink this, Abbie."

I shake my head as the smell of brandy hits me.

"It'll settle your nerves, calm you down. It's good for things like this." He passes me the drink and sits beside me on the sofa with his own brandy. "Are you okay?"

I shrug my shoulders silently. "Has he hurt you?"

I shrug again.

He pulls his head to one side, frowning sadly. "Come here."

He places his drink on the table, then takes my glass from my hand and sets it down next to his. He holds his arms out to me and I move over to him, closing my eyes as he pulls me into his arms. He adjusts the throw and passes me my brandy.

"Drink it, Abbie."

I breathe deep as he puts his arm back around me and kisses my head. I rest it on his shoulder and look up into his face. I take a sip of the brandy, grimacing at the taste.

"I don't like brandy," I whisper.

"Shush. Drink it." He closes his eyes, then speaks softly. "Sorry, that was bossy."

I nod my head.

"I've never cared for anyone before, and it crushes me to see you like this."

I can tell by the pained expression on his face that he means it.

He smiles. "Talk to me, tell me what happened. Let me help you."

I hesitate.

"Has he always been abusive?"

I stare at him, my silence answering his question.

"Why did you stay with him?" He looks bewildered. "Tell me."

I need to explain but I'm struggling. I hang my head down, embarrassed and ashamed of my own weakness.

"If I tell you, will you promise me that you won't judge me?" I look up as he nods his head at me. I close my eyes and breathe out. "He was okay at first, I suppose. A little controlling, but nothing too extreme. But once we were married, he changed." I shrug my shoulders and shake my head. Edward strokes the side of my face, tracing his finger along my cheek. I want to smile, but my face feels frozen.

"Hey, come on," he murmurs.

I try to hold back my tears, but I feel humiliated, knowing I let Adam do those things to me. I can feel myself slipping. I want to inwardly scream for being so stupid and weak. When I open my eyes, Edward's gaze is sad. "Talk to me, Abbie. Don't close down. I want to help you."

I look at him and realise that by blocking my thoughts and my feelings, I'm locking out the one person who cares for me, who's here now for me.

"I'm sorry, Edward." I take his hand and let out a sigh. "I just feel so ashamed!"

"No!" he says, suddenly angry with me. He shakes his head. "Don't you ever feel ashamed of yourself."

"But I do, I can't help it. I'm never going to be free of him."

Edward holds me close, and I want to stay like this in his arms forever. I feel safe when he's holding me.

"He's fucked with your head," he observes quietly.

I agree with a nod. "He was cruel, verbally and physically. Yes, he played mind games with me."

"And tonight?"

He chews his lip. I don't want Edward mixed up with Adam because of me.

"Just mind games, that's all," I say as convincingly as I can. "He didn't touch me, or hurt me."

"Really?"

I nod my head in agreement, but I'm sure he knows I'm hiding something.

"Tell me the truth," he says sternly.

But I can't. I lie, bend the truth, and tell him just a little of what happened. He jumps to his feet, his hands clenched in fists at his side. Then he runs his hand through his hair, shaking his head at me. I know that sign – he's frustrated and angry – and I'm not altogether sure what he'd do if he knew what really happened. I don't want to find out. I just want it to stop.

"Don't, please." I screw my eyes tightly shut.

"I'll fucking kill him," he breathes, his voice laced with aggression.

"No, that's what he wants. He wants you to bite, and if you do then he's won. He can't win, Edward, not ever."

I'm scared that Adam will hurt Edward, and I don't want them tangled up with each other. Edward is decent, loyal, kind, and I'm falling in love with him.

"Please!"

I take another deep breath.

"I can't understand why you stayed with him."

I bite hard on my bottom lip and taste blood. I close my eyes and let out a heavy sigh.

"I'd never been with anyone before," I admit quietly.

Edward seems shocked.

"You were a virgin before you married?"

I nod. "He used his charm; he was manipulative, and I didn't see it. I was naive. I wanted to wait." I run my hands over my face. "It started after we were married. He was only verbally abusive at the start, but then it gradually became more physical. He started to drink, and soon he was drinking heavily every night."

Edward breathes in hard, and I reach out to him.

"Please sit down," I beg.

He slumps beside me.

"I hated him touching me, but I couldn't stop him. I used to cry myself to sleep afterwards, while he lay there in a drunken stupor. I moved into one of the spare rooms, but that only made him worse. The more I defied him, the more abusive he became. I wanted to leave, but I had nowhere to go.

So I gave in, to stop the beatings, the arguments. I felt like I'd died inside, like there was hardly anything of me left. Then I fell pregnant, and I miscarried. After that I became depressed. He didn't care, as long as he had my money to spend. He went out all the time, and I stayed in with my own thoughts for company. I got pregnant again, and lost the second baby. That killed me inside. I even contemplated—"

I stop.

Edward stares at me, shaking his head. I feel the tears falling onto my cheeks, and my lip quivers as I remember the pain and loss.

"No, Abbie!"

I shrug my shoulders sadly.

"Why didn't you leave then?"

"I was trying to. I wanted to so much but I was weak, and I felt pathetic. I couldn't cope with what was happening, with my emotions or his abusive ways. He played mind games with me, said it was my fault that he treated me the way he did. He told me I was damaged and pitiful, that I was worthless because I'd lost my—"

I stop again, breathing in deeply. I can't tell him how I lost them, not yet. I can't face it. I start to cry harder and can't stop. "I began to believe him. I started to think that I'd done something wrong, and that God was punishing me and If you're told something enough, you eventually start believing it. I hid myself away behind a wall I'd built in my head, and I couldn't break free."

"So how did you? Start to break free, I mean."

"To be honest with you, I don't really know. I didn't plan it this way. I suppose it was a catalogue of events that just seemed to happen, until I ended up where I am today. My fate, maybe. Perhaps it was always meant to be this way. I started running again, and it seemed to help. It cleared my head and helped me to think straight. I ran until it physically hurt. I joined the running club, and that's where I met Joe."

Edward raises his eyebrows slightly.

"One day, Joe told me about a patient, and the story really stood out for me. It seemed to hit home, and it made me put my own life into perspective. Horrible things happen all the time, but there's always someone else worse off than you are."

"What was the story?" he asks.

"It was about a lady with a serious heart condition. She fell pregnant and was advised to terminate the pregnancy by her doctor.

He told her that the baby would kill her if she went through with the pregnancy, but she refused to have a termination.

She went against the advice of all the doctors and specialists, even if it meant that she'd die herself. She went into early labour ..." I sigh. "She died, and so did the baby. Her husband was grief-stricken, and after the funeral he took his own life. He left a note saying he couldn't carry on without the love of his life. It made me cry to think that two people could love each other so much that they couldn't live without each other, and I wanted that. I wanted to love someone, and to be loved like that. Does that seem wrong?"

He shakes his head sadly. "No, Abbie, it's not wrong."

"Joe said some nice things to me – that I should become a student nurse because maybe by helping other people I might be able to help myself. His words, and the story he'd told me, played over in my mind constantly. Something seemed to change inside me.

At first, Adam didn't know I'd applied, and when he found out he made me stop going to the club. I lost contact with Joe. But I was determined I wasn't going to give up my place. I told as many people as I could that I was starting at the hospital. It infuriated Adam, but he had to let me do it or he'd lose face. I threatened to tell everyone the real reason if he made me quit, and he couldn't take that chance."

I remember how I pay the price for doing and saying those things.

"I began to question the others things he was doing to me. He started leaving the house, staying out all night. Now I know why – he'd met Nicky. I'd already made my mind up by then that I was going to leave him. I was just waiting for the right time, and that came along that day in the hospital when I found out about him and Nicky. I took my chance and grabbed it with both hands."

I breathe deeply.

"You've helped me too, Edward, more than you'll ever know. You've made me sort of believe in myself. You care for me, and I care so much for you.

You've made me realise that one day I might be able to love someone." I hesitate, but I'm going to say it. "And I hope that someone is you!" I blush and close my eyes.

"Abbie!" He takes my hand. "I've never known anyone like you. You're so sweet and kind. I don't know how anyone could ever hurt you. I want to wrap you up and protect you. If he ever says another word to you, or lays a finger on you, then I swear to God I'll kill him."

"No, I don't want you to touch him. I knew this would be really hard, but I'm ready to do this. So please don't give him that satisfaction. I know exactly what I'm going to do."

"You do?"

"Yes, I'll get him where it hurts – money. That's what he's interested in. Adam wants money, he wants it desperately, so now I'll use that against him."

"But what about the house? Will he not get half of that? You're married."

"The house is in my name so, yes, he'll probably get half. But I'll make it so bloody awkward for him, believe me. I'm not giving in that easily. It was my parents' house, and I won't sell it without a fight. He'll be clever – I know him, and he knows all the ins and outs of the law."

"What does he do?"

"He's a solicitor."

"Really?" He looks shocked. "Then he should know better than to come round here threatening you."

"Yes, but he obviously thinks he's above the law. As far as I'm concerned, he can leave with what he came in with, and that's nothing." I try my best to sound convincing, although I'm not sure if I'm trying to assure Edward or myself.

"That's my girl!"

I nod firmly. I look at him. I feel safer and stronger, and that's down to this man sitting here with me. I believe it's true what they say: The love of a good man will make you stronger.

I'm not sure yet if it is love, but he cares, and that's enough for now.

He hugs me tightly to him.

"I'd better watch what I say in future," he says light-heartedly, trying to lift the mood.

I frown, puzzled. "You're nothing like him."

"I'm glad to hear it."

"I mean that with all my heart."

Edward kisses my forehead.

"I know you do. You look shattered. You should get some sleep. Are you tired?"

"I am."

"Would you like me to stay with you tonight?"

"Yes, please."

"I'll take the spare room."

"You will?" I look confused. "You don't have to do that."

"Yes, I think I do."

I smile at him, remembering last night and why he felt he couldn't stay in the same bed as me. He's such a gentleman and will never take advantage of me. I don't question him, but take his hand as he leads me from the lounge.

"Thank you for staying," I say softly.

"You're welcome."

He guides me along the hall and upstairs. We walk into my bedroom, and I smile at him, nodding at his scrubs.

"They're like pyjamas," I say gently.

He nods, then smiles. "You go and get ready for bed. I'll wait here for you."

I go to the bathroom, wash and put on my pyjamas. Back in the bedroom, Edward is sitting on the bed saying thank you to someone on his phone. He smiles at me and puts his phone down. I sigh, and my eyes start to droop with fatigue. He gestures with his head towards the bed.

"Get in, and no sulking. I meant what I said. I want you, Abbie, but not like this. When we make love I want it to be for all the right reasons."

I smile, and my heart crumbles as I climb into bed.

"And you call me sweet."

"Can I have a kiss before I leave?" he asks gruffly.

I nod and he leans forward, kissing me gently on the lips.

"Goodnight, Abbie," he whispers. Then he picks up his phone and leaves my room.

"Goodnight, Edward," I murmur into the darkness.

My eyes feel heavy from crying. I'm shattered as I fall asleep thinking about Edward.

A few hours later I wake up. I'm cold, really cold. I don't want to get out of bed, but I need a wee. I wander into the bathroom and use the toilet. I turn on the hot tap to wash my hands, but the water is freezing. A shiver runs through me, and I make a noise as my teeth start to chatter. I leave the bathroom and head back down the landing towards my room. I touch the radiator and it's stone cold. "Bloody boiler," I mutter to myself. It pleases itself as to when it works.

As I pass the spare room, I stop and look at the door, smiling to myself. It feels strange to know that Edward is inside. I know I should just go back to my room, but he's so close and I feel so drawn to him that I can't resist. I turn the handle and open the door slightly. I peek my head inside and peer into the darkness. Light spills in from the landing, casting shadows on the walls. I push the door open further and creep in. My shadow looms ahead of me, beckoning me towards the bed where Edward is sleeping. I smile again as I watch him sleep, this beautiful man who I realise is not only helping me; he's saving me too.

The dimly lit room appears seductive. I tip-toe closer, gazing upon his sleeping face. His mouth is slightly open as he breathes. My heart swells. I want to kiss his mouth. I bend and run my hand down the side of his face.

"Thank you so much. I don't feel sad, lonely or unhappy anymore," I whisper. I place my lips on his sleeping face. He moans and I turn to leave, not wanting to disturb him.

I jump suddenly, and squeal as he grabs my wrist, pulling me onto the bed and on top of him. I feel giddy as he locks me in his embrace, grinning at me from the bed.

"And where do you think you're going?"

I giggle nervously.

"You find this funny, Baxter, wandering into my room, waking me in the middle of the night?" He's holding me tightly around my waist with one arm, then moves my hair away from my face with his free hand, placing it behind my ear so he can see my face clearly. "You're cold," he says slowly. "Have you come to get warmed up?"

I tilt my head and kiss him gently. He moans, so I kiss him again, a little longer this time.

"Shush," I whisper. "Yes, and I'm not leaving until I'm warm."

He nods.

I continue softly, "I want you, Edward. Please make love to me."

He looks at me in surprise.

"Are you sure?"

"I've never been more sure of anything in my life."

I squeal again as he flips me off his chest and onto my back. He straddles me, pinning my arms above my head. He's so strong and I feel giddy. He releases my hands quickly, suddenly looking alarmed.

"Shit, I'm so sorry!"

I kiss him quickly, knowing what he's thinking.

"Hey, its fine. You're only playing with me, and I trust you."

"You do?"

"God, yes."

He looks at me playfully, and I can't stop myself from smiling. I bite hard on my lip as his face hovers over mine. His breath is warm on my skin, his voice seductive.

"You want me?"

I nod, because I do. I want him so much.

He grins wickedly at me, and I'm almost panting with desire.

"Good. Because I want you so bad … I'm going to send you to heaven and back."

I close my eyes. My core tightens, my face flushes, my pulse rises. His touch, his voice, has awoken my whole body. I've never been so nervous than I am right now.

Our eyes lock. His eyes are mesmerising; I'm unable to look away. They're inviting me, tempting me, captivating me. They're drawing me into his world of passion, intrigue and desire, and I want to go. I want to experience all he has to offer me.

He waits eagerly for my response. I nod yes, knowing that I have no defence, because my heart is telling me this is where I'm meant to be.

I whisper, "then make love to me!"

Chapter 12

"Do I need anything, Abbie?"

"I'm on the pill."

Edward raises his eyebrows, looking confused. "I thought—"

He stares, asking quietly. "Are you nervous?"

I nod as he strokes the side of my face, then kisses me tenderly on the lips.

"Don't be. I'd never hurt you," he whispers.

And I know he'd never hurt me, betray me or leave me. His words and his tenderness fill my heart with hope that I might find what I've yearned for but never had – someone to love me.

"I know, Edward, but I am." I lower my eyes.

"Shush. I'll be gentle with you, but you will tell me if I hurt you, won't you? You'll tell me to stop?"

I lift my eyes and nod.

"Good," he whispers. Then he gets up and stands at the side of the bed, holding out his hand to me.

I rise and stand in front of him, feeling nervous as that dark smile plays over his face once more.

"I want you naked," he rasps, tugging at my top. "Take it off!"

I start to remove it, my hands shaking with excitement. I pull it over my head and drop it to the floor. A light blush creeps onto my cheeks as my breasts are exposed to him. He places a finger under my chin, tilting my head up to look at him.

"Don't be shy," he whispers, moving his finger leisurely down towards my breast.

I gasp as he slowly circles my nipple, and it hardens at his touch.

"Mmm," he murmurs agreeably, moving swiftly towards the waistband of my pyjamas.

I tingle, and my blush deepens as he slides his fingers inside, feeling down towards my pubic bone and slowly teasing them over my hair.

"I like this. You're so soft." His voice plays softly in my ears.

I inhale sharply as he touches me. I close my eyes and he applies a gentle pressure, sending a shiver down my spine.

He moves his hand back to my waistband and tugs it. "Take these off slowly." It's almost a command. "I want to watch you, Abbie." His voice is husky.

I open my eyes, drinking in the look of sexual craving that insists I obey him.

He moves back slightly to watch. My hands are still shaking with nerves as I run a finger under my waistband and begin to slowly undress. His eyes scrutinise my naked body with a lusty appetite. I bite my bottom lip and he breathes out sharply, then beckons me with his finger to move towards him.

"God, you're exquisite," he murmurs.

His warm breath floats over my skin, sending ripples of pleasure everywhere. Our eyes lock, and he immediately pulls me close to him.

"I'm going to make you come, so slowly, all night long."

His words reach out to me, arousing my senses. I pull at the bottom of his scrub top and glide my hand over his chest. I raise myself onto my tiptoes, lift it over his head and drop it to the floor.

My eyes widen as I see him for the first time. His shoulders are broad, his chest and abdominal muscles defined. I place my lips on his chest, kissing him softly and slowly towards his neck while running my hands gently over his back and guiding him closer. I lightly trace them round to his chest and down towards his waistband. I'm mesmerised as I follow the V-shape past his hips then run my fingers inside, just as he did to me. He whispers my name sensually as I catch the head and start to slowly circle it. His eyes close and a moan of pleasure escapes as he breathes.

I'm aroused by the sound as I remove his scrub pants. He steps out of them quickly and my hand returns to his boxers, but he grabs my hand with one of his.

The other he places in my hair, gently twisting it around his palm, making my head tilt as he takes my mouth, kissing me long and deep. I moan, and my body erupts in goosebumps. I feel the pressure of his erection against me as he forces me to step backwards.

My legs suddenly hit the side of the bed. I stumble and he straightens me up, speaking intensely.

"Sit." His voice is low and determined. "Look at me, Abbie."

I look up at him and see a predatory look in his eyes.

"Open your legs."

God, he's making me feel as if he's going to gobble me up in one fell swoop, but I do as he asks, opening them slightly.

"Wider!" he gasps, watching me.

His hand slowly runs up my back. His lips kiss and suckle my neck, leaving me moaning breathlessly.

"Shush," he whispers as he slowly moves to my breasts. I gasp as my body tingles. He cups my breasts, and takes my left nipple into his open mouth, sucking hard. Then he moves to the right, nipping more firmly, making me jolt backwards. He pulls me back towards him, my breasts still held firm in his hands, while he continues to suck and nip, then soothing the slight sting with his tongue.

He lowers me down onto the bed, moving down my body, gently grazing my skin with his teeth while his hands move to my legs, lifting them onto the bed and holding my thighs open. My face flushes crimson as his head dips slowly down and between my legs. I hold my breath as he takes me with his mouth.

His hands move under my bottom to bring me closer to his mouth.

I'm in a trance, totally lost to this divine pleasure, then something suddenly takes hold inside of me, a sense of delicious, intense tightness. I try to move, but he holds me firm, pulling me closer to his mouth. I bite my lip as waves crash over my body, stronger each time. Oh God, I'm having an orgasm! I moan as my body tingles from head to toe.

"Edward, please!" I cry out.

He moves from between my legs, leaving me breathless, and places his hands under my arms. He moves me quickly up the bed. Then he opens my legs and swiftly moves between them. I feel him about to enter me. His voice is firm.

"Look at me."

I meet his gaze; his stare is sultry and demanding. He exhales sharply. "I'm going to fuck you so slowly you're going to beg me to stop."

"Oh God!" My heart races as he pushes slowly inside me. A bittersweet sensation overwhelms me, and it stings. I close my eyes, though I can sense him watching my face as he continues to move more slowly into me, stretching me, making me gasp as he pushes deeper this time. Then he pulls right out. I wince gripping the bed sheets.

"That stings," I whisper.

"Do you want me to stop?" His voice is soft.

"No!" I open my eyes, and he looks longingly towards me as I nod my head, yes.

He pushes deeper, until I can feel him completely inside me. I'm unable to take my eyes from his. I bite down hard on my bottom lip as he pulls out, then pushes back in slowly. The sensation is out of this world. He smiles, moving a little inside me, and my eyes go wide as he hits my sweet spot.

"Oh Lord!" I shout, unable to control myself as, he finds that same spot that I never knew existed until now. He watches my face as my orgasm builds. I rip at the sheets and my back arches up from the bed warmth invades my veins once again.

His breathing is ragged with excitement. He lifts my arms so that I'm upright, straddling him. I feel him deep within me. His hands slide around my back and pin me to his chest. His skin is damp against mine and I can feel his heart racing. He squeezes me tightly, holding me firmly in place.

"Hold on to me," he rasps, placing my arms around his neck. His hands move to my hips. He groans, thrusting hard, and I feel him push yet deeper.

"Move over me, Abbie. Fuck me!"

My heart races as I start to move. I feel immensely turned on, my taking him like this. His eyes close as I repeat the movement and he devours my neck and breasts as we move fast and hungrily together, losing ourselves in our mutual pleasure.

My body suddenly grows extremely sensitive. My hands and arms begin to shake as a burning sensation ignites my veins. I panic; I feel scared. I let go of his neck and dip backwards onto the bed, my body trembling uncontrollably as I struggle to breathe.

Edward is on top of me in a flash, whispering to me, calming me as he sees the fear in my eyes.

"Shush. You're okay, Abbie. You're just coming hard."

I nod mutely. He grits his teeth as he watches me climax beneath him.

His breathing is uneven. His body glistens with sweat as he continues making love to me, all the while moaning my name. His body tenses and his eyes roll as he's orgasms hard, aroused past the point of no return.

I can't take anymore; I beg him to stop.

"Edward, I'm breaking," I murmur, but he doesn't stop the rhythm that's shredding every nerve in my body. I'm breathless and torn. I feel like I'm going to shatter. "Please, Edward. God, no more." I throw my arms around him, squeezing as tight as I can, burying my head into his neck and begging him, like he said I would. "Please … no more!"

"Abbie … God, yes! Yes, baby, yes"

His words are driving me crazy. I'm totally at his mercy. I can't physically control what's happening to me. I cling to him as one orgasm stops, another starts, even stronger than the last.

"Oh my God! Edward, please. It won't stop!"

He moans loudly, gasping my name. His body becomes rigid, every muscle hard. I feel him pulsating and climaxing inside me.

We're covered in sweat, kissing frantically. We gaze at each other in awe. He breathes deeply, cupping my face with his hands and shaking his head.

"Wow," he mutters.

I nod, unable to answer him, hardly able to breathe. Our eyes are still locked together and we smile at each other.

He slowly starts to move but I shake my head.

"No, please. Stay. I want you to stay here forever. Don't ever move."

He smiles at me and kisses my lips tenderly.

I mean it. I don't want him to pull out of me. I'm falling in love with him. I want to tell him this. I gaze at him with tears in my eyes. I feel as though my craving for him will stop my heart. His beautiful green eyes look at me with lust, meaning and desire. I think I've died and gone to heaven.

I can't stop smiling as he murmurs my name, so softly that it stills my heart. He smiles, pulls out of me and rolls me to the side. Then he pulls me close to him, all the while kissing me, whispering my name. I move instantly, rubbing my hands over his wet skin and enveloping him with my arms. Then I drape my legs over his.

He kisses the top of my head and lets out a deep sigh of satisfaction. We lie in each other's arms, smiling and kissing for I don't know how long. We're not talking, just trying to get our breath back. I could lie like this for eternity with him.

"Abbie?" he says, eventually breaking the silence.

"Hmm," I say.

"Abbie!" he says again, raising an eyebrow at me.

"Hmm," I repeat sleepily.

"Can you not speak?"

I shake my head at him and he looks pleased.

"Are you okay?"

I nod, yes.

"Are you sleepy?"

I breathe out and it feels like such an effort.

He grins at me as I reply, "No ... I'm exhausted."

"Me too," he laughs. "I've never made love like that before. God, I think you're going to kill me!"

Ditto, I think. I giggle and yawn again.

"Sorry, am I boring you?"

I'm still giggling as I answer.

"No ... I just can't keep my eyes open."

"Really? It was that good?"

I nod happily. "Yes, Edward, really amazing!"

He has the biggest, cheesiest grin on his face that I've ever seen.

"Good answer, Abbie ..."

I pat him gently on his chest and he responds with a genuinely happy laugh that makes my heart swell and my smile widen.

"Do you want to sleep then?" he asks softly.

I nod, replying drowsily. "Please ..." I yawn again. "Please let me just sleep ... Let's just sleep and hold each other like this until morning."

He squeezes me tightly in response, laughing and stroking my hair.

I suddenly feel sore and tender as he holds me, one arm tightly around my back as I'm draped over his chest. I sigh inwardly to myself, knowing what the soreness is. I hadn't felt it while we'd made love. I must have blocked the pain out, but it's something I'm familiar with. And I know what it is because I've felt it many times before.

But I don't want to move out of his embrace. Instead, I suffer in silence, closing my eyes and wincing, because I don't want anything to spoil this moment.

I want to savour it for as long as I can. I just want to lie in his arms until the end of time.

He kisses my head.

"You sleep, angel," he whispers.

I screw my eyes tightly shut and don't answer him, feeling bad that I'm deceiving him by not telling him the whole truth about what happened tonight. I'm worried now about what he's going to think or say in the morning when he sees my body in the light of day. I should have told him the truth. I should have told him what happened, what Adam had really said and done.

I try to get the thought of Adam out of my head. I don't want to fall asleep thinking of him but I can't physically stay awake any longer.

Chapter 13

I'm being told what to do, but I'm screaming, "No!"

I feel like a robot, unable to make my own decisions. Everything seems surreal, as though I'm not really here, an onlooker, watching somebody else. But I'm not an onlooker; it's happening to me, and I don't want to be here.

I'm outside a church. There are graves next to the porch with names on. I stare in horror at the gravestone nearest to the doors:

Edward Scott. Brutally murdered, 13th December.

My hand flies to my mouth. I drop to the floor, unable to see any more as tears fall from my eyes. I scream, "No … no … no!"

A voice behind me fills my ears.

"I told you what would happen if you didn't fucking leave him. Now look what you've done. This is all your fault, Abbie." His voice is smug and contemptuous.

I try to stand quickly, shouting at him, "I'll kill you, Adam. I swear to God; I'll kill you for this."

He laughs and shouts back, "Get her in-fucking-side now!" Then he leaves and walks through the door to the porch.

I'm being dragged to my feet. I look down and scream in fear. I'm wearing a wedding dress. Oh my God, what's happening?

Uncle Patrick squeezes my hand tightly.

"You can leave if you want to, Abbie. It's not too late."

But I can't leave. I've nowhere to go, nowhere to run. He'll find me, no matter where I hide. A gust of wind howls through the old porch and a shiver runs down my spine. The church doors blow open and I can see him at the altar. My heart leaps into my mouth as he turns to look at me, his expression impassive. All the guests turn their heads slowly as the wedding march starts to play. I squeeze Uncle Patrick's hand, hoping that he'll take the hint and pull me away, that he'll understand that I need to leave, but he doesn't.

He smiles at me instead, nodding his head, and starts walking me down the aisle.

I stare at the guests, wanting them to help me, but they have no faces and they can't see my pain, my fear. I feel my wall rebuilding itself slowly, brick by brick, suppressing my emotions and suffocating me once again. My heart feels empty in my chest.

I've reached the altar. Adam snatches my hand from Uncle Patrick's and pulls it hard towards him so that I'm standing beside him. I want to run but I can't move. I feel myself slowly dying on the inside, unable to break free.

I hear a faint voice shouting my name. "Abbie, Abbie!"

I want to answer the voice, but I'm unable to. I can't force the words out of my mouth.

The priest starts to say the vows. I screw my eyes tight shut. I feel sick to my stomach. "Do you, Abigail Elizabeth Baxter, take …?"

I want to shake my head but I can't. He grips my hand tightly as I look into his eyes, and all I can see is a black void and the emptiness of his soul. I can't move. I'm terrified of what he might do if I disobey him again.

"She said, I do!" he snarls.

I stare at the priest, begging him with my eyes to help me, to save my soul, but instead he nods his head at Adam, smiling as he continues with the vows.

"To honour and obey … so long as you both shall live?"

Acid tears sting my eyes and fall onto my cheeks, but they're ignored. I feel the breath leaving my lungs, making me gasp for air. I panic as I feel my life being extinguished.

"I now pronounce you man and wife."

I inwardly scream, *No! Please God, help me. Somebody help me, please!*

Adam laughs callously, pulling my hand tight as he starts to move away from the altar and back down the aisle towards the open doors.

I try to pull free from his grip, but he's strong and holds me firmly as he drags me, pulling on my arm so that I have no choice but to follow.

I can still hear a faint voice calling my name. "Abbie!"

I want to answer but I can't.

He's dragging me fast now, trying to leave, but I can't let him tear me away from the sanctuary of the church. I'm frightened, so frightened of leaving, and of what he's going to do to me afterwards.

He shouts, "Walk, you bitch. Walk! I told you, I'm still your husband!" All the while, I can still hear that voice behind me. I try to turn and see who it is, who's calling my name, but he yanks me back and I stumble, falling to the floor. He lets go of my hand and I try to scramble free, but he grabs me by my hair and drags me to my feet.

"I said walk …" He pulls at my hair again, harder, seizing my face with his other hand. His expression is malicious and evil as he cruelly yells, "Until death us do part …" Then he laughs. "Until death us do part!" He keeps repeating it as he drags me towards the doors.

"Then kill me!" I scream at him. "I'd rather be dead than live another second with you."

"I might just do that. Remember, lover boy is dead because of you. Have I got to send you to him, and those babies you cry over?"

I start to weep in defeat because he's taken everyone from me.

"I know bad people, Abbie, and they'll do anything for money." He sniggers. "Well, it's your fucking money, and they'll revel in the thought of torturing you, raping you in turn and then murdering you." He laughs sadistically. "In fact, they might not even charge me for you! I know they enjoyed torturing Edward. They told me he died slowly."

I can't breathe, and he laughs like the devil, with no feeling at all. I feel like I've just died inside. I sob Edward's name.

Suddenly arms are around me. Then his hand softly strokes the side of my face.

"Hey, Abbie. Come on, wake up. It's a dream, just a dream."

I open my eyes slowly, seeing his beautiful face looking down at me. My heart misses a beat as terror and panic set in. I remember the nightmare, what Adam had done and the people he'd said he knew. Could he know people like that? I'm confused. I know he's bad, he's a monster, and he won't let anyone stand in his way, not now. He wants my money, and he wants to hurt me as much as he can. Will he use Edward to do it? I cannot, will not let him hurt another soul because of me. I recall his words, his threats: *until death us do part.* I picture Edward's grave, and my heart stops at the thought. Is it a warning to me? Is my dream, my subconscious, telling me what I have to do? That I have to let Edward go?

Between reality, dreams and Adam's mind games, I'm struggling to find reason. I know what Adam is capable of, the actions he threatened me with should I ever leave him. I should never have let it go so far with Edward. I should've told him to leave, but what can I do? I'm weak, scared, and hurting so much.

I stare at him with my heart breaking at the thought of what I'm about to say. I don't want to say it but I have no choice. Tears spill from my eyes as I slowly move out of his embrace.

"I'm sorry," I whisper. I start to get up off the bed, pulling the sheet around me. He looks at me in confusion and I screw my eyes tight shut. I can't look at him because I know he's going to hate me, and it's killing me. "I think it's for the best if you leave," I say abruptly.

"What?" he says, stunned.

I start walking to the en-suite.

"Abbie, stop!"

But I can't. I walk into the en-suite and lock the door. I sit at the side of the bath, sobbing. I feel sick and I'm in pain, pain like I've never felt before.

"Open the door."

I shake my head, even though he can't see me.

"Abbie, open the door!"

"I'm sorry, Edward. It's for the best."

"Like hell it is!"

I'm confused and messed up. I shout, "I'm sorry, but you need to leave."

"It was a dream!" he shouts back at me through the door.

And I want to believe him, but the past four years weren't a dream and I know deep down that if he stays the nightmares will begin again, and I won't tempt fate.

I shake my head, whispering repeatedly, "No, it's an omen."

I would sacrifice love to keep him safe. I can't stop crying and my heart is broken, but he can't stay. He has to leave, so I force myself to be stern.

"For God's sake, just leave!" Please, I mouth to myself, my eyes screwed tight shut.

"Do you really want me to leave?" he asks, his voice raw and hurt.

I shout as best as I can through my tears and pain, trying to sound convincing because I need him to go. It's one of the hardest things I've ever had to do in my life.

"Yes."

He's silent, and I know I can't take it back now.

I hear him moving around in the bedroom as he gets dressed. I rock myself on the side of the bath, picturing the hurt on his face, his confusion as he wonders what the hell is going on. I want desperately to go to him and hug him, but I can't; I have to let him go because I can't risk another life, another love.

He can't see my tears or my pain; he can't see that my heart is broken. I hear the bedroom door open, then his footsteps on the landing, then on the stairs.

He doesn't see that I'm scared, broken and crying for him. I hear the front door open, and I put my hand to my mouth to stop the sound of my grief from escaping. I know I've hurt him, but I'm hurting myself so much more by telling him to leave.

The front door slams with force, making me jump. I scream at myself, then whimper, "I'm so sorry. I love you!"

I try to catch my breath but I'm sobbing too hard. I'm so confused and mixed up by Adam's mind games. He's like a cancer growing inside me, eating away at me and slowly killing me.

I don't know what to do. Tears stream down my face as I run from the en-suite with the sheet still wrapped around me. I go to the window and pull the heavy curtains back. Edward's on the drive, running his hands through his hair and over his face. He looks confused and frustrated.

I bang on the window, shouting to him, "I'm sorry!"

He looks up at me, then he lowers his head and gets into his car.

"No, please. I'm sorry. Let me explain."

I bang repeatedly on the window, crying out to him, begging, whispering over and over, "Please don't leave, please. I'm so sorry."

But he can't hear me, and I have to watch him reversing from the drive, pulling into the road, leaving me. I watch him until he's out of sight, willing him to come back.

I grab my phone and ring his number. It rings and rings, then goes to his voice mail. *Scott. Leave a message.* Tears course down my cheeks at the sound of his voice, but I can't speak. I sniff, trying to speak, to say I'm sorry, but I can't get the words out. I can barely breathe. I sob into the phone, willing the words out of my mouth until the voice mail runs out.

I stand and stare at the empty drive, then at the road. He's gone. I drop my phone and fall to my knees, crying so hard that I can't stop.

My heart is aching and I've a burning lump in my throat. I try to swallow it down but it's stuck there and hurts so much. I'm still whimpering, "I'm sorry, so sorry."

I try to ring him again, but this time a voice says, *This mobile number is not receiving calls. Please try again later.*

That's it. It's over.

A haunting wail leaves my throat, lingering in the room as if it's coming from somewhere else. But it's not coming from somewhere else, it's coming from me, and it's the sound of my heart breaking, crying for him to come back. I cry until I've nothing left but that strange wail.

I'm cold and I struggle to get to my feet. I start to feel the pain again in my shoulders as I steady myself; the back of my neck and arms hurt too. I look under the sheet at my body, seeing bruising appearing. I've hand prints on the tops of my arms where Adam grabbed me, banging me against the wall. I pull the sheet back over me, wincing.

I can't do this anymore. My body can't take much more, and my heart, well, that's dying. I stumble towards the bed, get in and cuddle my babies' rabbit close to me. I've lost everyone. I can't stop crying or making that noise. I've tried, but it won't stop. I eventually fall asleep, exhausted.

I wake, confused and startled. My heart's racing and I'm sweating. I've been dreaming about Adam again, and what he's done to me over the years. He's back in my head, in my face – and in my life – and it's the same dream. He was chasing me, shouting what he was going to do to me. He grabbed for me from behind, catching my hair, then I woke. My head is so fucking screwed up.

I leave my room, like a zombie, heading towards the bathroom, where I walk into the shower switching it on and letting the water run over me, as I sit on the shower floor cradling myself, staring at the extent of the bruising on my shoulders, and the deep purple fingerprints on my arms. I stare, feeling numb.

I'm in the bedroom patting myself dry with a towel, not really remembering leaving the bathroom. I feel as though I'm in a trace and have stepped back 4 years. The bruising, the mind games. Adam.

I take some clean pyjamas out of my drawer, seeing Edward's jumper. I remove it, closing my eyes hugging it to me. I can smell him, tears well as I regret what I've allowed myself to do by telling him to leave. Allowing Adam to once again control my life.

I pull his jumper over my head and start making my way to the front bedroom. I enter gazing at the bed, then crawl into the side where he slept, pulling his pillow close to me and cradling it, wishing desperately that he was still here. But he's not. He left me. Because I told him to leave. My lip quivers, because I can't blame him for not staying or answering my calls. I blame myself.

My heart is heavy, and I'm drained, knowing that in life you cannot always choose which way you fall, though I know I've fallen badly.

My eyes start to close once again, as I feel myself drifting backwards, my wall crushing and suffocating me as it starts rebuilding itself slowly, brick by brick. Adam he makes me feel as if I'm going mad, that I can't control my own emotions, my own thought – but that's what happens when you let someone get inside your head, them constantly lurking in the shadows, reminding you. There's no pill I can take, no more than there's a cure for cancer, but I need to stop this disease from spreading before it rots the very inside of me.

Chapter 14

I've finished packing two small bags, and start making my way downstairs, leaving them next to the front door, then continue towards the cellar, as I reach up for the bolt to unlock it, I notice it's not bolted. I raise my eyebrows, not remembering if it was bolted before or not. My dad put that lock on when I was a little girl, to stop me from going down there, as I'd once got locked in and was terrified. That feeling hasn't gone. I'm still scared as I turn the light on and carefully make my way down the worn, stone steps. And I wonder how many people have walked up and down these steps for them to be so worn and dipped in the middle.

It feels cold as I reach the bottom and stretch up to pull the light switch that hangs above the bottom step, the large room is dimly illuminated. The walls are whitewashed and the stone beams have cobwebs hanging from them. The boiler sits on the wall next to a window, with the old Belfast pot sink sitting underneath with one huge tap in the middle of it.

I make my way over to the boiler, still shivering and a little jumpy, and glance through the window at the stone steps that lead from the door at the end of the room to the outside. They're covered in reddish-brown leaves from the trees at the side of the house. The gate at the top hasn't been bolted and is banging against the railings; it sounds scary as the wind hisses through the cracks around the old wooden door.

The black-leaded range is full of dust and bits of rubbish that have blown in from outside. I shudder, thinking about the servants that lived down here back in the day when the building was a grand gentleman's house. I'd hate it. Adam was always down here, storing things, his things. I left him to it, although now that I look around it's practically empty.

Out the corner of my eye, I notice a padlock on one of the doors that leads into what used to be the servant's bedrooms.

I make my way over, curious as to what's behind. I turn the knob, rattling the door, but the padlock's large and doesn't shift.

I suddenly jump, hearing a cry from outside, then a bang. I turn towards the window, my heart racing. It's Marmalade, banging her paws against it.

"Shit, you stupid bloody cat!" I practically shout, as it stares back at me through the glass, ignoring me.

I walk back to the boiler turning the thermostat to the winter setting to keep the pipes from freezing. Then I check the wooden door that leads to the outside; I hear Marmalade meowing at the back of it. "Go home," I mutter, as I replace the safety chain back, pulling it to make sure it's secure, then pull the light cord, leaving the cellar, virtually running up the stairs.

I enter the hallway and breathe a sigh of relief as I slam the door shut and replace the bolt, knowing I don't have to go down there again until I return. I finish emptying the fridge and take out the rubbish. I take care to bolt the gate at the top of the steps and then head inside to the lounge.

I sit, just waiting on the sofa, feeling as though I'm in a dream, a trance-like state, numb and empty, ever so empty. I can't eat, I can't sleep, and my dreams have returned. They're bad, really bad. Adam is there every time I close my eyes and when I eventually do doze off, I dream, feeling every punch, every screaming match, every belittlement, until I walked away defeated.

The cruel mind games, and, of course, the loss, the loss of …

My lip quivers – it's as if I've a DVD on repeat in my head.

Then I open them to see Edward's face and I break again and again. I can't cry anymore. I've no tears left. I think I've cried a river with everything that's happened.

I stare at the flowers Edward sent me and read the card incessantly, attempting to find the humour in what he wrote, picturing his smiling face and raised eyebrows as he wrote the card, no doubt with a hint of scepticism.

Please keep me.

I pull my lip in hard, thinking off the irony – that this time I've kept the flowers but told him to leave.

I can't describe how I feel, apart from lonely; my head's full of memories that will haunt me for the rest of my life. I've been in a daze all day, wondering whether I've made the right decision to go away and leave all this behind me. But deep down I know I have. I can't continue my life like this, letting Adam creep back and spoil any chance of happiness I may ever have. I know it's over between Edward and me – he'll not return my calls; and I can't go to him because I don't know where he is, though I'm desperate to apologise. He must hate me so much. I know I hate myself.

I've ordered a taxi that'll be here soon. I've not even had the courage to phone Alison to tell her I'm going away. Instead I sent a text, knowing that if I spoke to her she'd sway me into staying. She keeps ringing my phone, but I know she'll want to come round.

But I can't stay – I have only one option now, and that's to leave. I will not allow Adam to hurt anyone else because of me. I want finally to be free of him and to try to start rebuilding what's left of my miserable life.

My phone is still in my hand and I keep willing it to ring, just once, just one more time, so that I can explain why I did what I did. I want to tell him that I love him – and I truly do – and that I'm sorry for hurting him. I see his face smiling at me while we made love and it breaks my heart over and over again. I've been holding my phone so tightly that it's as if my fingers are frozen around it. I stare down at the screen, repeatedly reading the message that I wrote to Edward, but I find myself unable to send it because I know if I do that it's over between us.

Edward, I'm sorry I asked you to leave, and that I've hurt you. I'm sorry I've had to say this in a text, but you will not answer my calls. I've screwed up big time, I know. I'm leaving tonight before I hurt anyone else – mostly you. I never wanted it to end, especially like this, and I'm so sorry. But please know this: no matter how much you're hurting, I'm hurting twenty times more. I can't say or tell you how or what I feel for you as that would be unfair, because you are better off without me and my fucked-up life.

I will never forget you, or what you've done for me, and I will treasure the memory of the beautiful night we spent together as long as I live.

All my love, Abigail. xx

My hand hovers over the send button as tears start to stream down my face and bounce off the screen. I hear the taxi pip his horn from the drive as I close my eyes and press send. I place the phone in my handbag, before wiping away the tears from my eyes with the back of my hand. I walk involuntarily towards the front door, picking up my bags on the way. I open the door, walk through it and lock my past inside.

I make my way down the drive into the cold, wet night. The driver takes my bags and places them in the boot. I climb into the back, not speaking. I nod and he returns the gesture with a sympathetic smile.

"Where to, Miss?"

I take a deep breath.

"Potters Hotel, please."

"The lakes, Miss?"

I nod my head as I put on my seatbelt and he doesn't say another word, as if he's picking up on the vibes that I don't want to talk.

He pulls away from the drive and I stare at my house through the back window as we head towards the main road.

The lights change and I sit quietly in the back, staring out of the window at the harsh weather that's now pelting the taxi.

My phone rings. I take it from my bag and look at the number. It's Gran. I've told her the truth about Adam this time, and my break with Edward, knowing I can't keep hiding, or lying, not now, especially to the people I love.

"Hi sweetheart. Have you set off?"

"Yes."

"Are you okay, Abbie?"

"No, not really, Gran, but I can't carry on like this."

"I know, darling; I just wish you'd have let me come with you."

"I just need some time on my own ..."

Although I'm desperate for a hug from her and her wise words telling me that everything will be okay, that my heart will mend and that I'll stop feeling like this.

"I've booked you a room, Abbie. Will you please ring me when you arrive? Then I'll know you're safe."

"I will. Thank you, Gran."

We say goodbye and I hang up. I feel defeated, empty and very lonely. The driver looks at me in his mirror. I put my head to the side and continue looking out of the window into the dark bleak winter night. I close my eyes and fall asleep listening to the rain beating at the windows, thinking of Edward and how different things could've been if it hadn't been for Adam.

I'm woken suddenly by the driver's voice. "Miss, we're here."

I open my eyes and nod my head. He leaves the taxi and makes his way to the boot to remove my bags. I get out and pay him the fare. He smiles at me then drives away.

I stand in the car park with my bags, bewildered as to how I ended up here. The wind is howling around me and it's freezing cold. I'm getting soaked to the skin from the rain that's now torrential.

I look towards the hotel. It's large with steps leading from the car park to a covered veranda over the entrance where a sign hangs: Potters Hotel.

Five stars are lit up underneath. Another sign to the side of the revolving doors advertises the Michelin-starred Bird Cage Restaurant. Open to non-residents, by reservation only. I walk up the drive towards the steps, noticing an abundance of very expensive cars parked in private bays. I raise my eyes upwards, knowing this is something Edward would have chosen.

I pull in a deep breath and walk through the revolving doors and into the reception area. It's enormous, contemporary in style, and the warmth immediately hits me. The brightness makes me squint as my eyes adjust to the glare. It's noisy with lots of people walking around. The dining room is visible and is crowded with diners smiling and laughing with each other. I step back suddenly as a couple walk past me quickly, practically running. The woman nearly bumps into me and she smiles, then giggles.

"Sorry," she says. Her partner winks at her and pulls her towards the lifts with a grin.

I merely roll my eyes. I don't want to stay here – it's too busy. I'd asked my gran for something small and quiet, out of the way. She'd told me what the hotel was called after she'd booked it, and I'd imagined a cosy little bed and breakfast, not this. I think I know why she booked this particular hotel; she knew it would be busy and probably thought I'd not feel so lonely, but none of these faces is the one I want to see. It's strange how you can feel so lonely in a place full of people. I want to turn around and leave but it's too late; I've been spotted by the woman at the reception desk.

"Good evening, madam." Her voice is laced with confidence and familiarity as I walk slowly towards the desk. "Have you a reservation?"

I nod towards her as I put my bags on the floor. "Name, please."

"Abigail Baxter."

She goes to the computer and casts her eyes over the reservation list. She spots my name and smiles at me, then hands me a key-card.

I reach into my bag to get my purse. She smiles sympathetically and I wonder whether it's because of my bruised face. I automatically put my hand to my cheek to cover the mark, but she just smiles kindly again.

"Miss Baxter, the room has been paid for, for as long as you want it."

I raise my eyebrows.

"Will you be taking dinner with us? We're serving until 8.30," she says as she points in the direction of the dining room.

My eyes follow to a packed dining room. I don't want to eat there or mix with people at the bar – it's too busy. I can't be bothered to smile or strike up a polite conversation just so it's not awkward.

And I'm sick of pretending that my life is fine when it's not; it's been torn apart, and it was my own doing this time. I'm getting really good at hurting myself. I'm beginning to wonder whether I even want to happy, because all I do when I am is cock it up. I want to run in the hills and never come back.

I return my eyes to hers; she's still waiting for my response. I shake my head.

"Miss Baxter, are you okay?" she asks.

I manage a weak smile, shrug my shoulders and then nod.

"Yes, sorry. I just need to go to my room, please."

"If you'd like to wait, I'll get the porter to take your bags up."

"No …" I pause, knowing I'm being rude, but I just want be left alone. "I can manage, thank you." My tone of voice a little harder than I'd intended as I take my key-card from her hand.

"I'll show you how it works."

"Please, I'm fine; I'll figure it out. Thank you," I reply sharply.

Then I pick up my bags and make my way to the stairs. I'm on the third floor. I walk up them robotically and finally reach room 324.

I try to figure out how to open it, pushing the key-card in and out of the slot every which way possible; on the third attempt it opens and I walk in.

It's a suite with a luxurious king-size bed. I stare at the bed, thinking, *For one.*

I shake my head, feeling sad, lonely and miserable as I throw my bags on the bed.

I look at my phone. 7.25 p.m. No messages or missed calls. I sigh. I need to ring my gran to let her know I've arrived safely but I've no signal. I walk around the room holding my phone up and then down. I try the bathroom and the corridor. I open the French doors to the balcony and nearly get blown off my feet; it's raining heavily, the wind is still howling and it's started to thunder. I have two bars so I ring her quickly before I lose the signal.

"Hi Gran!" I shout, struggling to hear her for the weather. "I'll have to be quick. I've no signal. I got here safe and I'm okay. I'll ring you tomorrow."

She's trying to tell me something. "Abbie."

"Yes."

"Can you hear me?"

"Faintly but be quick – I'm losing the signal; it's on one bar."

The line's really crackling; words are being spoken but I can only make out a little of what she's saying.

"I've … at house … wants …"

"Gran, I didn't understand that. What did you …?"

My signal's gone. I try repeatedly to ring her back but the storm is now on top of me. There's a boom, then a crash. There's lightning over the lake and it makes me jump as I try to get back into the room.

I struggle to close the French doors against the wind. I'm soaking wet as I push my full bodyweight against the door. Leaflets in the room blow around and the wind screeches through the last bit of open space in the door before I finally manage to close it.

I place my phone on the bedside cabinet and try the room's landline, but it's dead.

I make my way into the bathroom. I'll ring her tomorrow, first thing. I turn on the hot-water tap for the enormous bath tub and put in some bubble bath that's on the side. I pull my face as I inhale the scent – it's lavender, which I'm not fond of, but it's meant to help you relax and sleep.

I remove my jacket and hang it on the radiator to dry, exposing the jumper I'm wearing; I'm just staring at it as I start to run my hand over the soft wool – it's Edward's. I hug it to my face; it smells fresh with a hint of his aftershave – his smell. I inhale deeply, screwing my face up and holding back the tears as I pull it over my head. I take it into the bedroom, fold it neatly and place it on my pillow. I've worn it constantly, even in bed, wanting to feel close to him. I wish desperately he was here with me. I remove my T-shirt, jeans and pumps, only leaving my knickers on while I wait for the bath to fill. I've no bra on as the straps hurt my arms and back. I stare at my bruised body in the mirror, until I can't bare the sight anymore.

I remove my knickers and get into the hot bath. The heat from the water hits my tender skin and I let out a cry as I slowly winch myself down into the tub, hoping it will soothe my weary body.

Tears sting my eyes once more as I lie there until the water goes cold.

I wrap a large towel around myself and dab at my skin gently, trying to dry it as I walk back into the bedroom. I pick up Edward's jumper and put it on. Then I take the knitted rabbit from my bag and climb into bed, sad, shattered, aching, and knowing this is all I have left of my children, and my Edward.

I pull the duvet over my head, hugging the jumper and rabbit close to my heart, sobbing and hiding from the world once again.

Chapter 15

I wake feeling warm and thirsty; my throat is sore and dry. I get out of bed and make my way too the minibar, taking out a bottle of water and drink it, coughing as I try to swallow the liquid.

I sit back on the bed and throw the duvet over to one side, taking another drink; it makes me cough again and I feel the pain in my throat and back as I glance out of the window. It's still dark outside. I can't see very much apart from the spotlights in the hotel grounds, but at least it's stopped raining.

I glance at the clock. 7.30 a.m. I've slept for a good few hours, although I'm not sure exactly what time I went to bed.

My tummy starts to rumble and I've a bad headache. I'm not sure if it's down to the room being too warm or that this is day two of not eating. I'm still sore and tender but I need to get some fresh air.

I get up and start pulling clean underwear, my running pants, trainers, and a hoodie from one of my bags. Then I make my way into the bathroom with them. I wash, clean my teeth and put my hair up in a ponytail. I put my knickers on and try my bra; it hurts but I don't think I can run without it. I suffer the pain, wriggling a little to try to make it more comfortable. I dress in the rest of my things and leave the room. On the stairs, I catch sight of a man on the next flight down. My heart jumps. He's tall with dark hair and he's wearing a suit. He looks very smart. He turns as he hears me on the stairs behind him.

"Morning. Early run?" he asks with a smile. His tone is friendly.

I just stare – it's not the same smile, not the one I want. I nod and continue walking behind him. He stops at the bottom of the stairs and looks up at me. He seems nice, kind.

"Can I tempt you with a coffee before your run?" He gestures with his hand towards the breakfast room.

"No, thank you," I reply, shaking my head. I move my eyes in the direction of a woman walking towards us who's dressed equally as smart.

"Jack, there you are," she says, smiling towards him. She nods her head at me.

"Another time then maybe?" he says to me.

She looks at me, and he smiles. "I'm here for a few days, and you?" he asks.

I don't answer; I just smile politely and walk in the direction of the exit.

I stand outside for a few minutes. I pull my hood up over my head and zip up the pocket that holds my mobile. I breathe in the cold morning air, thinking of Edward and willing my phone to ring, but I know it won't.

I sigh deeply, thinking how that man had looked like Edward from behind. I take a deep breath and start to run from the hotel grounds along a path at the side of the lake. It's starting to get light. I push myself, trying to get rid of the thoughts in my head. I thought that man on the stairs was Edward. I thought he'd come for me, that I could say sorry to him, for hurting him, explain why I did what I did. I start to run faster and faster, but my legs are hurting and I'm slowing down. I try to push myself harder again, but I can't; I'm exhausted. I haven't run far, about a mile, and I put it down to the fact that I've not eaten. I sit on a bench facing out towards the lake and catch my breath. It's started raining again.

I close my eyes but all I can see is Edward's face, and I imagine the sadness and confusion in his eyes as I told him to leave. And as I think of him, of us together, making love for the first time, tears flood my eyes as I'm reminded of how I felt with his arms around me, holding me and loving me.

I suddenly pull my lip in tight, remembering the dream, then my telling him to leave. It's too late; the floodgates have opened once again.

I pull my legs up onto the bench and in towards my bottom and curl my arms around them, holding them to me, hugging myself. I sit alone, crying. People walk past me but I don't move. A lady's voice speaks.

"Are you all right, sweetheart? You're getting soaking wet."

Her voice is full of concern but I don't respond or look at her. I sit very still in my own little space, cocooned in my own sorrow.

I start to shiver. I'm cold and wet. I've stopped crying but I don't know what to do. I want to run, hide, go back to the hotel and climb into bed, fall asleep and never wake up, as if my life's been one long, miserable dream. But it's not. I've already run, and now I'm hiding. And, yes, my life is miserable.

I feel numb. I open my eyes, get up from the bench and walk along the path. Lots of people are now out, busy with their lives, talking to each other about Christmas and how many shopping days there are left. Children laugh and giggle, excited at the prospect of Father Christmas coming down the chimney, and I stare at them, wishing that my life, for even a second, could be like that. I stop and rub my face with my hands. I take a deep breath, although at this moment in time I want to scream from the top of my lungs and not stop until someone says, "Everything is going to be okay."

I start to run, and pick up speed. I'm running quite fast and I know what I'm doing – I'm trying to hurt myself physically so that the pain in my head will stop. But it's not working this time; the pain in my body hurts just as much as the pain in my heart. I don't feel able to pull myself out of this state but I don't want to go back to that dark place. I don't want to suffocate myself with that brick wall again. I want Edward. I want him so much that it hurts to breath.

I stop in my tracks as my phone vibrates in my pocket. My heart pounds as I unzip my pocket. I'm hoping, wishing and praying it's Edward. I catch my breath, pulling my phone from my pocket quickly and swiping the screen.

"Hello?"

No one answers, so I repeat louder. "Hello?"

I hear a snigger. I'm taken aback and reply harshly, "Who is this?"

"It's a fucking good job you told him to leave."

My eyes are wide and bile has risen in my throat at the sound of his voice. "Are you listening to me, bitch?"

I want to scream at him and my face screws up in revulsion.

"You …" I shout back but he shoots me down before I can continue.

"I'd listen, and listen fucking good, Abbie."

I cut him dead as anger begins to radiate from me. I've lost everything because of him and I don't care anymore. I shout back over him and I don't stop this time until he's silent. "Fuck you, Adam!"

People are staring at me but I have tunnel vision; all I can see is his face and the things he's done to me. If these people knew what he was capable of, they wouldn't stare; they'd applaud me.

"Go to hell, Adam. Where you belong!"

"You fucking listen to me, Abbie—"

"I said, NO!"

I'm just about to cut him off when he starts again, his voice now manipulative.

"I know where you are. Christmas in the lakes. Hmm, yes, it's nice this time of year."

I freeze; my heads whizzing. I feel sick. How can he know where I am? I start to shake and my eyes are darting around, trying to find him, see if he's followed me.

"I've done what you said. I've left him – now leave me alone, Adam."

He starts to laugh; he knows I'm scared.

I close my eyes as his tone changes, like it always does when he thinks he's got the better of me.

"Do you honestly think I'd leave you the fuck alone, Abbie? I want what's mine. I've worked too hard for this and you're not fucking getting away with it."

I can't continue like this, not anymore, and I don't know where my next sentence comes from, but I shriek, "No, you damn well listen to me. You've taken everything from me, and the one thing you want now is my money." I take a deep breath and shout with determination in my voice, "Go to hell, you will never see me or my money again. Have you got that?"

I hear someone in the background and it sounds like his secretary, Kimberly's voice.

"Mr Lord, telephone call on line one, sir."

"I said I did not want to be disturbed. Get out and shut the door," he blasts back at her.

I breathe a small sigh of relief as I know now that he's at work and not here in the lakes. And he knows I know.

His voice is again manipulative as he continues angrily, "You listen, you little bitch. I meant what I said – *until death us do part.* And you know I mean what I say. Haven't you got that through your thick head yet?"

My reply is heartfelt. "Drop dead, Adam. You'll have to kill me first. And don't ever, ever ring me again."

He's still screaming at me, his voice aggressive. "Fuck—"

I hang up and stare at my phone. My hands are shaking with fury, adrenalin, fear, God knows what, but I've done it. I've said it and I meant it. He's dead to me and I don't think I care anymore what he does.

I'm still bewildered over how he knew where I was. Then it dawns on me – he's always known where I am.

"Bastard. He's tracked my phone!"

It starts to ring again. It's the same private number. I drop it to the floor quickly, like it's on fire and burning my hands. I stamp on it repeatedly, and I can't stop. It's like I'm trampling him out of my life.

A lady smiles at me in sympathy; she's overheard my side of the conversation. She walks towards me, smiling, and she looks familiar. She reaches me and takes my hand in hers, and I suddenly feel calm as she speaks.

"I think its broken, sweetheart. Let it go."

I look at her and she says again, kindly, "Just let it go."

I smile, holding my tears of frustration and anger back. I nod my head.

"You go and do what you have to do, and be strong." Her voice is serene; it calms me. She kisses the side of my cheek before walking away.

I'm staring at the back of her, trying to digest what I've just said to Adam. What she just said to me. She's a stranger, but I feel like I know her. It's as if she knew what I was feeling. I think about her – she's not much older than me, reddish-brown hair, kind eyes. She made me feel so tranquil. I put my hand to my face where she kissed me and a tear hits my cheek as a flush of emotion runs through my body.

I shout to her, "Mum!"

She turns slightly, saying something, and I'm sure it's "I love you."

She smiles at me as I wipe the tears from my eyes and hold my hand to my heart. And then she's gone.

It couldn't be, could it? Was it my mum? It felt like her, and I feel different. I stroke my face again, still feeling that kiss on my cheek.

I smile, closing my eyes briefly before starting to walk back to the hotel, feeling strange, thinking about my mum, and wondering after all these years whether it was her. I'm trying to rationalise what I saw, what I heard, and now I'm worried I'm going mad. But I feel quite different now – stronger, and surprising calmer than normal, because I really do want to believe it was my mum; but of course my head is telling me different, but I still look towards heaven and whisper, "Thank you, whoever you were. And I love you too, mum!"

Chapter 16

I enter the reception area. I stop, taken aback by the brightness of the lights, and squint. Then the warmth hits me. I slowly glance at the clock – it's 10.30 a.m. I've been out nearly three hours, but it doesn't seem that long. I feel weird; nervous yet calm.

I'm shivering. I hold my hands, trying to stop them from shaking. They feel like icicles and my clothes are soaking wet. I must have walked back from wherever I was in a trance.

I can't stop thinking about my mum. I can't explain what I think I saw or how it's made me feel; it all seems quite surreal. Warmth begins to spread through my veins; it makes me feel strange and a little scared, as if I'm not in control of my body.

I stare at people talking to each other in the reception area. Their lips are moving but there's no sound coming from their mouths. I start swaying. The brightness of the room begins to fade.

I hear someone shouting, "Miss, are you all right?"

Everything around me is going black; the woman from the reception area approaches me.

"Miss …"

My legs suddenly give way and I find myself falling towards the floor. My eyes start to flicker. I can hear a muffled voice – a woman's.

"She was standing there one minute and then the next she was on the floor."

I open my eyes slowly, feeling dazed. Two figures are crouched over me but they're not in focus.

Another voice answers.

"She's coming round, give her some air."

They both move backwards, but remain near to me on the floor.

"Jenny go and get Nathaniel ask him to bring a chair please."

"Okay, Michele."

She gets up moving away.

"Miss? Miss Baxter? It's Michele from the reception desk. Are you all right? Do you think you can stand?"

I look at her, a little puzzled, but I nod. She smiles at me, then directs her attention to someone else.

"Michele, the chair."

"Thank you, Nathaniel. Just leave it there. Can you help me with Miss Baxter, please?"

"Yes, of course I can."

"Miss Baxter, are you okay to stand if we help you?"

I nod and they both help me to my feet and onto the chair.

"Jenny, please get a glass of water for Miss Baxter," Michele says.

I'm a little bewildered and she's noticed.

"You fainted. Just sit for five minutes and then we'll help you to your room."

I sit on the chair and Michele ushers away the onlookers. Jenny passes me a glass filled with iced water.

"There you go, miss. Just sip it so it doesn't make you sick."

I nod my head in response, feeling a little silly with all the attention I'm getting. I sip the water and start to feel myself coming around.

I raise my eyes towards Michele and mouth, "I'm sorry."

She shakes her head.

"Well, don't be, miss. You can't help fainting. Do you feel up to it, I mean going to your room?"

"Please."

"I'll help you. We'll take the lift."

She holds out her hand and I smile at her, thinking how many nice, genuine people there are in the world, people who just want to help; I'd never really noticed it before. I've never let anyone help me, always trying do everything by myself.

She guides me towards the lift. The doors open and we enter. We start to go up and my tummy churns; I feel sick but it quickly wears off.

We reach the third floor and Michele continues to hold my arm as we head for my room.

"Miss Baxter, may I come in for a minute, please?" She asks as we reach the door.

I nod and she follows me in.

"Gosh, it's quite warm in here. I'll open the window for you and let in some fresh air."

A light breeze enters the room; it brings me to my senses.

"Thank you for helping me, Michele," I say.

"You're welcome, Miss Baxter."

"Abigail, please."

"Abigail, I hope you don't mind me asking, and please don't get offended, but are you okay? I mean, really? I think I know what the problem is – man trouble?" she asks.

Normally, I would've told her to mind her own business. Instead, to my surprise, I reply, "Yes, complicated man trouble, but I'm sorting it out."

She doesn't probe any further, but asks, "Have you eaten, Abigail?"

I roll my eyes.

"I thought not. I'll ask the porter to bring you a warm drink and some …" She smiles. "Toast as well? I'll leave you to change out of your wet things. Half an hour shall we say?"

"That's kind. Thank you again."

"No problem, Abigail. And if you want anything, anything at all, just ring down to reception. The phones are working now."

"I will, Michele."

She smiles towards me as she's leaving my room.

I walk into the bathroom and think about running a bath. Then I change my mind – it's already warm; perhaps a hot bath isn't a good idea. I remove my wet clothes and start the shower instead, adjusting the temperature so it's just right.

Washing is still uncomfortable.

I tip my head back under the shower and apply shampoo, massaging it into my scalp. I start to think of my mum again, wondering if it was her, and what she meant by *let it go*, although I probably already know – she meant let my past go and move on, which I'll try to do. Though where I'm going, I've not yet decided.

I wipe the soap from my eyes and start thinking of Edward; my heart pains. I'll never see him again. Then a saying comes into my head: *It's better to have...* but I can't finish it to the end, for wondering if that person who wrote the quote had ever loved. I think not, because who would want to live their life feeling like this? I certainly don't.

I hear a knock at the door – it's the porter with my toast and coffee.

"Just a minute, please," I shout, grabbing the dressing gown that's hanging behind the bathroom door. I put it on and run a clean towel over my hair and face as I'm walking towards the door.

There's another knock.

"I'm coming!"

I open the door, hiding behind it, just peeking my head around. Then I look up. I stare, dumbstruck. My heart's racing.

He's staring back at me.

I swallow hard as I feel tears well.

"May I come in please?"

I step backwards, still unable to speak as he comes into my room and closes the door behind him.

There's another knock.

"Room service."

He opens the door.

"Thank you. I'll take that," he says as he removes the tray from the porter. He takes some money from his pocket and places it in the man's hand before he walks past me putting the tray onto the coffee table.

I can't speak; I just stare at him. I close my eyes, not believing he's here, not understanding why he's here.

His voice as he speaks is almost a chant.

"Why, Abbie, why?"

I run my hands over my face, trying to push the tears back into my eyes, asking myself the same question.

"Answer me, Abbie. Why? Why did you tell me to leave?"

I bite my lip hard. He shakes his head.

"I'm struggling to understand you."

My reply is faint. "I know."

"Then *why?*" he shouts.

I jump and he looks shocked at my reaction but continues to shake his head. "Did you not think I'd be upset after you told me to leave, Abbie?"

"I'm sorry," I say weakly.

"You keep saying you're sorry but you've still not answered my question."

"I said I'm sorry … and I am, Edward," I blurt out nervously.

He stands, watching me.

I need to tell him the truth, get this out before I bottle it. I hold my head down; I can't look at him because I know I lied that night and hurt him badly. My hands begin to shake and I'm desperately trying not to cry. Seeing him here in my room, standing in front of me, confirms how much I feel for him. I don't know where to start, and I begin to babble.

"I know a lot of bullshit comes out of my mouth." I raise my voice in frustration. "You want me to tell you? You want me to tell you the truth?"

He nods.

"Because I'm scared. Of Adam. Of what he's going to do to me …" I close my eyes. "And I was scared that he was going to …"

I can't do it. The words make me feel sick and I know I'm bottling it. I can't even think about what he was going to do to me, what he threatened to do to Edward, let alone speak it.

I look at him dumbstruck and his expression has changed, as if he's a little shocked. But I'm not surprised because I've told him nothing, not really, about that Saturday night. I honestly believe he thinks I'm fickle, telling him to leave as I did.

Eventually he speaks, "Scared? Scared he was going to do what, Abbie?" He pauses. "What is it you're not telling me? You have one dream, then you tell me to leave?"

I desperately want him to hold me, but I feel as though I've lost that right to his love. I lied to him. I've hurt him too much.

He continues to stare, waiting for me to answer.

"I'm sorry," I say meekly.

"Tell me, Abbie," he says frustrated.

My lip quivers. I want to put my head back in the sand but I can't keep running. I have to face up to what I've done. I need to explain or I'm going to lose him forever.

Then her words suddenly float into my mind, making me feel stronger.

Do what you have to do, and be strong.

I pull a very deep breath, dragging the words from the pit of my stomach. They nearly choke me.

"Rape me," I whisper as bile raises into my throat.

I've said it.

His face immediately drops. He runs his hands through his hair and stares at me.

"What?"

I sniff.

His eyes are fixed on mine. "And you thought it best not to tell me. Why?"

He starts pacing around the room.

"You said he never touched you, never hurt you." He turns quickly towards me. "Did he hit you – hurt you – touch you?"

I shake my head hard. He's really angry; I'm not sure whether it's with me, the situation or Adam.

"No, he never touched me. He tried but I fought, and I fought him hard."

"So he hit you? Tell me the truth Abbie."

I nod my head. He closes his eyes, shakes his head and takes a sharp intake of breath. I think he's holding back his temper.

"Then you'd better tell me what really happened, Abbie. And don't lie to me this time. I want the truth!"

He's firm and I tell him what really happened that night. Everything this time, all of it, the sordid little details as well. About him ringing me, tracking my phone and knowing where I was; about my smashing the phone.

When I'm done, he's silent. He stares, shocked. I swallow hard.

"Speak to me, please."

He takes my head in his hands and rests his head on my forehead.

"I'm sorry, so sorry," I whisper.

He moves his head to look into my eyes; he looks hurt.

"Stop it, Abbie. Stop saying you're sorry. He's really fucked with your head."

I nod, slipping my hands under his jacket and around his waist, holding him to me, feeling scared but relieved.

Edward wraps his arms around me, drawing me closer to comfort me. He holds me tightly but I flinch. He notices and pulls back.

"Are you in pain?" he asks.

I shrug but he knows I am.

"Let me see."

I shake my head, feeling uncomfortable, not wanting him to see the bruises, bruises that made me feel so weak.

His voice is calm but firm. "Let me see, Abbie."

I close my eyes, feeling torn. I open them to find him just staring and waiting, although he looks as if he's losing patience.

"Abbie, let me see. I'd rather you show me than me having to look myself, because either way I am going to see."

I nod my head. I know I have to show him this time and try to make him understand why I didn't tell him.

"Okay."

My hands shake as I slowly unfasten the dressing gown and hold it over my breasts. I feel so ashamed of myself.

He gently takes my robe and stares at the hand prints and bruises on my arms. He looks livid.

"Anymore?" he asks through gritted teeth.

I nod.

"Where?"

I close my eyes as I can't bear to look at his face. Then I turn slowly, waiting for his reaction. He shouts when he sees my back and neck.

"Fucking hell! I'll kill him. I'll fucking kill him!"

His fists are clenched and he bites down hard on his bottom lip.

"I should've told you the truth, Edward, I know."

He shakes his head in disbelief.

"I should've shown you but I was scared that he would do this to you, and I couldn't bear that—"

His hand raises immediately to stop me talking, and he seems frustrated as he starts shouting over me.

"And you think I can fucking bear this, what he's done to you? You let me make love to you, the way I did …?"

He looks totally shocked.

"You told me to leave, knowing that he'd done that to you?"

I suck in my lip hard and nod my head, whispering, "Don't shout at me … please. I'm sorry."

"Fuck-ing-hell, Abbie!" He's fuming. I've never heard him yell or swear like this.

"Do you honestly think I would've left you, knowing he'd done this to you?"

I close my eyes, wanting to scream, "This is such a mess,' but I open them and look him in the eyes.

"I know I've hurt your pride, Edward, and I'm sorry I asked you to leave."

His eyes widen.

"You think you've hurt my pride when you asked me to leave? You hurt more than my fucking pride, Abbie."

I step back from him, shaking my head, trying my best to explain why I did it.

"I never wanted you to leave; it broke my heart."

He looks dumbstruck and I don't think he believes what I'm saying.

"I'm trying so hard to understand what's going on inside that head of yours, Abbie, but I'm struggling."

"I know, but believe me, I didn't want you to leave." My voice is almost begging him. "I had no choice."

"No choice?"

He looks completely bewildered but I'm so flustered that I can't say what I mean.

"No! Because—"

Then I stop, holding my head down, frustrated. I'm scared of saying what I really mean because I don't want him to reject me if he doesn't feel the same.

"Because what, Abbie?"

I lift my head to look at him and he's practically scowling; I can't blame him.

"Just tell me."

I jump and his face suddenly changes, as if he's hesitant about continuing. He chews on his lip and starts to speak again. But this time his tone is apprehensive.

"Are you scared of me?"

I'm shake my head immediately. He can't think that,

"God, no!" I blurt, holding my hand to my heart and shaking my head. "Because …"

I look into his eyes and they look sorrowful but baffled.

I pull in my lips, whispering, "I'm falling in love with you and I know he'd use that to hurt me, to hurt you. And he can never hurt you, not ever! I will not allow it."

He stares at me, stunned, then closes his eyes and takes a sharp intake of breath as he pulls me back into his arms holding me gently, as I slide my arms under his jacket, holding him to me tightly, not wanting to let go. I can feel his heart racing against my bare chest.

He moves back slightly then takes my hand.

"Look at me, Abbie."

I look up and see concern.

"You'd sacrifice your own happiness for me?"

I nod, knowing I would gladly sacrifice anything for him. His eyes look glazed over, but he doesn't speak, and I don't know what he's thinking. Tears sting my eyes again.

"Edward, I wouldn't blame you if you left and didn't want to be here with me. I'd understand," I whisper.

He continues to gaze at me and I feel as though I'm losing him.

I close my eyes, whispering once again, "Am I losing you?"

He leans forward towards me and gently kisses the top of my head. Then cups my face and looks into my eyes so intently that it's spellbinding. He breathes in deeply, before speaking.

"No … never, Abbie." Then he kisses me tenderly on the lips.

I smile into that kiss. My heart skips at those three words and that single kiss, because they mean more to me at this moment than anything.

I return my head to his chest listening to his beating heart, knowing for the first time in my life that I'm exactly where I want to be. Here, with him.

Edward Scott – the man I love.

Chapter 17

We've stood holding each other for I don't know how long. I feel more relaxed now as Edward keeps stroking my hair, kissing me and cuddling me gently. I've not spoken; I just smile. I'm unable to process everything that's happening. I keep squeezing him and sighing into his chest. He makes me feel as though I can face up to anything, especially Adam. I love being here in his strong arms and this feeling of safety. I feel needed and wanted by him, knowing everything is going to be okay.

"Miss Baxter," he says, gently pushing me out of his embrace, "are you going to get dressed?"

He reaches towards the floor and picks up my dressing gown.

I shake my head, hugging him tightly to me, not wanting to let go.

"No. Five more minutes please, Edward."

My tummy rumbles.

"When did you last eat, Abbie?"

I look up at him, pulling a silly face.

"Umm … Sat … ur … day."

He shakes his head. "Saturday Abbie?"

"Umm … yes." I smile sweetly. "I couldn't face food."

He kisses me fondly on the cheek, then passes me my dressing gown. As I put it on, he gestures for me to sit on the sofa and points towards my breakfast.

"Get your coffee and toast."

I sit down and pick up my coffee. I pull a face as I taste it. Edward just raises an eyebrow at me.

"Abbie, drink it."

"I can't."

"Why?"

"It's cold."

He walks over to the phone, picks up the receiver and dials a number.

"Room 324. May I order room service … A large pot of hot coffee, toast and jam please." Another pause. "Thank you."

I smile at him as he walks promptly over to my bags and removes knickers, a bra, T-shirt and jeans and places them on the bed. His eyebrows suddenly raise as he spots something on the bed.

"Abbie, is this my jumper?"

I nod shyly. He smiles.

"Come on, let's get you dressed."

"What?" I say, stunned.

"You heard me, Abbie. Let's get you dressed."

"Edward, I think I can manage to dress myself."

He grins. "Maybe, Abbie, but I'm here and I'm going to take care of you from now on."

And what can I say back to that? I stand and walk over to him, smiling, my heart bursting with love from his kind gesture, but I stick to my guns.

"Thank you, but I can dress myself, Edward. I'll be okay."

"Oh, I know you'll be okay, Abbie, from now on."

I raise my eyebrows at his remark. He nods his head to confirm he means what he's saying.

"Because I'm never letting you out of my sight. You understand me? I'm going to take care of you, Abbie, and no one will ever hurt you again."

I smile at his bossy words, but I know he means them endearingly. I think of my mum and those words that she spoke to me.

Do what you have to do, and be strong.

And that's exactly what I'm going to do – to keep this beautiful man, this kind, honest, bossy, beautiful man.

I laugh slightly.

"Miss Baxter, do you not think my intentions towards you are honourable?"

"Of course I think your intentions are honourable, Mr Scott, but I'm sure I can manage to dress myself. Thank you so much for the kind offer, though."

He grins before replying, "Well, come on then before your breakfast arrives."

He watches me putting on my knickers, then my bra. I wince as the straps hurt my shoulders. He walks towards me, his eyebrows raised.

"See, let me help."

He slides his hand under the strap, gently smoothing it down.

"Turn around, Abbie."

And I do. He takes the straps at the back to fasten the clasp; he inhales sharply. I turn and put my hand on his while he closes his eyes. And I know what he's thinking as he reaches for my T-shirt and places it gently over my head.

"Put your arms in."

I do as he asks. He picks my jeans up and tells me to sit. He bends down in front of me and pulls them over my feet, then tells me to stand and pulls them up my legs, moving his hands gently and slowly. Then he fastens the button and zip and hugs me carefully.

There's a knock at the door.

"Room service."

Edward gets my breakfast from the porter.

"Come, sit, Abbie. Eat your toast while it's hot." He pours the coffee and passes me a cup. "Drink it."

He's taking care of me like he said he would. It's nice, and it's him, and I couldn't be happier. I sit smiling while he watches me.

"Okay?" he says.

I nod.

"I'm just going to change. See you in ten?"

"You have a room?" I ask, puzzled.

"Yes. I booked it after I spoke to your gran. She told me where you were staying."

"You spoke to my gran?" I reply, shocked.

"Yes …" He looks confused. "Did you not listen to your messages?"

"No, I couldn't. Nothing came through and I'd no signal because of the storm."

"I see." He looks puzzled. "Your gran telephoned you – you spoke to her while I was there at her house."

"Yes, I did but then we got cut off."

My eyes open wide, realising what he's just said.

"You went to my gran's house?"

"Yes, after I received your text message on Sunday …"

He stops looking sad.

"Your message really got to me. What you wrote. I tried to ring you but your phone was switched off. I went to your house but you weren't there so I went to your gran's and she told me you where here."

My eyes raise towards him as I remember what I wrote.

"It got to you?"

"Yes, Abbie, it got to me." He breathes out. "Are you going to repeat everything I say?"

"I don't know. It got to you? You went to my house, to my gran's house? You phoned me?"

I'm more than a little surprised and he can tell, but he laughs.

"Yes, for the third time."

"What did my gran say to you?"

He stops laughing, and just looks at me with his eyes slightly closed.

"That you were sad."

"I was more than sad, Edward."

"I know, Abbie. That's why I came. I'm sorry you asked me to leave and I'm sorry I left. And I'm so sorry I didn't answer when you rang me."

"May I please ask you something, Edward?"

He nods.

"When you told me I'd hurt more than your pride ..." He nods. "What did you mean?"

He smiles, taking my hand and then placing it on his heart. I smile back and he doesn't have to tell me what he means because I know.

I close my eyes, whispering, "Will you please kiss me?"

"I thought you'd never ask."

He responds eagerly and takes my mouth. We kiss passionately. It's long, tender and beautiful, and when we pull away I'm still smiling.

"Edward?"

"Yes."

"Were you angry with me?"

He looks torn.

"Please, I need to know, and we promised to tell the truth to each other."

"We did." He sighs. "Yes, I was angry with you. Angry that you told me to leave. Angry at myself for leaving when all I wanted to do was break down the bathroom door, then shake you, scream at you ..." I raise my eyebrows, knowing I can't blame him. "I didn't want to frighten you, but I was so frustrated and angry. I didn't understand what was going on, so that's why I left.

"I couldn't answer your call when you rang me because I was scared I'd say all the wrong things to you in the heat of the moment. I pulled over near the traffic lights where we first met, remember?"

I nod.

"I listened to your voicemail; you were crying, unable to speak. I turned the car around and drove back to your house. I pulled up outside and looked up at the window where I'd seen you last, but then I couldn't get out of the car. I felt mixed up and for the first time in my life I couldn't control my emotions. So instead I drove home.

"I sat in my lounge, in the darkness and silence, just wondering, *Why*?

I thought you might've made a mistake, that I'd made a mistake. Was it too soon for us? All those thoughts were whizzing around at top speed in my head and I couldn't justify them, I couldn't find an answer.

All I could see was your beautiful face smiling at me while we made love for the first time ..."

I've tears in my eyes and I try hard to hold them back. I breathe out heavily but a tear falls onto my cheek.

He shakes his head. "Don't, Abbie ..." He breathes out too. "If you cry, I'll not be able to carry on, and I think I need to be honest with you."

I nod and suck in my lip. "It wasn't my pride that was hurting or the fact that you'd told me to leave. I realise that now. It was the thought of never seeing you or being with you again. That's what hurt so much."

I hold my hand to my mouth.

"God, I'm so sorry. But do you understand why I did what I did? I thought the nightmare was true at the time. And Adam's a monster, Edward. What he's done and what he's said are nothing compared with what he could do."

He looks annoyed.

"So you don't think they were just threats."

I shake my head.

"No, sorry. But, honestly, I don't know what to believe anymore, not from him. I think he's mad, lost the plot. And he's bent, I'm sure of it."

I continue shaking my head.

"No, he *is* bent. I think deep down I've always known that, Edward."

"Do you not think the police are best dealing with him then?" he asks.

But I know what he really means. He's not asking me; he's telling me.

I shrug my shoulders because I'm sceptical and, truth be known, I'm scared and ashamed of my past.

I know I want to do it, but do I want my past raking up. Would I be strong enough to deal with Adam's mind games?

I sometimes wish I had a magic wand that I could wave and make the past four years disappear. *Puff* – just like that. But this is the real world and as much as I'd like it to happen it's not going to.

I know I don't want to ever feel that low again, like I did when I lost my babies, or like I've felt over these past days without Edward, because that's painful, so painful, when your heart is crying out and broken for what you can't have back.

I close my eyes and take a deep breath to psych myself up. I'm not at all sure what's brought on this sudden urge to go to the police and report Adam. I'm not just doing it because I want Edward back and so that all this will stop. I'm doing it because I want Adam to be punished for what he's done, to me and to my babies, and to make Nicky see him for what he is – a monster. Because that's what he is. He can't ruin that unborn baby's life by being its father, because he's not capable of being a father. He has no love, no heart, no soul, and he holds no remorse. And a monster like that should never, ever, have the right to be a father.

I'm angry and I know that this is what I should have felt years ago. I'm cross with myself, knowing that I've been brainwashed by him, thinking all this time it was my fault. Why did I not see it earlier? It's taken all this time for me to realise this.

I always thought in terms of wanting someone to love me, but I've had love all my life. The love of my parents, my gran, my grandad. So, today, I look with open eyes, eyes that now see clearly, and what I'm seeing, I'm liking. Because love has always been there for me; I suppose I'd just forgotten it.

My seeing that lady whom I'd thought was my mum, and that kiss on my cheek, which I can still feel, has made me understand that.

I was loved and just because they're not here with me anymore doesn't mean that they've stopped loving me. Then there's my gran, who desperately want her granddaughter back, and Edward – I want to spend the rest of my life with him, if he'll have me.

Edward is giving me a second chance, a chance to mend my broken heart, and I'm going to take it. I want to love him, and let him know that I love him. And I want to be loved back by him.

I make a promise to myself.

I, Abigail Baxter, am no longer going to bury my head in the sand. I will not run away anymore.

Edward smiles, still waiting for me to answer, and I know at that very moment in time, what I'm about to do – Fight. I feel the binding chains snap then shatter.

I nod, pulling in a very deep breath, speaking so confidently that I almost don't recognise my own voice.

"Yes. The police. They can deal with him now."

Acknowledgements

A massive, huge, thank you! To everyone who has bought and read, Broken and Breaking Free.
Thank you to my friends old and new, and especially Sandra. Everyone should have a Sandra in their life, because my life is so much better with her in it.
I would also like to add a special thank you to my copy-editor Louise. To Paul for doing such a fantastic job with the art work on my book-cover designs. I couldn't have done it without you all.

Adele -x-

Mending

Book 3 of the Abigail's Fate series
By Adele Lea

Coming soon
Available on Amazon bookstore.
Paper back and kindle edition.

22896206R00133

Printed in Great Britain
by Amazon